OTTO PENZLER PRESENTS
AMERICAN MYSTERY CLASSICS

THE CAT SAW MURDER

Dolores Hitchens (1907–1973) was a prolific mystery author who wrote under multiple pseudonyms and in a range of styles. A large number of her books were published under the D. B. Olsen moniker (under which her "Cat" series was originally published), but she is perhaps best remembered today for her later novel, *Fool's Gold*, published under her own name, which was adapted as *Band a part* by Jean-Luc Godard. She was among the most important early authors of domestic suspense who helped define the genre for generations to come.

Joyce Carol Oates is the author of more than 70 books, including novels, short story collections, poetry volumes, plays, essays, and criticism, including the national bestsellers *We Were the Mulvaneys* and *Blonde*. Among her many honors are the PEN/Malamud Award for Excellence in Short Fiction and the National Book Award. Oates is the Roger S. Berlind Distinguished Professor of the Humanities at Princeton University, and has been a member of the American Academy of Arts and Letters since 1978.

THE CAT SAW MURDER

DOLORES HITCHENS

Introduction by
JOYCE CAROL OATES

AMERICAN MYSTERY CLASSICS

Penzler Publishers
New York

This is a work of fiction. Names, characters, places, and incidents either are the product of the author's imagination or are used fictitiously. Any resemblance to actual persons, living or dead, businesses, companies, events, or locales is entirely coincidental.

Published in 2021 by Penzler Publishers
58 Warren Street, New York, NY 10007
penzlerpublishers.com

Distributed by W. W. Norton

Cover image: Andy Ross
Cover design: Mauricio Diaz

Paperback ISBN 978-1-61316-213-2
Hardcover ISBN 978-1-61316-212-5
eBook ISBN 978-1-61316-214-9

Library of Congress Control Number: 2021904962

Printed in the United States of America

9 8 7 6 5 4 3 2 1

THE CAT SAW MURDER

INTRODUCTION

Magic is mysterious, and mystery is magical: we are enthralled by that which we don't (yet) know, and many of us are under the spell of a near-visceral compulsion to learn the truth—"solve" the mystery.

It's a natural instinct, to wish to *know*. Problems exist to be solved but mystery is ever elusive. Even if we know *who* has committed the crime, we need to know *how;* we need to know *why.* Beyond that, we crave to know *meaning.* In magic, the ingenious magician is one who not only knows how to perform magic but knows how to deflect his viewers' avid attention from the workings of magic itself, which are (of course) illusory—the magician is the "illusionist." Of magic it is commonly said that the "magic" exists exclusively in the eye of the enthralled beholder; expose the mechanism behind the magic, you have reduced it to mere trickery—disillusionment.

Mystery/detective novels of the Golden Age (1920-1939) are more akin to magic than to mainstream literature in which an exploration of human personality in a recognizably "real" world is the point, as well as a cultivation of language as an end in itself; in the classic mystery/detective novel as executed by Agatha Christie, John Dickson Carr, and Ellery Queen among others, a brilliantly facile sleight-of-hand obscures from readers "clues" cleverly seeded in a prose narrative that, upon a second, closer reading, leap forward as premonitory. So *that* explains it, we think, marveling. As in Edgar Allan Poe's "The Purloined Letter" the most inspired clues, as they are likely to be invisible, are before our eyes.

All mystery/detective novels begin with a crime, usually a murder, which precipitates everything that follows. To compose an adventure of detection of some length it's necessary for the author, as the master magician, to deflect the reader's immediate attention from clues that will give away the mystery too quickly, as the reader's attention must be directed toward, yet also away, from the individual who will be unmasked at last as the "guilty" party. Ideally, readers should be surprised by the unmasking, yet recognize it as plausible, indeed inevitable. If inadequate clues are seeded beforehand, the reader will feel cheated; if clues are too obvious, the reader will feel cheated. (The game-like nature of the genre was brilliantly highlighted by Ellery Queen's innovative "challenge to the reader"—interrupting the prose narrative to declare that, given the assemblage of clues available at that point, the attentive reader should be able to solve the mystery himself.) Like magic, mystery/detective fictions are variants on formulas, read by aficionados familiar with the conventions of the genre, which can come to be addictive: because Mystery is never solved, but only shifts to new circumstances, mysteries can be explored forever.

In genre crime literature nothing precedes the crime: there are no significant "back-stories," no complex social circumstances. The discovery of a body sets in motion a sequence of actions each related to its predecessor and successor in a causal relationship; the randomness of life is anathema to the Golden Age mystery. For the author, as a puppet-master, the skillfully composed mystery begins with its ending, and is imagined backward; all forward motion—"plot"—moves inexorably toward that ending, the "solution" of the crime or crimes. Along the way there will be an ample supply of "clues" both legitimate and misleading; there will be a (hopefully colorful) cast of "suspects" with "motives." The ideal Golden Age mystery is a "locked-room" mystery in which ingenuity is the point, demonstrated by the (unknown) murderer and the sleuth who tracks and eventually names him, at which point the fiction dissolves to the sort of ending characteristic of fairy tales: nothing beyond this naming of the "guilty," no lingering consequences of murderous crimes, no permanently traumatized victims, no anxiety about whether criminal justice will be fairly meted out, or meted out at all. As in *The Cat Saw Murder* the ideal sleuth is an amateur for whom no employment of forensics or the resources of professional law enforcement is an option and who must rely upon her own ratiocination: "There was the puzzle of the crime, which allured [Miss Rachel's] mathematical mind as would a problem in algebra."

The sleuth, like the reader, is presented with a situation, usually of escalating criminal acts, but, unlike the reader, the sleuth can construct a coherent path through the underbrush. By the end of the novel we are dazzled by an illumination of just one, crucial and seemingly inevitable storyline, which "solves" the mystery; in an ideal specimen of the genre, a second reading will reveal how cleverly the author has arranged his revelations amid much that is distracting.

The Cat Saw Murder is a particularly eccentric example of such a genre work in that there are two "mysteries" running concurrently: the mystery of *who* has committed a curiously awkward, quasi-bungled murder at a most inopportune time, and the mystery of *who* is narrating the story, from a future perspective in which the mystery has (evidently) been solved, and one, or two, or three individuals are engaged in narrating it. The primary mystery is a conventional one involving murders in close quarters, with a limited cast of characters/ suspects, as in a formulaic locked-room mystery; the secondary mystery is more intriguing, for its solution must lie beyond the scope of the novel's time-span, in a future devised by the unlikely sleuth, 70-year-old Miss Rachel Murdoch.

The first in a series of mysteries by D.B. Olsen, one of the pseudonyms of bestselling Dolores Hitchens (1907-1973), *The Cat Saw Murder* (1939) inaugurates what has become a curious publishing phenomenon—the "cat mystery," now a multi-million-dollar-a-year industry. (Given the mythology of cats, originating in ancient Egypt where cats were allegedly worshipped as gods, it is not surprising that the cat, of all animals, is imagined as the Doppelganger of amateur detectives, usually women: where dogs are extraverted and eager to please, cats tend to a brooding sort of introversion, and a marked disinterest in "pleasing"—exactly the sort of personality suited for dispassionate detection and the unmasking of deceit.) In twelve mysteries published between 1939 and 1956, bearing such playful titles as *The Cat Wears a Noose, Cats Have Tall Shadows, Cats Don't Smile, Death Walks on Cat Feet,* among others, the fragile-bodied but sharply observant Miss Rachel Murdoch confronts murder after murder with astonishing composure for a maiden lady of advanced years; in *The Cat Saw Murder* Miss Rachel is fearless, at times reckless in the pursuit of solving the mystery of who brutally killed her niece in Miss Rachel's very presence (she has been drugged with morphine), and goes on to kill again, with a gruesome corpse-maiming as a bonus. One of a devoted pair of elderly sister-spinsters, Miss Rachel is the lively sister, the inquisitive sister, the one whom the author favors:

> Even at the age of seventy some traces of what had been Miss Rachel's stunning beauty remained. The hairline—though the hair was white and thinned—was a perfect widow's peak and set her small face off into the shape of a heart. Her eyes regarded Miss Jennifer [her sister] with a dark aliveness, like the movement of water in a little pool which feels the current of the stream. Her hands broke her toast with definite grace. [3]

Miss Rachel will prove to be a delightful amateur sleuth, more than a match for her professional counterpart, the socially maladroit and somewhat bumbling Detective Lieutenant Stephen Mayhew, who has been called to the crime scene in the coastal town of Breakers Beach, California; the informal partnership of Mayhew and Miss Rachel, whom he condescendingly calls "the old lady," gives to *The Cat Saw Murder* an air of uplift, as in romance, or young adult fiction, in which unlikely individuals become bonded in a singular heroic effort.

Indeed, Mayhew behaves less like a police detective than an amateur sleuth whose homicide investigation involves inveigling a naïve young woman to act as a decoy to attract the murderer—with near-fatal results for the young woman. He is something of a cinematic "character"—mercurial, short-tempered, a sexist who "dislikes fat women who wear red nail enamel" [212], a bully who "throws" an annoying suspect into a corridor, and slaps the face of a traumatized young woman. He is so narrow-minded that an attempted suicide by an (obviously innocent) older woman is "tantamount to a confession." [191] Exotically described as having "blue-black hair, bushy black brows and a brown square face as emotionally mobile as a nicely carved wooden mask . . . . [Mayhew] needs only a good nasty growl to complete the picture of a black bear." [47] Eventually Mayhew will feature in two independent Olsen mysteries but he is not nearly so interesting or original a creation as Miss Rachel.

One of the novelties of *The Cat Saw Murder* is that the account of the mystery is jointly narrated, by both Miss Rachel and Mayhew, from some undisclosed future time; while the homicide case is past tense, the narration is present tense, a distinction likely to distract some readers with frequent time shifts, and an obscure perspective, in which Detective Lieutenant Mayhew seems to have acquired an informal personal relationship with Miss Rachel. (It will give little away to inform perplexed readers that Miss Rachel, Mayhew, and Mayhew's young wife Sara are well acquainted, having bonded together in the strife of the homicide investigation of *The Cat Saw Murder*; at some peaceful later time the three are piecing together their individual memories of the case, which Mayhew has called "the damnedest case that he ever met up with" [1]. If the reader keeps this in mind Olsen's frequent time-shifts are not so jarring.)

The cat that saw murder is Miss Rachel's "black satin" Samantha, an elegant creature with "golden eyes" and a "soprano miaow" whose life is endangered since she happens to be an heiress, having inherited a small fortune from Miss Rachel's elder sister. (This is a subplot, not integrated into the larger mystery.) Readers uneasy at the prospect of a preternatural feline acting as a sleuth, or as a companion of a sleuth, should be assured that Olsen's cat is not possessed of extraordinary gifts, and Miss Rachel is not an especially besotted cat-owner: at one point she is uncertain that the cat is even Samantha. (Among much that strains credulity in the novel is Miss Rachel's bizarre notion that a strange cat has been substituted for Samantha, as it is unlikely that Miss Rachel wouldn't immediately take Samantha away after two attempts are made on the cat's life.)

Beyond feisty Miss Rachel, bear-like Detective Lieutenant Mayhew, and Samantha the black satin cat, characters in *The Cat Saw Murder* are but functions of the plot, sketchily presented as physical beings of a repellent sort: among the suspects are Mrs. Turner ("Her bony cheeks were flushed with anger; her big jaw jutted at him . . . she had the beak and eyes of a bird of prey and her neck was wrinkled and grayish as a buzzard" [65]); another unpleasant (female) suspect is "tall, big-jawed" [36], still another has a "stout bosom" [61]. Miss Rachel's niece Lily, whose function in the plot is to get herself murdered in an early chapter, is a slovenly, mammalian figure, clearly repulsive to the author as to fastidious Miss Rachel herself:

> Lily Sticklemann was getting perilously close to forty but she tried desperately, though not cleverly, not to show it. She was a big woman with very white skin, prominent teeth and mountainous masses of pale hair . . . Her figure was not svelte. It bulged, in spite of an excellent corset . . . If Miss Rachel might properly be said to resent anything, she resented the fact that Lily was so obviously and persistently stupid. It was an involved stupidity that attempted to simulate cunning; that loved its little mysteries; that was coy; that was dull. [9]

Significantly, the frowsy Lily is not Miss Rachel's niece by blood, only by marriage: she confesses to Miss Rachel that she has been cheating at bridge, but so ineptly that she has been losing badly, and is now in serious debt; she offers Miss Rachel a most unappetizing liver sausage sandwich from which "she withdrew a long yellow hair . . . and dropped it into the sink, where it lay disconsolately upon soiled dishes." [21] A fount of dismaying manners, Lily is soon murdered with excessive brutality, in the sort of awkward circumstances that would be unlikely in actual life but are characteristic of murders in "locked-room" mysteries in which there are numerous suspects in close proximity, each of whom will have to be interrogated by the sleuth.

The novel's suspenseful scenes establish Miss Rachel as not only a cerebral sleuth but one willing to risk herself physically; to determine who may have murdered her niece, Miss Rachel manages the acrobatic feat of lowering herself into the apartments of suspects in their absence, a practical endeavor described in detail:

> There was such an opening in the ceiling of Miss Rachel's closet, and when she saw it her heart gave a bound of pure sleuthly joy . . . To get into this place without leaving an obvious stack of chairs, or a similar means of mounting, seemed at first quite a problem, and then it became exceptionally easy. Miss Rachel simply pulled each drawer of the built-in chest slightly outward, so that its edge gave a firm foothold, and then upon this arrangement she mounted daringly upward . . . It was as black in the attic as the uppermost depths of Hades might be presumed to be. [161]

Despite her frail physique Miss Rachel is clearly not hobbled by her gender, no more than by her genteel caste and reasonable disposition.

As sheer entertainment, its wild improbabilities overlooked, *The Cat Saw Murder* is deftly executed; Miss Rachel is an engaging, even endearing amateur sleuth, and "black satin" Samantha a highly promising companion for further adventures. D.B. Olsen was a skillful storyteller whose mysteries are due for reexamination, particularly in the light of women's crime fiction and contemporary "cat mysteries." Beneath the surface narrative, fast-moving as a stream, is a deeper sort of tragic wisdom, appropriate for the darkening era of 1939 as for our own:

> Mayhew was disturbed by the evidence of the severed hand more than he liked to admit. He had been in contact with violent death many times, death both planned and accidental and most hideous, but outright, cold-blooded torture was rare to him. He found himself wondering about the hand and about the man who had owned it: what frozen superhuman control or babbling frenzy had possessed him in his hour of agony, and above all, what the purpose of the torture might have been. [133]

What the purpose is not a theme taken up by most mystery/detective fictions, beyond the pragmatic and expedient purpose of creating a mystery to be solved by an impresario sleuth. In *The Cat Saw Murder* it is particularly satisfying that the 35-year-old plainclothes detective Mayhew is aided by teaming up with the 70-year-old Miss Rachel; only by joining forces can these two seemingly antithetical individuals put an end to what would be a succession of brutal murderers by a crude and unrepentant murderer.

—Joyce Carol Oates

THE CAT SAW MURDER

Chapter One:
Lily Is Frightened

Detective Lieutenant Stephen Mayhew has been heard to complain that the murder of the Sticklemann woman was the damnedest case that he ever met up with; that solving the thing was like working a jigsaw puzzle upside down and backward; that it got progressively worse as it dragged along; and that it set him at such insane tasks as pulling hairs out of Miss Rachel's cat and forcing a timid fat woman to scream. He has said, with embellishments, that he hated the thing from beginning to end.

But Miss Rachel from the wisdom of her seventy years thinks otherwise. Though she admits Mayhew's pose of truculence, she thinks that it was a camouflage for happiness. She says that Mayhew's eyes shone and that his step was springy in spite of himself. She has an idea that he ate well during that time, and slept like a top. She is as sure of his grin at finding the pin at the window as she is of putting it there. It was a small and ordinary pin but it set awry the first careful intrigue of the murderer. It must have pleased the lieutenant.

As for Rachel herself: there was shock and grief, and a time when the cold fingers of death had almost clutched her. There was the puzzle of the crime, which allured her mathematical mind as would a problem in algebra. At only one time was she really desperately afraid and that was during the night that she spent in the attic listening to the murderer search her room below. The attic was windy and chill, and so black that Miss Rachel felt disembodied in darkness. Until she sneezed. Then she became very much present in the flesh—a breathless thing all ears to hear if the person below had caught the sneeze and were coming up after her. The wind blew on her through the musty attic; the black pressed like a fist into her eyes; and she didn't dare stir for fear of making a sound.

A minute ticked away. Perhaps two. The whispering rustle below continued as someone went through her belongings. Miss Rachel breathed again.

Then the cat opened her mouth with a small wet sound in the dark and Miss Rachel was struck anew with terror. Was the cat getting ready to yowl—or just to yawn? Miss Rachel waited.

But Lieutenant Mayhew would object that the story shouldn't begin there—not properly. It should start at the beginning, before even he had barged into the picture.

So the scene fades back and back, until . . .

The Misses Murdock were having breakfast.

In the bleak spaciousness of their white breakfast room the little table looked woefully astray, as though it had wandered out of a kitchenette apartment somewhere and didn't know how to get back. The Misses Murdock themselves seemed somewhat lost. They were tiny and gray and very old; two quaint figures in gingham, wrapped in woolen shawls against the cold of the large unheated house and perched upon their chairs at the little table, munching their toast and sipping milk.

Miss Jennifer gazed with her usual mild reproach at the towering white walls, and through the doorway into the vastness of the kitchen beyond, and shivered. The shiver was also usual, as were the words which followed:

"We ought to give up this place, Rachel. Rent it out to a big family—lease it to someone. It's big enough for forty people and much too big for just the two of us." She pulled the shawl up to cover a transparent blue-veined ear. "Cold in the mornings too. If we had a small place we might afford to keep it warm."

Miss Rachel, sitting opposite her, showed neither surprise nor worry at this complaint. She gave no immediate answer save the lifting of white brows above her dark and brilliant eyes. Even at the age of seventy some traces of what had been Miss Rachel's stunning beauty remained. The hairline—though the hair was white and thinned—was a perfect widow's peak and set her small face off into the shape of a heart. Her eyes regarded Miss Jennifer with a dark aliveness, like the movement of water in a little pool which feels the current of the stream. Her hands broke her toast with definite grace.

Miss Jennifer did not much resemble her sister. She was a plain elderly woman, as she had been a plain girl, and she held no truck with facial preparations. She looked neglected.

Miss Rachel spoke a single meditative reminder. "Our father built this house, Jennifer."

Miss Jennifer stared irritably at her milk. "I know. So we stay. Even though we freeze, we stay. Keeping up the Murdock tradition. If it were only possible to break up a tradition and stick it into the stove and get heat out of it—that would make me happy."

Miss Rachel seemed pained. "It's been home for more than forty years, Jennifer. No other place would ever seem right to us after all that time. You yourself would balk at moving when the time came. I know you would."

Jennifer softened grudgingly, still unhappy. "So I would, I guess. Come to think of it, I can't really picture us ever living anywhere else. We're used to this old house. A modern place with a lot of mechanical contraptions would probably frighten us to death. But lately I've felt the cold so badly. It's like a barn in here. My feet are frozen."

It was then that the telephone rang. The harsh jangle was caught up and multiplied by the big echoing rooms so that its summons burst upon the Misses Murdock like a towerful of bells. Miss Jennifer choked on her milk.

There was a moment of watchful questioning silence. Then Miss Rachel touched her lips with the tiny blue linen napkin and got to her feet. "I'll go," she said calmly, as though to have the telephone ring before eight o'clock in the morning were the most ordinary thing in the world.

Jennifer was looking gradually more and more alarmed. "Who could it be at this hour? Not the grocer, surely."

"I'll soon know," Miss Rachel said quietly, and went out.

Miss Jennifer sat straight and still until her sister returned, not eating but staring with worried annoyance at the wall and picking up toast crumbs with the tips of her fingers.

Miss Rachel came back as unhurriedly as she had gone. "It was Lily," she said in reply to the question that Jennifer looked at her. "She asked me to come to see her at that place where she's living. Today."

Miss Jennifer munched toast with her teeth and the telephone message with her mind, assimilating both gradually. "Whatever for?" she wondered.

"She didn't say," that lady replied coolly.

Miss Jennifer's face betrayed the beginnings of amazement. "She wants you to come all the way down to Breakers Beach to see her—and didn't say why? The woman's much stupider than I thought, to expect you to do that. All that long trip down there and back . . ."

"She wanted me to stay with her for a few days." Miss Rachel meditated on the view from the window.

"Now, that's more odd yet! Stay with her? She's never asked us before." The thoughtful look in Miss Rachel's eye caught Jennifer's attention. "You wouldn't dream of going . . .?"

Miss Rachel seemed to watch the city stirring to life at the foot of their steep hill. There was a moment of stillness in the breakfast room. Then: "I'm tempted to do it," Miss Rachel admitted.

Jennifer almost shook with alarm. "Rachel! To *stay* at Breakers Beach? Why, that wet sea air wouldn't be good for you! You might get pneumonia, or asthma, or whatever you catch on beaches. Oh, you mustn't!"

"Nonsense!" Miss Rachel put in calmly. "I need to get out, to get away from here for a while. You yourself were suggesting a change just a few minutes ago. Now weren't you?"

Miss Jennifer shook her gray head. "Not that kind of change. Just a short move, I meant. Not all the way down to the——"

Her sister cut her off again. "Don't be a goose. Breakers Beach is just an hour from Los Angeles on the electric train. It isn't as if Lily were living in Timbuctoo, or Naples—though goodness knows I almost wish she were. Just the names of those places . . . However, it sounded interesting—going to the beach, I mean. You and I never go anywhere any more. Do you realize that, Jennifer?"

Miss Jennifer put her lips together firmly and looked reproof at her sister. "At our age we shouldn't expect to. We're *elderly,* Rachel. We need quiet and rest. I'm content not to go gallivanting around the country. I know what's best."

"Is it best?" Miss Rachel's white brows rose like a child's. "Or doesn't it seem more like—like dying, to just sit waiting for the end?"

Miss Jennifer hmmmph'd through her nose. "I'm not waiting for the end, as you put it. I'm comfortable, or I would be if this house were warmer, and I know it's sensible to stay at home. If you're getting restless again by all means take a trip to the beach. I will say this—it probably won't be as harmful as that spell of movie-going you had all this winter. Murder mysteries!"

Miss Rachel blushed a little. "They were interesting," she defended faintly.

"They must have been! After you'd seen that third one—what was it now, *The Purple Horror?*—you were as jumpy as the cat. Well, go to the beach and find out what Lily wants. It's money, I'll wager. Isn't it always?"

At this moment a soprano miaow sounded from the kitchen and a black satin cat walked through the door. She regarded the Misses Murdock with reproachful golden eyes and switched a plumy tail, the gift of her Persian father, in mild annoyance.

Miss Rachel looked at the cat with amusement. "She isn't jumpy, no more than I was. She's a little angry because she wants breakfast."

"*You* were jumpy," Miss Jennifer insisted, getting up to pour milk into the cat's saucer. "Here, Samantha. Drink your breakfast."

Samantha put a pink tongue into the milk. Miss Rachel, still watching her, spoke in a tone elaborately casual. "You know, of course, that I'll have to take Samantha with me."

Jennifer spun around, still holding the milk bottle. "Take the cat? *The cat!* Are you all right, Rachel?"

Rachel arranged her delicate face to indicate extreme sanity. "Now don't be so annoyed. Nor so forgetful, either. You know Samantha has to be with me. You'll remember, if you put your mind to it, how she refused to eat a bite when I was in the hospital last year. When I got home she was simply skin and bones. She's dreadfully attached to me and she will have to go to the beach."

"You're going to take her?"

"Yes, indeed."

Miss Jennifer sighed. "You're so stubborn, Rachel. What on earth would you carry her in?"

"There's that old picnic basket. In the hall closet, isn't it? Put some cloth in the bottom of it—your old white petticoat, for instance. Get that, Jennifer."

Miss Jennifer opened her angular mouth sadly. "I still don't think—" she mourned.

"I'm going to pack a few things. Not many. I'll probably only be there a few days." Miss Rachel stood up from her chair again, slim but not bony in her gingham, and smoothed a stray lock of white that had dropped from the neatness of her crown. "Just a very few days," she comforted Miss Jennifer. She had no way of knowing then about the pin and the drafty attic, nor even about Lieutenant Mayhew. But she was starting on her way toward all of them.

She went upstairs to her bedroom and took her old-fashioned valise out of the far corner of a closet. Into it went a silver-backed comb and brush, a jar of facial cream, a tiny box of powder. Her nightgown, smelling delicately of lavender, came out of a chest of drawers in the corner. After some meditation upon the failings of even the best of beach rooming-houses, two sheets and a pillowcase, also smelling of lavender, followed the gown. A wrapper went in, a pair of bedroom slippers, an extra dress, and other articles which Miss Rachel considered necessary.

She reviewed the row of dresses that hung upon her rack in the closet and elected to wear her gray taffeta, the one with the jacket. She wasn't consciously thinking of dresses, however. She was mentally reviewing Lily's rather startling message over the telephone.

"Come down here, Auntie. Please," Lily's hoarse voice had begged. "I'm in a sort of a mess and I need advice badly." That had been the main part of it.

Lily wasn't the only one who awaited Miss Rachel's coming. The pin and the attic and murder were waiting also, in their appointed place and time. As well as that big brown-faced man, Lieutenant Mayhew. He was haggling information out of a pickpocket that morning and probably, if he'd been asked, would have said that he was fairly happy. Later, when the Sticklemann case got under way, he was heard to declare himself as going completely crazy.

But Miss Rachel thinks now that he enjoyed it.

Lily Sticklemann was getting perilously close to forty but she tried desperately, though not cleverly, not to show it. She was a big woman with very white skin, prominent teeth and mountainous masses of pale hair which she wore in a long bob. It was a style of hair-dressing which she had noticed as being very becoming to young women. It was not becoming to Lily. It emphasized the droop of her cheekline and the smallness of her light blue eyes. And her figure was not svelte. It bulged, in spite of an excellent corset. It wore an iron-ribbed look about the waist. But Lily was undismayed.

She stood impatient in the interurban depot at Breakers Beach, happily unconscious that she was large or looking middle-aged. She saw the eye of a naval chief petty officer stray her way. She debated whether to wink at him, thought better of it and simply smiled. The chief petty officer looked away in a hurry.

A smug expression overshadowed the other things in her face without obliterating them: worry and anxiety and a wavering resolve. Behind her smile, still turned on in spite of the chief petty officer's coldness, Lily was making up her mind to something. The moment that Miss Rachel Murdock should see her, that calm old lady would know it.

If Miss Rachel might properly be said to resent anything, she resented the fact that Lily was so obviously and persistently stupid. It was an involved stupidity that attempted to simulate cunning; that loved its little mysteries; that was coy; that was dull. It had never, to Lily's open amazement, even taken either of the Misses Murdock by surprise. It had caused them, in the privacy of their home, to discuss freely the shortcomings of their niece.

Such discussion did not weigh upon them with any self-reproach. Lily was not truly their niece by blood. She was the adopted daughter of their dead brother Philip, a stray out of the world of humanity whom Rachel and Jennifer had loved wholeheartedly as a child and were faintly ashamed of as a woman.

Miss Rachel sighed within herself as she alighted from the interurban train and saw Lily standing in the station. The long untidy bob was a new coiffure and Miss Rachel recognized it at once as being infinitely worse than the boyish shingle which had preceded it. The tangled mass of hair seemed to symbolize

Lily's tangled life: her ineffectual romances, her fads, her changing ways.

Miss Rachel was reminded, as she always was on seeing Lily, of Lily's marriage some ten years before. Lily had come, arch and playful and mysterious, to visit them. She had been in her thirties then, a not unhandsome woman though already leaning to stoutness. After her had trailed a man whom she coyly introduced as her husband—a lank sullen-faced man with reddish hair and an ungainly step. Mr. Sticklemann had been vague and not given to friendly overtures to elderly spinsters. It was Lily who offered the invitation for them to make a return visit.

Miss Rachel and Miss Jennifer had duly called a week later, being conscious of what they owed to Philip's memory.

Behind the clutter and confusion of a run-down electric repair shop, they had found Lily in a small apartment. The electric shop was Mr. Sticklemann's and his sister's. Lily made a self-conscious remark about refinancing the place. Mr. Sticklemann grunted, watching Miss Rachel. Conversation had petered out. Sometime during the latter time of their call a face had looked briefly in upon them from the direction of the shop up front. It had been an angular dark face topped by an atrocious black bonnet. The face had not smiled; it had regarded them with its sharp malicious eyes and had gone away. "That's Anne," Lily had hurried to say. "She's been out, I think. There's so many things—ah, *we* I mean—need, and so . . ." Lily's laugh had been as nervous as her fat white hands, fumbling a handkerchief. "Anne likes to shop," she finished, not looking at her aunts.

Miss Rachel had known in that moment how Mr. Sticklemann and his sister Anne must be devouring Lily's money. It had left a sense of mental nausea in her mind.

Lily had been wildly, foolishly proud of her marriage for some months. Then had come hints of rupture, of quarrels with Anne about money, and at last an admission that Mr. Sticklemann and his ever-present sister were gone. There was indeed a question as to Mr. Sticklemann's right to have married Lily at all, but she hadn't known of that, of course, until the last. Then the knowledge that she had lived, unknowing, without legal wedlock with Mr. Sticklemann, and Mr. Sticklemann's use of the fact, had cost her money.

Mr. Sticklemann had died a year later, almost to the day. Miss Rachel sensed from Lily's lifted spirits that a steady drain upon her purse was done.

Since then, Lily had had a series of beaux of startling variety. Fat, thin, poor or well off—there had been dozens of them. Only of late there queerly had been no news of new romances.

Miss Rachel stepped through the depot door, her basket on her arm.

Lily turned on what she believed to be charm. She was bright; she was enthusiastic. She caught her small wriggling aunt and kissed her before everyone. How were her darlings? So good of one of them to come down to see their Lily girl! Looking so well too. Such a *dear* little jacket! Uuuuuuuh—the basket—lunch? *No?* Could she peek just an ittsey-bittsey bit? Oooooo! *The cat!* Dear old thing—still keeping well?

"Very well," Miss Rachel assured her, sighing. Miss Rachel detested public fuss.

Lily petted her again and went off on a wake of strong perfume and the stale odor of Turkish cigarettes to find a porter. Miss Rachel smoothed a ruffled gray taffeta shoulder and watched her go. Lily was plainly worried about something, as her call had indicated—but not too worried—and she was deciding whether to settle it with Miss Rachel's help or in her own way. If the latter, it would be a haphazard way with much lost motion and dull pretense. Miss Rachel wondered what was up.

Absently she felt of the catch on the basket. It was secure, and the vibration of a strong contented purring caressed her finger tips as she touched it.

Lieutenant Mayhew has wished that he might have had the gift of second sight at this point. He maintains that he would have sent Miss Rachel straight back home: cat, baggage and all. Today, he thinks, he could have had the pleasure of knowing that two thoroughly disagreeable people were in prison. Cruel and ruthless people who deserved much worse than they got.

Miss Rachel made him let them go.

Chapter Two:
Poisoned Meat

Miss Rachel, thinking not of murder, was a quaint and attractive picture that drew the eye of more than one in the waiting room. Her heart-shaped face under its widow's peak of snow was serene; her gaze was mobile and intelligent; her posture erect. She abhorred the hats that most elderly women affected—the pill boxes and poke bonnets and turbans too high on their scant hair—so that she herself wore something entirely different. Her hats were of no particular style. They sat well down on her ears; they were snug; and their brims flared narrowly just above the hairline to frame her face. She wore taffeta a great deal because she liked its rich rustle and not because it was considered proper for old ladies. Her shoes were narrow and had style. She might have been anybody's grandmother, for she had the mellow placid look that so many grandmothers have—and several people in the station seemed to be wishing that somehow she were theirs.

Lily came back smoking. Her smile had faded into a look of frank speculation. A porter followed her. He found Miss

Rachel's valise in the pile at the baggage room and called them a cab.

The cab driver hummed briskly, he flung the car into space with a roar and things went past the window with some speed. They passed a motor officer drowsing at a corner. Miss Rachel thinks he opened one eye at them. The day was very warm.

Seacliff Boulevard runs the length of the bluff above the beach. There is a narrow park on its seaward side, then a sheer drop to the Strand with its concessions and gaudy amusements, and then the Pacific. Miss Rachel found herself looking out upon a flat blue brilliance that hurt the eyes.

There were buildings set down below the bluff and facing the beach—rows of rooming houses and concessions and motion-picture palaces and little restaurants that opened onto the cement promenade with the beach beyond. Miss Rachel did not, however, connect any of these places with herself or with her niece until Lily leaned forward and told the driver to turn down toward the beach at the next corner.

The man nodded scornfully without looking around, turned his projectile on two screaming wheels, dived, and braked to a shuddering halt at the edge of the cement walk that edged the beach. Miss Rachel reswallowed her heart. She still thinks that she knows what a test pilot feels like.

"I'm living right on the Strand this season. It's so exciting!" Lily babbled into her ear. She widened her little eyes. "Right in the middle of everything here—people going by all night—and you can hear every wave that breaks on the beach! It's the real thing, Auntie!"

"A bit noisy, isn't it?" Miss Rachel wondered, recovering and keeping her eyes on a small boy beating a drum. What would be his little sister was blowing something that looked much like a fife. They tramped back and forth with military precision, bumping into people but giving an impression of the Spirit of '76.

"Oh, a little, I guess," Lily deprecated. "But, of course, we can't have everything, and I always do say it's the beach you come down here for. So why not be right on it? The people are interesting too. And oodles of them! Hear the waves? See them out there?" Lily chuckled round her cigarette and helped Miss Rachel to alight. She paid off the driver with a dribble of silver. "Never mind. I can manage the bag. It's only a few steps down the walk."

They picked their way through strollers in street clothes and past active groups of bathers going and coming from the beach. Samantha miaowed once when a fat man jostled her basket.

"Beg pardon, madam," the fat man bowed.

Miss Rachel was mutely thankful that the cat was shut in. If she had been able, Samantha would have gouged him.

"Here it is, darling! Not fancy at all, I'm afraid. But comfortable. Come right up here . . ."

Miss Rachel stopped; she stood perfectly still, so that Lily on the steps turned round to see what was keeping her. The mouth that held the cigarette was tight, but Lily made it smile. "Surprised? I said that it wasn't fancy."

Miss Rachel put out a little foot to take one slow step. "It—it's so different, Lily. Somehow—I remember your last place."

"Oh, that! Away out in the sticks."

"But it was nice. Lily—it isn't that anything's gone wrong about your money? What Philip left in trust for you? You still get an income from that, don't you?"

"That measly bit? Yes, I get it. But don't judge this place by its looks. Rents are higher right here on the water. This place costs me as much as any of them did. Come on in. It won't bite."

It might not bite, Miss Rachel thought, mounting the warped steps, but it looked remarkably ready to fall in upon its tenants. For years the wood had had no contact with paint, and sea winds and fogs had weathered it colorless. The backbone of the roof had an oddly broken look. The window screens sagged outward and were red with rust.

There was but one story to it, and a hall ran its length down the middle of the house.

From the bright sunlight of the beach they stepped into musty gloom. Miss Rachel put out an exploring hand.

"It is dark in here," Lily was admitting. "They ought to keep the lights on all day. Watch your step here! There's a worn place in the carpet that will trip you if you aren't careful. I nearly broke my neck here last week. Didn't really hurt me any though," she hastened to add.

They went past several doors, darker rectangles in the half-light of the hall. One of them was opened a crack. Against the darkness of the wood Miss Rachel clearly saw the ghostly paleness of four fingers. Someone was standing there, staying quite still behind the door until they went past. Not hiding, exactly. The hand in view showed that they didn't care whether their presence were known or not. They waited in an empty hall.

Miss Rachel walked a bit faster. Lily's corseted bulk had halted up ahead and there was a rattle of a key in a lock. A widening crack of light shone into the hall. Lily gestured Miss Rachel in ahead of her.

"This is the room I got for you, Auntie. It's like the rest of the house, not elaborate or anything fancy. But I think you'll find it comfortable. My room is right next door, toward the back. On the other side of you is Mr. Leinster. He's young but he's very quiet. I don't know the people across the hall—they came just yesterday. A girl with what seems to be her mother. They're quiet too. Were last night, at any rate. All you'll hear during the night is the sound of the waves, with maybe snatches of the merry-go-round music from the other end of the Strand."

"Oh, this will be fine, Lily. I'm sure that I'll enjoy my visit here. When you called this morning——" She watched Lily's face to see if it betrayed any of the alarm that the woman had expressed in her message. It didn't. Lily was being quite casual in lighting another cigarette. "When you called and asked me to come down, the idea really appealed to me. Jennifer thought I shouldn't come . . ."

"Dear Aunt Jennifer!" Much feeling was got into the three words.

"But it seemed a good chance to get away for a bit. We stay too close at home lately, so I came. Besides—you mentioned some trouble."

"Did I?" Lily opened her blue eyes as widely as possible. "Over the telephone? Hmmmmm . . . let's see. Oh, yes. That! I just remembered." She made a small chuckling sound deep in her throat. "Did I sound dramatic? I was a little—well, *worried*. You know how little things can upset you sometimes; mountains out of molehills, I guess you'd call it. It wasn't much. I'm sorry if I frightened you, Auntie, or made you think anything serious was wrong. You wanted to come down anyway, didn't you? I mean, just to visit?"

"Oh, yes. Yes." Miss Rachel set about arranging the things from her bag. Lily wasn't telling then. Whatever the mess was she was keeping it down, keeping it hidden. She loved her little mysteries until they exploded on her, which they usually did. Then it was "Wolf! Wolf!" and a great call for help. Lily had never heard of the boy who kept sheep and wore out the patience of his would-be rescuers.

Miss Rachel laid out her silver toilet set on the dresser, trying not to notice the thick layer of dust that already occupied that article. When she looked up, the distortion of her own image in the cracked glass startled her. She jumped.

Lily was watching the smoke from her cigarette with elaborate interest. She began speaking almost at once of the band concerts on the beach. "Every night except Mondays," she explained, "and they have really marvelous music. Mr. Malloy—he lives here too; a wonderful man!—he really taught me to enjoy the concerts. You know me. Not much for such stuff, though I've always admired good jazz. But after Mr. Malloy talked to me about them and we listened together—maybe it was the moonlight." She laughed on an oddly girlish note that brought Miss Rachel round with instant attention. There was a pink blush on Lily's cheek; her mouth was coy. Miss Rachel knew the symptoms of old. She went back to her unpacking.

"Mr. Malloy loves moonlight. He makes it seem romantic too. Knows poetry—all that stuff. He's educated. You'll like him."

"I'm going to meet him? Tonight?"

A kind of anxiety tempered the girlish blush. "Oh, you'll meet him. I want you to very much. He's really nice, not like some of the others I've introduced to you and Aunt Jennifer. Some of them weren't so hot, come to think of it. Though Mr. Malloy says not to brood on the past, ever!"

"I suppose he's at work now?"

"No. He's away. Somewhere—I don't just—" A little frown, much smoke. "But he'll be back. I know he will. Then you'll get to see him."

Miss Rachel obliged by looking mildly eager. "He's very nice, you say? Hmmmm. What does he do?"

"For a living? Oh, he—he works. Just different things. You know how it is now. He has been at some of the shops on the Strand. He used to be an actor; gives him an air, you know."

"Older than you are?"

"Some. Fifty-three, I think. Gray hair, and he's tall. You wouldn't notice his age. He's awfully good-looking. Still has his profile. I have a picture of him in my apartment. Leave your things and I'll show it to you."

They went into Lily's room next door. It was in total disorder. Lily without maid service was something to dream about.

There was clothing everywhere—limp and soiled, the most of it. The bed, unlike the one in Miss Rachel's room, was of the variety that belongs properly turned up into a wall cubicle during the day and allows the room the appearance of a parlor. The bed was still down, with its covers a bagged roll in the middle. There was a chair beside the bed. On it was an old cake carton with crumbs in it and an empty glass with milk rings down the inside surface.

It was the curtains at the window which most attracted Miss Rachel's disapproval. They had been cheap stuff to begin with; now they were soiled and old and in one of them was a great triangular tear that gaped, showing the faded wallpaper below the sill. Miss Rachel looked quickly at her niece. Lily was rummaging through a mountainous drawerful for Mr. Malloy's photograph. Miss Rachel took a pin from behind the lapel of her taffeta jacket and went to the curtain to fix it.

Dust rose into her nostrils in a little stinging cloud. The material was rotted with age and refused to hold the pin. Miss Rachel, working quickly lest Lily be annoyed, thrust the pin into the wooden sill of the window. It held in the wood. The curtain seemed whole again.

She looked beyond at the pane. The window was closed. It had been closed for so long a time that a faint drift of cobweb showed against the dirty glass.

Lily was holding out the picture of Mr. Malloy. Miss Rachel saw the head and shoulders of a man obviously near fifty, with gray hair, much nose and chin and a supercilious stare.

"Good-looking, isn't he, Auntie?"

Miss Rachel chose a more formal term. "Handsome. Yes, he is."

"I wish he were here, so that you could meet him. You'd realize how fascinating he can be."

"I'm sorry he isn't here. Perhaps he'll be back before I leave. Do you think that he might?"

Again the little frown bunched Lily's brow. "I wish I knew. It seems odd, his going away like he did without telling me. Though no doubt he had a perfectly good reason. However, this isn't getting us our lunch."

She opened a door on the far side of the room that led into a cubbyhole kitchenette. "I've got stuff for sandwiches. Come on in."

Miss Rachel followed her into the small dreary room. "It seems a bit stuffy in here, don't you think? Could we—could we open a window?"

Lily glanced at the small spotted pane of glass above the sink and laughed brightly. "That window's absolutely a false alarm—never been able to get it open. See?" She tried it strongly with her fat white arms without getting it to budge. "I guess they put it here to help people develop their muscles."

Lily began buttering slices of bread and spreading them with liver sausage. She hummed a tune. Once she withdrew a long yellow hair from a sandwich and dropped it into the sink, where it lay disconsolately upon soiled dishes. Miss Rachel put out a feeler: "If anything's worrying you, Lily, I'd like to know. In your telephone call——"

Lily put on an expression of bewildered innocence. "What's that, Auntie? The telephone call? Oh, you mustn't keep fretting about that! Does it still worry you?"

"A little," Miss Rachel admitted. "You sounded—afraid."

Lily stopped humming. Miss Rachel sensed her concentration, her careful choice of words. "Well, there is one little thing. Nothing awfully important. I've about decided that I can take care of it." Miss Rachel had already realized this last. "It's just—just a little money matter. That's all."

The thing was beginning to sound familiar. Miss Rachel trod gently. "Some money that you owe someone? Is that it?"

Lily shoved a plate of sandwiches on the table and indicated a chair for her aunt. Her face was blank. "Yes. It's money I owe."

Miss Rachel looked intently at her two slices of bread with the gray greasy filling bulging out between. "Very much money?" she asked.

Lily munched her sandwich and obviously considered whether to tell the truth or lie about it. Then: "About a thousand," she admitted.

There was a time of silence. "That's almost as much as you get in a year, isn't it?"

"Just about."

"Were you—were you wanting me to help you, Lily?"

"I had a wild idea about it this morning. That's when I called you. My memory must be playing tricks on me. I didn't remember till later that your money's in trust the same as mine is."

Miss Rachel, sifting wheat from chaff, decided that this last wasn't quite the truth. Lily's memory wasn't that poor—it had had too many reminders on the same point in the past. "Yes, it's in trust," Miss Rachel said carefully, as though the subject were new. "I put it there myself some years back. You see, Jennifer and I made very poor investments with the money Father left us. Philip put his into his business—you get the benefit of that, Lily. But Agatha was the only one of us who ran her inheritance up into real money. She was very shrewd that way."

Lily laughed roughly and bitterly. "And Samantha gets the benefit of *that!*"

Miss Rachel put out a gentle hand. "Try not to feel resentful, Lily. Remember, it was Agatha's money. She got quite—quite strange, near the end. She mistrusted everybody. She told us many times every day that the cat was her only friend, and she lavished all the affection of her poor soul upon the animal. It seems cruel, to you, to need money, and have it belonging to a cat. But there's nothing we can do but wait. It doesn't matter to Jennifer or me any more. We have enough for our needs."

"You should! You get all the income from what Agatha left!"

"No. Not all. Just enough to pay for Samantha's care. Be patient, Lily."

Lily breathed hard through her nose and gave her aunt a long look. There was tired anxiety in that look, and a growing resolve. "It doesn't count anyhow," she said. "I'll get along."

Before she prepared for bed Miss Rachel let Samantha out into the back yard for a little while.

There was no moon. In the narrow yard under the shadow of the bluff the dark was like velvet. A faint clatter echoed from the direction of the Strand—the chatter of guns in the shooting galleries, the faded shout of ticket sellers at the concessions, the merry-go-round's calliope. The rustle of the surf washed over all of it. Miss Rachel smelled the cool sea air and found it good.

A little breeze came up; it veered about, bringing with it the odor of fried fish from the restaurant next door where she and Lily had had dinner. And then—something else! Miss Rachel stiffened, there on the small back porch. She turned her head, drawing the air strongly into her lungs. A look of fright came into her face. She caught at her heart where it seemed to go pounding up into her throat.

She had trouble then making her voice work. "Here, kitty, kitty!" She stooped, holding out her hands.

The cat did not come at once. For a long moment Miss Rachel stood there in her awkward position, her limbs trembling as if in sudden cold.

Then Samantha came, emerging out of the night. Her eyes drifted goldenly up the steps as if they were alone, then the light from behind Miss Rachel caught the glisten of her fur. She rubbed Miss Rachel's wrist with a hard little ear. Miss Rachel took her into the hall and held her up. Between the cat's jaws hung a bit of red—raw meat, quite fresh—and it had been well slashed with a knife.

Miss Rachel pried apart the reluctant jaws. She put the cat down and turned the piece of meat to the light. The slashed places gaped, and in their depths showed the reflected glitter of some undissolved crystalline stuff.

Miss Rachel went to her room, the cat following at her heels as she liked to do. Miss Rachel put Samantha into her basket. The meat was a puzzler. At last she emptied her jar of facial cream, forcing its contents down the drain of her washbasin. She put the meat into the jar, screwed the lid on too tightly for any hungry animal to get it off and dropped it through the window to the sand.

Lieutenant Mayhew has complained that he should have been called in at this stage of the game; that it was already shaping up pretty ominously, with possibilities sticking out all over it. He thinks that he might have done something—he isn't sure what. But he is certain that his detective's nose would have smelled a rat.

Miss Rachel objects that you can't smell a rat that was *almost* killed, and that it wasn't a rat anyway, but a cat. She has pointed out, too, that the one thing out of the whole mess that they understood from the beginning was why the cat was given the poisoned meat.

They knew the motive for this minor crime all along, and it helped the rest of the case not a bit.

Chapter Three:
MISS RACHEL RECEIVES A LETTER

MISS RACHEL was conscious, in that first moment of wakening, of several things: of the moonlight like a white hand pressed against her window, of the somber ticking of her little clock, of the wet boom of the surf, of her own heart beating fast and hard. And also—*that other.* She looked about the dimness of her narrow room. There was no one in it but herself.

It had been outside her door then, that scratching, clawing sound. Fingernails, she knew somehow, scrabbling at the lower edge of her door from the hall.

"Who's there?" she called into the night. There was no answer and the scrabbling sound suddenly stopped. Her little clock ticked; the surf thundered. A minute went by in moonlight.

Miss Rachel sat up and the cold caressed her. She put out a foot, listening. It was a while before her courage sufficed to get her to the door, to get the door unlocked and to peep through.

It was Lily, lying in the hall upon her face. She was plainly out of her corsets, her body loose inside the dingy wrapper and the disarray of her hair hiding her features.

She was, however, not dead. Even as Miss Rachel bent down

to touch her, she moaned and stirred. Miss Rachel heard her own voice echoing faintly down the dim-lit empty hall. She was hoarse with a kind of tight drying of her throat, and the words shook. "Lily! Lily! Get up!" She caught at the wrapper but Lily rolled suddenly, pulling the fabric from her fingers. "Lily—answer! Are you hurt?"

Suddenly there were other people in the hall. They came ghostily from either direction, the draft blowing their night robes. The first to reach them was a tall middle-aged woman whose gauntness showed up strongly against the feeble yellow of the light at the end of the hall. She bent close to Lily, staring hard. For a panicky moment Miss Rachel had the illusion that she knew this woman's name, that she could speak it if she would. It was the fright she'd had about Lily of course. When the gaunt woman turned her eyes upward, and Miss Rachel read the anger and scorn in them, the illusion faded.

"What's the disturbance here? What's happened to Mrs. Sticklemann that she's lying on the floor?"

Lily moaned an unintelligible reply.

"I'm the landlady here. I can't have things like this going on. This is a respectable house." She bent her gaze down again and once more Miss Rachel felt the odd little urge to call her something, some name almost forgotten. But she knew this woman's name and there was nothing familiar in it. Lily had told her the landlady's name. This then was Mrs. Turner.

At that moment someone quite young, with a small oval face and long hair like a skein of yellow silk, bent down beside Miss Rachel. She was so clean and shining, and the odor of her was so faintly fragrant, like flowers with dew on them, that Miss Rachel—even in the midst of her fright and perplexity about Lily—had to notice the girl. There was another woman with her, just stepping into the hall from the doorway opposite Miss Rachel's. She was an older woman; her eyes were wide and yet bitter, and her hair was gray. The girl helped Miss Rachel turn Lily, and so saw her face. She stood up at once and said something to the older woman in a low tone.

They both drew away and the girl looked as if she had touched something she would rather not have. But when she saw Miss Rachel's frail arms vainly working against the looseness of Lily's bulk she bent down again and helped to lift her.

Two others, a man and a woman, came from the front part of the building, but they stayed back and did not help. Mrs. Turner lent a grudging hand. "If it's a fit," she warned harshly, "take care that she doesn't bite you. They'll do it."

They got Lily into her bed and everyone left the room except Miss Rachel. Lily was not totally unconscious—her eyes roved the room, which had the light on when they entered it. She seemed lax and stupid. A red abrasion showed plainly on her chin, as though she had been struck a glancing blow by a hard fist. A series of marks darkened in the flesh of her throat and became fingerprints. Her breathing filled the room.

There was no attempt to talk for a long while. Miss Rachel watched the window, The moonlight faded and changed, and things outside began to show softly in the gray of dawn. Some billows of fog went by on a morning breeze. A light flashed on in the back window of the restaurant next door and a faint clatter of pots rang out. Miss Rachel could smell coffee being made.

She looked at Lily after it had become quite light in the room and found the big woman's eyes upon her. Miss Rachel leaned from her chair to touch the blankets gently. "Are you feeling better?"

Lily's look was stony. "I'm all right."

"Can't you tell me what happened? I'd like to know."

"I can't tell you."

Miss Rachel sat back, rebuffed. "I don't mean to be prying, Lily. I only wanted to help you, if I could."

"You can't help. Nobody could. I'm in it up to my neck."

Miss Rachel leaned forward again, just a little. "You can't be sure. There might be something that I could do. Let me try." Lily looked at the ceiling and did not answer. "You mustn't think that I want to—to interfere with your affairs. I don't, really. If it's something you can handle alone, well and good. But if it isn't . . . You see, Lily, I can never quite forget that you were Philip's little girl. None of the rest of us ever had any children . . . . Once you fell down the stairs at our house. I picked you up and bandaged your knee. Do you remember?"

There was still no answer. Lily looked away toward the window, and Miss Rachel caught the reflected glitter of tears.

"It might help some just to talk it over. It looks as if someone has—has attacked you. Does it have anything to do with the debt you owe—the one you spoke about?"

Lily jerked her head once in mute assent.

Miss Rachel went on very carefully. "And about your living here in this odd place. It's so different from the other places where you've lived. I could understand your being here as a makeshift, till you found something better. It's only a makeshift house. . . . Are you trying to save money to pay off your debt?"

She had been careful, but she knew by Lily's expression that she had blundered. The woman turned over at once; she was defensive, and her eyes were angry. "I like it here," she flung out. "And that's why I'm living here—because I do like it. It has nothing to do with the debt I owe. Nothing. So forget it."

Miss Rachel apologized. She felt that she had overstepped

some invisible bounds that she should have regarded. "I only wondered," she murmured. "Please don't be angry."

Lily softened and reached for Miss Rachel's fragile hand. "I'm not angry, Auntie. I'm sorry if I sounded cross. It's just that sometimes you remind me of my father. In the way you look at things, I mean. He was always talking about good taste and distinction—stuff like that. He wouldn't have liked this house. You know he wouldn't. But I know when I'm happiest. I was—*am,* I mean, happy here. And I'm going to stay. It's awkward just now because these people I owe the money to live here also. But I'll pay them off. And I won't move."

Miss Rachel tightened an already anxious grip. "But you're in danger here. You mustn't stay! Even if it's—pleasant here, you mustn't. There's *danger.* I feel it! Please come away."

But Lily shook her head. "No, Auntie. I can't go. There's a special reason why I must stay. I can't explain; but I can't leave, either."

"Then at least we must see about raising some money. I'll go back to the city today. I didn't realize that they were so—so eager . . ." It seemed an inadequate word with which to describe the feelings of Lily's creditors, but Miss Rachel was too tired to think of another.

Lily was shaking her head again, her hair making a limp montonous movement on the pillow. "No. Don't do anything. There's nothing you could do to help."

"I might be able to get a thousand dollars."

Lily looked up with her face stark. "It isn't a thousand any more, Auntie. They—they want two thousand now."

Miss Rachel didn't attempt to answer that one. There didn't seem to be much that she could say. Her thoughts went sick on her; she sensed that this time Lily's trouble was much deeper, more sinister, than her other affairs. Lily had been attacked either in her room or in the hall, and she had been choked almost to insensibility. Her debt had doubled itself sometime during the hours that Miss Rachel had slept. It was very confusing, and it was frightening.

The cold crept down Miss Rachel's back as she sat by Lily's bed. She remembered with sudden nostalgia that today was the day for the cleaning woman at home, and that Jennifer, capped and aproned, would be meeting Mrs. Brannigan at the door of their big house in a little while. She wished herself there, instead of in this stuffy forbidding room with Lily staring at the ceiling through her tears.

She had an urge to go home. But Lily had been Philip's little girl in those lost years when Miss Rachel was young, and that same little girl—somehow mysteriously transformed into a gross woman—needed help now. She looked through Lily's eyes; she pleaded with Lily's voice. Miss Rachel became lost in reverie, remembering what had been.

It was Lily who roused her from her chilled remoteness. Her hand, touching Miss Rachel's, startled because it was so cold. "Go back to bed, Auntie, and finish your sleep. Everything will be all right. Run along."

Miss Rachel rose, feeling stiffness and tiredness echo along her bones. Lily did not turn her head to watch her go. . . .

Miss Rachel wooed slumber, curled in her covers in the big sagging bed, but slumber refused to come.

A faint mewing at last allowed her an excuse to rise. She got from bed and released Samantha from her basket. The black cat arched herself prettily, closed her eyes to yawn, looked an apology in the direction of her mistress and walked about the room on her silent small feet, sniffing at things. Miss Rachel put on her clothes.

When she stepped out into the hall with the cat under her arm she came face to face with the young girl and her mother, whom she had seen in the hall during the night. The girl was dressed simply and smartly in white, with her gold-colored hair drawn into a knot upon her neck. She was very straight—as straight as an Indian, Miss Rachel thought, though she had never seen in the flesh a specimen of the red race. The girl's mother, beside her, looked subdued and tired. Her mouth was tight with some repressed emotion. She was of the same height as the girl but the girl's young straightness was lost in her—she was bent as a crooked tree.

Miss Rachel hesitated, expecting them to ask after Lily. They murmured a brief greeting and went past her to the door.

Miss Rachel found Lily's door in the gloom and tapped; and presently her niece opened to her. Lily had her throat bandaged with a strip of rough cotton—for concealment, Miss Rachel thought—and the mark of tears was plain on her face. "Come in, Aunt Rachel. Here's a chair. I expect you're getting hungry—it's after nine. I have some things for breakfast. I'll fix them right away."

Miss Rachel disclaimed any appetite. She had noted the ink-stains on Lily's thick fingers and the envelope propped up on the dresser. The envelope bore Miss Rachel's name in a wide scrawl. She went up to it timidly. "Is this for me?"

Lily gave the envelope a reluctant glance. "Yes. It's for you. I was going to give it to you after breakfast, but I might as well do it now." She picked up the envelope and looked at it curiously before she gave it to Miss Rachel. There was still evidently some thought in her mind about it. "Here you are, Auntie. Keep this thing safe somewhere. It's not to be opened unless something happens to me." She looked her aunt directly in the eye, and for once Miss Rachel found no dissimulation in her face. "I mean *in case I die.* Then you must open this and read it."

Miss Rachel clutched the envelope. "Lily, are you really afraid of someone? Do you *know* that you're in danger here?"

Lily shook her head in a pleasant determination. "I think not. Not real danger. But they're getting rough. You know that."

"Lily . . ." But Lily's bland immobility beat back Miss Rachel's pleading. She felt as if she might as well be talking to the wind. But she had to go on. She begged Lily again to come away.

Lily wanted breakfast. She laughed, not wholeheartedly, and propelled her aunt toward the kitchenette. They ate toast and fried salt pork and scrambled eggs. Lily gobbled her food with relish, but Miss Rachel could not bring herself to be hearty.

If anything worried Lily it seemed to be Mr. Charles Malloy. She was feverishly voluble on that one subject. Mr. Malloy had been gone for nearly three weeks. "I'd know the minute he returned," Lily confided. "His door is right across from mine, and I would hear him. But he hasn't been there—not for all this time. I've missed him."

Miss Rachel's brilliant eyes looked at her in understanding. "You're very fond of Mr. Malloy, aren't you? Are you and he engaged?"

Lily put down her fork and caught some egg off her lower lip with the tip of her tongue without seeming to know that she was doing it. Something more than surprise looked out of her eyes at her aunt—alarm, staring fright, amazement. "You do say such things!" she got out finally, and licked her lips absently again. She was recovering. "Shoo, Auntie! Don't try to tease! We're very good friends—friends—"

Miss Rachel did nothing save raise her neat brows a little. It seemed to frighten Lily all over again. She tore some bread nervously. "Give the man time! We just barely know each other! After all . . ."

She couldn't leave the subject alone, nor could she stop watching her aunt. "What made you say that, Auntie? It's funny—awful funny! Mr. Malloy's been nice to me. We've gone to the movies together and the dances and band concerts. He's a nice man." She managed a gusty chuckle, scattering a little breathful of crumbs across her plate. "Engaged! Oh, Auntie! If you knew how funny that sounds. We're *just friends*. . . ."

Miss Rachel looked through the kitchen window at the stained stucco wall of the building next door. She kept her eyebrows down where they belonged. She was thinking to herself, patterning her thoughts to Lily's chatter. She was wishing that Lily wouldn't go on so. Lily was lying, and Miss Rachel knew it. . . .

In the salty warmth of noon Miss Rachel went to the sunroom to write some letters.

Surf House—the place boasted a name on a board over the door—had no lobby for its tenants' use, but what would have been the right-hand apartment coming in was glassed in on the side next the beach and furnished with a cheap wicker settee, a writing desk, some forlorn veneered rockers and a fern stand. The view was good. Next the steps was a wide cement walk, then the sandy beach with its mushrooming of bright umbrellas, and to the horizon the blue sparkle of the sea.

A little girl of perhaps five years was playing with some papers at the writing desk. She was a slight child with light-colored hair and a sharp sallow face and too much knee and elbow. She regarded Miss Rachel with casual dislike.

"I'm Clara," she announced, staying at the desk.

Miss Rachel acknowledged the introduction with a pleasant smile. She asked if she might use the desk for a few minutes.

Clara looked sidewise, turning her head as a bird might. "I might let you have the desk," she said shrewdly, "if you'd give me a penny."

Miss Rachel felt in her handbag. "And what will you do with the penny if I give it to you?"

Scorn came into the sallow face. "I'll bet I know what you're thinking. You think I want it for candy. Don't you?"

"Oh, no. I wasn't thinking of candy at all. I just wondered what you'd do with your penny when you got it."

"Well, it won't go for candy. No, sir!" Clara sat very straight, her thin back like a rod. "Candy makes your belly ache and your teeth fall out. I know that, all right. But I'll tell you a secret—I want the penny to get my mama something." The sullen look vanished in a toothful smile for a moment, then it returned and the child's eyes grew hard. "You won't tell? You'd better not! It's going to be a surprise, when I get enough money."

"I shan't tell. Here's a penny."

The little girl took the coin and slid out of the chair. She appraised Miss Rachel frankly. "You're not a bad-looking old lady, you know it? Even if your hair is white."

"Thank you," Miss Rachel said gravely, seating herself. "Don't you like old ladies?"

"Not most of 'em. I guess I could like you though. You don't seem cross or cranky. Do you like little girls?"

Miss Rachel looked into the narrow face. "I like them very much," she said. "I used to wish I might have one of my own."

"Didn't you get one?"

"No. Never."

The wary eyes softened for a moment. Then: "I'm sorry. My mama says we can't have everything." Clara went awkwardly toward the door. "Good-by." She went through the door, then popped her head inside again. "You won't tell?"

Miss Rachel reassured her, and the head disappeared.

Miss Rachel wrote two notes—one was for Jennifer—and put them into envelopes and addressed them. She fumbled in her purse; she added something to one of the envelopes. Then she rose to leave.

The door to the apartment across the hall opened and a woman came through it. She was deep-bosomed and tall; her clothes were handsome; her face stared boldly forth from above her furs. There was something arrogant in her walk. She took several steps, looking directly at Miss Rachel. Her gaze took in Miss Rachel's tiny hat, her warm jacket, her handbag and the letters in her hand. "Good morning!" she said in a rich purr. "Are you going out?"

Miss Rachel, meeting her gaze, found something venomous in it. "Ye-es," she stammered. "I am."

"And so am I," said the big woman smoothly. "I'm Mrs. Scurlock. It's nice to have someone to walk with. Shall we go?"

Miss Rachel tightened her clutch on the letters. She wished desperately for a way out. There wasn't any, outside of downright rudeness. Miss Rachel was unaccustomed to that practice. "I'll—You'll have to wait. I must go back to my room for something."

The dark face composed itself. "I'll be glad to wait for you. I'll be right here when you come back."

Knowing Mrs. Scurlock as he later came to do, Lieutenant

Mayhew has been heard to ask Miss Rachel why she didn't go back and hide under her bed. But Miss Rachel disclaims any such urge. She simply went and got the cat in her basket and rejoined the big woman by the front door.

It had been warm inside the old house but out-of-doors the wind was cool. They went down the amusement zone together and found it very quiet at that time of day. Some people were eating lunch in the restaurants and some were lying on the beach, but the concessions were deserted. The two women did not talk. Mrs. Scurlock looked purposeful and calm and determined. Miss Rachel looked like a mouse thoughtfully considering a new kind of trap.

They came to a postbox and Miss Rachel deposited her letters. She turned to tall big-jawed Mrs. Scurlock. "It's all that I came out for. I'll have to go back now."

Mrs. Scurlock took it very agreeably. "I only came for the air myself," she said. "I must be getting back too."

Chapter Four: Murder

Mrs. Scurlock slid a big hard hand under Miss Rachel's elbow and helped her to turn around. Miss Rachel had been helped before—at street corners by various gallant gentlemen who overlooked her bright alertness, and in the midst of traffic by hearty Irish policemen with grandmothers of their own at home—but she had never been taken in hand before with such heavy suavity or such compelling force. Her small feet pattered obediently beside Mrs. Scurlock's calm stride, and though she was not one to give way to fear, her heart had started to pound thickly and fast.

She was escorted home in ominous silence. They were met at the steps by a tall man, colorlessly blond, whose clothes were too extremely cut and whose eyes sat too closely together in his long head. He brightened when he saw them. He arranged his face to smile.

"Well! Who is your new friend, Donna? Won't you present me?" He massaged his yellow gloves and bowed.

Mrs. Scurlock, very much in control, hoisted Miss Rachel to

the first step. "This is Mrs. Sticklemann's aunt. Miss Murdock, I'd like to present my husband, Mr. Scurlock."

It had the sound of being well rehearsed. Miss Rachel's hand was clutched in a yellow glove and her eyes looked at many teeth. "So glad to know you, Miss Murdock. We're quite well acquainted with your niece. She'd said so many charming things about you—made us anxious to get to know you! You are a picture, if I may say so. A picture out of Grandfather's album. Haw, haw! Don't mind my raving, do you?"

Miss Rachel experienced such an intense dislike for him that she did not trust herself to speak. She murmured a nothing in his direction. The two of them seemed somehow to surround her and she was wafted into the hall. "Won't you step in and see us for a minute?" Mrs. Scurlock purred in her ear, much as the legendary spider must have addressed his fly. "We'd love to get better acquainted. Wouldn't we, Herbert?"

Miss Rachel wriggled tentatively. Mrs. Scurlock's grip was iron. "Indeed; very much indeed," Mr. Scurlock answered, getting his key.

Miss Rachel clutched Samantha's basket; she was ready to risk a feeble bleat for help and make a bolt for it. But it was at that moment that Lily barged into their little group. She had come up soundlessly in her house slippers. Above the rough band of cotton on her throat her face blazed. She reached out and plucked her small aunt from the hands of Mrs. Scurlock.

"Leave my aunt alone," she said harshly. "She isn't in this."

The Scurlocks surveyed her in their separate manners: Mrs. Scurlock bold and angry; Mr. Scurlock with an uneasy sneer. He fitted the key into the lock. "Aren't you forgetting?"

Lily shook her head. She swallowed hard and the cotton

band moved. "No. I'm not forgetting. But my aunt's out of it—clear out of it. Get that?"

Mrs. Scurlock's odious eyes dwelt on Miss Rachel's face. "It wasn't that way in the beginning," she murmured. "We were all going to co-operate. Like friends." She laughed.

Lily gave her a glare and marched Miss Rachel away. "Don't listen to them," she said fiercely. "Don't pay them any attention."

They entered the stillness of Miss Rachel's room. "Who are they, Lily? Are you really acquainted with such people?"

"Acquainted is no word for it. I'm saddled with them. I owe them money, the more fool me."

Miss Rachel read Lily's bitter face. "Is it the same money? The debt we were speaking of before?"

A wary look crossed Lily's countenance; she breathed hard for a moment without saying anything. Then: "Don't ask me, Aunt Rachel. I can't explain. All I want you to do is to forget this. And keep out of those people's way—for God's sake!"

Miss Rachel looked round the shabby room suddenly, as though she saw it for the first time. "What keeps us here?" she whispered. Lily asked her sharply what she had said. Miss Rachel tried her hand at lying. "I was thinking that I didn't like those people—the Scurlocks. They're so oily and smooth and strong, and—*evil.* And dangerous, Lily."

Lily looked away. She fumbled in the pocket of her wrapper for a cigarette. Over the little flame she regarded her aunt. "They think they're pretty hot," she sneered. "They think they've got me over a barrel. But I'll get the best of them yet. You'll see if I don't."

"I wouldn't trifle with them. If you owe them money it would be best to pay it and have done with them."

Lily blew out a great mushroom of smoke and flipped her burned match toward a corner. "Let's eat," she said flatly. "I called the delicatessen and they've sent over some stuff. It looks good."

It seemed to Miss Rachel that she had done nothing except eat since she had arrived at this sinister house. If there were pleasures to be had at Breakers Beach she had seen remarkably little of them. She and Lily had spent most of their time in Lily's room. Lily scarcely seemed even to wish to talk. She sat perfectly still most of the time, or sprawled on the bed, with her eyes vacant. There was a look of waiting about her—an appearance of puzzled expectancy. She came to life only at mealtimes. Her appetite never failed her.

Miss Rachel put the cat in the closet and went to Lily's room.

Again—was it still and so often a coincidence, Miss Rachel wondered?—she met the girl and her mother in the hall. The older woman drew back when she caught sight of Lily, and the girl stood quite still with her head high. They waited, silent and constrained, until Lily went past them. Lily gave them no heed beyond a brief glance. It was not well lighted in the hall—only a dim reflection from the glare of the beach illumined the scene through the open front door—but Miss Rachel marked how the older woman turned her head with a sick expression to avoid Lily's cigarette smoke, and how the girl looked at her mother with her eyes full of pity.

They came into Lily's cluttered room. "Do you know those people?" Miss Rachel asked.

Lily shook her yellow mop. "No, I don't. They're new here. Didn't I mention they came in only day before yesterday? I don't even know their name."

"The girl's very pretty, isn't she?"

"Sort of, I guess. A little on the skinny side."

"There's something rather familiar about her face. Does she remind you of anyone we know, Lily? I can't think of who she does resemble—but it's somebody . . ." Miss Rachel puckered her brow in thought.

"I hadn't noticed. Come into the kitchen and we'll eat."

They had lunch. Lily filled herself and was pleased. Miss Rachel pecked her food like a feverish hen. . . .

Miss Rachel did not wait for night to let Samantha out for exercise. She put her into the yard at about five o'clock.

Miss Rachel sat for perhaps a half-hour, watching the cat at play, then she rose from the steps and called Samantha. And the rock slide began.

A few pebbles moved at the top of the bluff and gathered more rubble and much speed as they rushed fan-wise down the slope. The cat looked behind her, curious at the sound. Miss Rachel called again. Some large stones came thudding down, pushed from the top. The cat arched herself and spat. A stone struck her tail; she howled in fury and ran to Miss Rachel.

A look of cold anger came into Miss Rachel's usually placid face. She stood and watched the top of the bluff. A minute passed—two—and then something showed between the green leaves of the shrubbery. Something light-colored and glistening. It rose and became a line of hair across a human head. Blonde hair, but the eyes did not show themselves. They peered hidden through the leaves. In another moment the head was gone. . . .

Evening came down drearily and brought a rolling fog in from the sea. The old house on the beach was shut off. It might have been a ship a thousand miles from land. Fog pressed wetly at Miss Rachel's window—it was like cotton batting held up against the glass. There was no seeing through it, and even sound was dimmed. The air was thick and damp to breathe and had a strong smell of the sea in it. Even within the four shabby walls of her room Miss Rachel could feel the increased reverberating thunder of the surf. Under the fog the tide was rising. It shook the loose pane with a ghostly rattle, a sound that attracted the attention and disapproval of the cat. Her golden eyes reproached her mistress for their bleak surroundings; she miaowed once, forlornly.

At 8:30 Miss Rachel put down a book to take her tonic, which she had forgotten in the agitation of the night before. The label said definitely: *Take at bedtime, two tablespoonfuls;* and as a sop to her conscience, Miss Rachel took four. It was a harmless though bitter medicine. After her double dose there was little left in the bottle.

"It tastes worse than ever!" she told herself half aloud. "And I'm glad that it's almost gone!"

She put on a shawl, went through her door and locked it and was almost to Lily's door before she realized that the cat had followed her into the hall. Two amber eyes glowed at her feet.

Miss Rachel picked up Samantha and marveled as always at the cat's heaviness and the sleekness of her fur.

Her first errand was with Mrs. Turner. At the end of the hall she stopped before the landlady's door. From the room inside came the smooth-running hum of an electric sewing machine. At Miss Rachel's tap the hum stopped, and Mrs. Turner opened the door. "Yes?" she said sharply.

Beyond her the room looked warm and comfortable, with the sewing machine in the middle of it and yards of curtain material thrown over the sewing table. "Yes?" she said again.

"I need some towels," Miss Rachel requested.

The woman swung on her heel and went out of sight behind

the door. When she returned she bore one single towel across her arm. She held it toward Miss Rachel. "Laundry's tomorrow," she said curtly.

Taking the towel, Miss Rachel went back to Lily's door to say good night. The hum of the sewing machine rose behind her, fiercer than ever, as though Mrs. Turner resented being taken from her curtains.

Lily had a headache. She was lying down on her perpetually disordered bed with a wet towel on her forehead. She was fretful and she looked tired, but when Miss Rachel would have gone to her own room again Lily begged her to stay. "I'm lonesome," she admitted roughly. "I'd like to talk too. Maybe I've been a fool, keeping all of it to myself. I've been thinking—maybe it wouldn't hurt to listen to what you think of it. Want to listen?"

Miss Rachel settled herself in the depths of a large dirty leather chair and took the cat on her lap. "Of course I'll listen. Tell me anything you wish to."

Lily sighed with a rasping sound. She prodded the wet towel and licked her lips. "I'll start off by admitting that it's mostly my fault. I can see now what a nut I've been. You will too, before I'm done. But perhaps you'll figure a way out that I couldn't think of. Gee—my head!" She moaned a little. "Hand me that box of aspirin and get me a glass of water—will you, Auntie?"

The aspirin and water were brought. Miss Rachel waited for Lily to go on.

"Damn this headache! I could scream! And with this mess I'm in—it's too much!"

"Maybe I can help."

"I hope so. Anyway, I'm in debt. I told you that much. I didn't tell you that it was a gambling debt, but it is. I still can't understand why I didn't win, or rather, why I couldn't keep on winning. At first my luck was wonderful."

"Your—luck?"

Lily turned her head sharply to regard her aunt. "What makes you say that—that way?" she demanded.

Miss Rachel looked very innocent. "Oh, I don't know, really. Something you said, I guess. About not winning—you seem so sure you should have."

Lily laughed bitterly, but a look of something like shame came into her face. "Charles—Mr. Malloy, that is—had a system of winning at bridge. I guess, if I were you, I'd call it cheating. I didn't think of it that way at the time. These people had won almost fifty dollars from me, playing in the evenings in their apartment. I was mad, and I wanted to get my money back. It didn't seem any harm to use the kind of cards that Charles had. He explained how to read the backs of them when they were dealt." Again her glance crept to her aunt's face. "You think I'm terrible, I bet. Maybe I was."

But Miss Rachel was not thinking that Lily had been terrible. She considered it an almost incredibly stupid trick. If it had been the Scurlocks with whom Lily had played she could guess how long they had been fooled by Lily's system.

Lily went on in a more sober tone. "Well, it went fine at first. Charles and I were partners against them for several evenings. We made the stakes high and we won. Then Charles got a temporary job in a novelty store on the Strand. It was evening work and we couldn't play with these people any more. I liked the idea of winning. It seemed so easy that way. So I talked to Mr. Leinster—he's the young man in the apartment on the other side of yours, and real friendly too—and he said he'd be my partner. I couldn't somehow explain to him about the cards. He looks like kind of an honest guy. So I thought I could do it alone perhaps. But we didn't win—*we lost.* We kept on losing. Then Mr. Leinster got worried and said that he couldn't afford to lose money like we were. Auntie, I just *knew* we had to start winning sometime! Why, I knew every single card and who held it! If I could just have thought faster sometimes when we were playing. . . . Well, I told Mr. Leinster to please stay in the game as a favor to me, and I'd stand all losses for the two of us. He didn't like that, but I begged. So we went on playing every evening, but still we didn't win. I got sort of desperate—it was like a nightmare!—and I had got to owing them a lot of money. Oh, Auntie, the stakes went up and up till they were terrible! I tried and tried to be careful, to think it all out. But bridge can get you all mixed up if it's played fast like they— But, Auntie, aren't you even *listening?*"

It was true that Miss Rachel looked remarkably drowsy. She struggled up when Lily spoke to her; she tried to seem alert. She was so desperately eager to know with whom Lily had gambled. It was the one fact that the big woman had persistently kept back.

Minutes ticked by on Lily's battered clock. When she spoke again, it was in a different tone and upon a different subject. "Auntie, there's one thing I'm very sorry for. I wonder if you knew. . . . Of course I really wanted to see you, but there was another reason for asking you down here. I'm ashamed now. You see, I knew you'd bring the old cat. I—did you dream it was I who—who——" She choked on something like a sob; her voice drifted to silence in the room and was washed out by the muffled thunder of the surf.

Miss Rachel wanted to look up but her eyes were swimming with sleep. She wanted to open her lips and tell Lily that she did know, that she understood and that she forgave. But the words wouldn't come. Her head seemed heavy and stupid, and the room was swinging slowly out of focus, its lines distorting themselves into odd angles.

A pleasant fluffiness was billowing up into her thoughts; a lethargy weighed her limbs. She felt the cat stir gently in her lap and lift her head. Had there been a scratch of sound from the direction of the door?

The clock ticked evenly and sounded far away.

Looking at the room was like looking into the depths of a distorting mirror. Lily's cloth had slipped down over her eyes—queer that in a moment of clarity Miss Rachel saw this—and Lily had let it stay that way. It hid the tears that were so unusual for her.

She knew that Lily was waiting for her to speak but the heavy tiredness held her back, kept her lips still, kept her from telling of this strangeness that had overtaken her.

The cat lifted her head again and at the same moment Miss Rachel felt a draft blow cold along her neck. The door was opening; air was coming in from the hall. It seemed a part of the other strangeness—the door opening so silently to admit—*whom?*

Without lessening the helplessness of her body, her senses came suddenly alive for a moment and sight and sound were painfully clear. Her head was falling forward, and yet she saw Lily, still lying with her eyes covered, saw the little clock with its hands pointing almost exactly to 9:00. With the air from the hall came sounds—the sound of a rocker squeaking in the room across the hall, where someone sat with the moving chair on a loose board, and the sound of Mrs. Turner's sewing machine like a lost bumblebee at the end of the corridor.

The machine stopped for a moment. So did the rocking chair.

Then both started again, the machine humming and the chair complaining.

The draft slowly lessened. Someone had come into the room and was closing the door.

"I must warn Lily," thought Miss Rachel somewhere in the depths of her. "I must *say something.*"

Yet she could not. She was falling asleep, falling into a blue fog where nothing mattered.

The blue fog swallowed her. She was asleep.

It was while she slept, there by Lily's bed, that murder was done.

Detective Lieutenant Stephen Mayhew is a very large man who never seems especially happy. He is well over six feet tall; he is a good deal over two hundred pounds; and all of him appears to be obsessed by melancholy. He has blue-black hair, bushy black brows and a brown square face as emotionally mobile as a nicely carved wooden mask. He has a habit—Miss Rachel is sure that it is nothing more—of hunching himself forward at intervals into an attitude that suggests he is ready to spring upon whatever and whomever is in front of him. He seems to like to frown, and his black brows do it very well. Mr. Leinster has made the unpleasant suggestion that Lieutenant Mayhew needs only a good nasty growl to complete the picture of a black bear.

Miss Rachel doesn't like that. She says that Lieutenant Mayhew is really very much misunderstood—that if he kept proper hours and ate home-cooked food and were under a good woman's influence, he would be quite a different fellow. Lieutenant

Mayhew has been heard to wish for the first two of these. The latter he had, until recently, avoided.

The first time that he had laid eyes on Miss Rachel he took for granted that she was dead. It was only when the medical examiner, Dr. Southart, applied his stethoscope to her breast and announced that she was still alive, that Mayhew took much notice of her. He had been looking over the bloody mess on the bed.

"She's barely alive. I'd say, frankly, she's dying. But there may be a chance. Call another doctor—Aaronson will do—and a couple of nurses. Get hold of one of those women in the hall and put her to making coffee. Strong coffee. Find out from whoever runs this place if this is her room as well as that dead one's. If it is, get her another. Sully, you and Thomas carry her out of here. I can't examine a dead woman and revive a dying one at the same time."

Dr. Southart prodded the limber rubbery stethoscope back into his bag and moved away from Miss Rachel's chair. It was the first good look Mayhew had had at her.

"Where's she wounded?" he asked the doctor.

"She isn't, apparently. Drugged, for sure. Dying of morphine poisoning, I'd say. If Aaronson and the nurses don't hurry we'll be out of a job before they get here."

Mayhew bent down to look more closely at the small huddled form. "She's a little thing, isn't she?" he asked. "But Lord, if she isn't cut somewhere, how'd she get that awful mess of blood on her?"

"The blood came from the other woman. She's a sight if I ever saw one. Try beating somebody's head in as thoroughly as hers is, sometime, and watch the blood fly. That neck wound alone must have spouted like a geyser. The cat—hello! Where's the cat? I saw one when I came in."

Mayhew's deep eyes picked out the ball of black fur in a far corner. "There's the cat."

"The cat's a mess too—or it ought to be."

Mayhew went toward the golden eyes; they retreated under the dresser. He bent down to stare. "You're wrong. The cat's as clean as a pin," he said thoughtfully.

Chapter Five:
Something Odd About the Cat

The doctor shrugged. "No reason why she shouldn't be, come to think of it. She was probably frightened and spent all of the time that the murder was going on, in under the dresser."

"Might have," Mayhew agreed cryptically. He turned then to look at Sully, who had come from the hall.

"A dame outside says that the little old lady had the room next to this one. Shall we take her in there?" He approached Miss Rachel's huddled figure and made as if to pick her up.

"Yes. Get her out of here. I'll go with her till Aaronson comes. That on the bed will keep."

Thomas, the literal-minded fingerprint expert, spoke up. "It won't keep for long," he reminded the doctor.

Dr. Southart gave him a glance as sharp as one of his own scalpels. "Is somebody making coffee?" he demanded. "You, Edson, go through this dump and round up some rubber tubing and a water bottle. I'm going to rig up a proctoclysis outfit."

Edson, Mayhew's assistant, who was wall-eyed and vague and always curious, wondered what a proctoclysis outfit was. The doctor told him. Edson went out looking very uncomfortable. Things got busy in the room with the murdered woman. A camera was set up and pictures were taken of the corpse from several angles. Fingerprints were dusted and photographed. Next door a battle began: a battle for Miss Rachel's life against morphine and coma and death; and the last had almost got her.

Mayhew poked about Lily's room avoiding the puddled blood that was drying now to a sticky consistency. He at once noticed that the window was open with the screen unfastened and hanging ajar. He went outdoors by way of the hall and the rear door. By the light of his flash he found many deep marks made by a tool along the lower edge of the screen framing. These he decided to keep a careful eye on until a moulage impression could be taken. He went back to the Sticklemann woman's room that blazed with light and was thick now with cigarette smoke.

The doctor, relieved by Aaronson of the care of Miss Rachel, was going over the body carefully. "Beaten very thoroughly with something quite heavy and sharp," he muttered.

"A knife?" Edson hazarded after a moment's thought.

"My God!" Thomas expressed amazement. "How'd you ever get into homicide? The doc says somebody beat her over the head and you want to know if it was done with a knife! Did you ever hear of anybody bein' *beat* with a knife? Knives are to stab with, or wouldn't you know?"

"So they are," Mayhew grunted. "And quit yapping about it. Go on, Doc."

"A lot of wounds—a whole lot. The skull must have a dozen fractures. It looks like too much of a beating simply to get her killed. May be a grudge case—revenge, or so forth. See how deep these gashes are—" he pointed with a long delicate finger—"I'd say this woman had an enemy."

"So it would seem," Thomas murmured with a smirk. He was not to be subdued, even by so black a stare as Mayhew's.

"She could hardly have died at the first blow." Dr. Southart looked about him at the splatterings of blood. "She probably lost consciousness right away, however. That would account for there not being any gashes on her arms. She'd put them up, you know, if she were conscious. She's had plenty of time to bleed, with her heart still pumping. I'd summarize it by saying that she lost consciousness from the first blow, was beaten and lost a lot of blood, and was finally finished off by that crack over the temple. I think most of the head wounds followed after death. The neck wound would account for a lot of this blood—it cut into an artery. Of course this is preliminary. I'll get out a full report after the autopsy."

Mayhew nodded his thanks to the doctor.

He was thinking that a lot depended upon the little old lady next door. If she were revived, even for a moment, she might be able to tell them who had killed Mrs. Sticklemann. If she died without speaking their work would be harder, but Mayhew had little doubt that the case would work toward a successful conclusion. His work always had.

Remembering Miss Rachel, he decided to go to see how her case was progressing. But when he stepped into the hall he found his way blocked by a tight group of people whose voices died as he appeared. They looked at him mutely with a kind of horrified eager attention and he sensed a concerted holding of breaths.

Mayhew towered among them with his face betraying no emotion save a studied ire. "Is the person here who discovered these women?" he rumbled out, and looked from face to face.

A tall gaunt woman drew back and a small buxom one

came forward. She clutched a brown coat protectively across her bosom and looked fearfully up into the dark face of Lieutenant Mayhew. "I—I did," she got out after several swallowings.

"Tell me about it. Quite briefly, please." Mayhew dismissed the others with a glance, but they lingered in fascination.

The small stout lady before him fluttered her hands, tried to go on speaking and stopped to look sick. A man as round and red-cheeked as she came close to her and patted her shoulder. She breathed hard, managed to get on with it. "The cat," she said with difficulty. "It was simply yowling in there . . ."

"Yes. Go on," Mayhew prodded her.

She became apologetic in the midst of her fright. "I don't usually dream of going into anyone else's place." She glanced at the lingering faces of the others with a bewildered pleading. "But the people in there didn't answer my knock, and the poor cat kept crying and *crying!* So I just opened the door the tiniest crack and called the kitty. But she wouldn't come at first. So I peeped in. And there—" She clutched her stout little husband for support. "There they—were!"

"Your name, please?" Mayhew dragged out a worn little book and a stubby pencil.

"Timmerson." The little man took charge of the situation and of his wife. He adjusted his second chin and his glasses. "Mr. and Mrs. Rodney J. Timmerson," he elaborated. "We live here. We have the first apartment on this other side of the building, next the sunroom. We've been here a long time. Ask Mrs. Turner. She knows we've been here the last year, since she's come."

"We won't talk any further tonight," Mayhew told him. He raised his voice to the others, scattered the length of the hall. "I'll want all of you tomorrow morning. Keep yourselves available."

Grumbles answered this instruction but he gave them no heed. He went to Miss Rachel's door and tapped lightly. A dark young head with a white cap on it poked itself into view.

The nurse was very pretty; her eyes smiled as well as her mouth. "You wanted something?" she asked briskly. "I'm afraid you can't come in."

"How's the little old lady doing?" Mayhew asked her. "Any hope?"

She pursed her good-looking mouth in an attractive gesture of uncertainty. "Doctor Aaronson says it's too soon to tell. He thinks there's a good chance for her. It's morphine, and she's awfully old, but the doctor says she's responding. Anything else?"

Mayhew shook his head. "Nothing."

"Then excuse me. The doctor's going to do an intravenous." The dark head withdrew itself; the door closed.

Mayhew looked absently at his watch. It was nearing one o'clock in the morning. . . .

The fogginess lifted for Miss Rachel just for a moment, like a curtain going up at the opera; there were lights and sound and people moving about. She made a feeble effort to sit up and somebody in starched white leaned over to help her. Another somebody held out a cup and hot coffee stung her mouth. She gasped, and moved her legs. They ached as though she had been doing much walking, but she remembered nothing.

She sat there, clinging to a white arm, feeling very strange and befuddled and weak. Amid exclamations of annoyance from both the doctor and nurses, the cat, seeing her up, made a quick leap and landed on the counterpane. Samantha purred loudly, kneading the covers with her claws, then she came close to Miss Rachel and curled into a black ball against her knee. Miss Rachel reached out to touch the silken fur.

There was something odd—odd and different, about the cat. She couldn't place what it was for her thoughts were dreamy and blurred and she wanted dreadfully to sleep again. But Samantha—she oughtn't to be . . . whatever it was . . .

Then Miss Rachel was lying back upon her pillows again. Someone was saying, "You must keep awake for a while. Don't sleep." But her eyes drooped nevertheless, and her mind went blank as though a shutter had closed in it.

She was destined to tell Lieutenant Mayhew of her vague impression about the cat. She was also to see that big man sit in patience while she rummaged through her memory in an effort to put her finger on that vanished thought. But now she was not worried, and murder did not perplex her. She slept, and did not dream. . . .

Lieutenant Mayhew took a leaf out of his shabby notebook and drew lines upon it. Two long lines, parallel, bisected the center of the sheet. Mayhew wrote the word *hall* between the two lines.

He went on from there to divide the space upon either side of the parallel lines into five approximately equal squares. Then, having what sufficed him as a plan of the old house, he set about writing names into the squares. He was seated at the desk in the sunroom. The light was intensely bright upon his work. Outside, beyond the promenade, a few early bathers braved the sea. It was not quite nine o'clock in the morning following the discovery of Mrs. Sticklemann's body.

Having his plan drawn and what names he knew properly located, he sent Edson, who was on the wicker settee doing his nails with a pocket knife, to bring him the Timmersons.

They wandered in wearing both dignity and innocence. "You asked to see us, sir? About what happened last night, no doubt . . ." Mr. Timmerson left his voice hanging on a clothesline of doubt. Behind his glasses his eyes were wide, but their lids fluttered with something like dismay.

Mayhew turned his big body in the chair and gave them a cold stare from beneath heavy brows. His big hands reached out, scooped up the little book and held it menacingly—almost as if it held proof of the Timmersons' guilt in this matter—and his black glance was accusing. Some of the Timmersons' innocence melted. Mrs. Timmerson caught at her bosom and fell into a chair.

"That's right." Mayhew's tone was easy; it was more comforting than his look. "It's about the murder. I have called you before any of the others because you were the first, most likely, to have seen the scene of the murder after the murderer left it. What you may be able to remember about your discovery—even seemingly unimportant things—may prove to be of significance. Sit down and relax, and tell me all you know about it."

Mrs. Timmerson brightened a little. Mr. Timmerson found the edge of a chair. He stretched his two chins, felt of them and cleared his throat. "The time is important, isn't it? Let's see—about eleven, wasn't it, Maria? Or was it?"

"No," she was saying with careful emphasis, when Mayhew broke in upon her:

"Let's start farther back than that. Begin right after you had dinner and cover the whole evening, especially the time of the murder. Try to think of anyone who could prove what you tell me." He fished, got out his stubby pencil and was ready to take notes.

The Timmersons stared at him in a silence that moved

through stupefaction to alarm. "The time of the murder?" Mrs. Timmerson gasped. "But we didn't do it!" And Mr. Timmerson gobbled: "We've got to account for our time—we're *under suspicion* then?"

Mayhew was annoyed at their fright but his frown did not help them any. "No one is under suspicion yet," he rumbled at them. "We simply want to know of the movements of all of the people who live in this house. That's obviously important."

Mrs. Timmerson thought that one over. "Then—you think that the murderer is somebody who lives here? Another tenant?"

Mayhew's black stare gave her no answer. "Let's get back to the original subject," he told them. "Please tell me what you did last evening."

Mrs. Timmerson hesitated between indignation and disappointment, then she adjusted her skirt nicely, as though getting ready for an audience, and spoke. "We went to a motion picture," she said firmly.

"Before that?" Mayhew demanded.

"We—we had dinner. And just walked on the Strand a bit."

Mayhew swung his stare at the person of Mr. Timmerson. It might have been a stage light for the response it got. Mr. Timmerson immediately came alive and went into his act. "My wife is correct—entirely correct, Officer. We had dinner about six—yes, six. Then we walked a short while, watching the people. They're interesting, don't you think? You—ah, uh—don't? Well, then we went to a show."

"When was that?"

"The time, you mean? Oh, about seven o'clock, I think."

"You can prove, I suppose, that you were at the theater?"

"Prove it, man? Look here, are we or are we not——"

But Mrs. Timmerson was being brightness and light; she

broke in with a smile. “But certainly we can prove that we were at the theater. Don’t you remember, dear, the trouble you had about that bill? The cashier ought to remember that.”

Mr. Timmerson choked; he glared at his smug little wife; he breathed as if something were in his windpipe that shouldn’t be there. “Don’t mention *that!*” he got out at last.

“Tell me about it,” Mayhew said promptly. To Mr. Timmerson’s discomfort Mrs. Timmerson went on to tell the lieutenant that Mr. Timmerson had tendered a counterfeit bill at the theater and that there had been quite a fuss about it.

Under Mayhew’s keen eyes Mr. Timmerson blushed and stammered that he hadn’t manufactured the thing—if that’s what he was thinking.

Mayhew shepherded them in their talk and they got on. He learned that the Timmersons had come home from the show at about nine-thirty o’clock. Mr. Timmerson’s eyes grew wide with remembered horror. “It was right then that we heard the cat. It was howling just dreadfully!”

“And no one else seemed to have noticed it?”

Mrs. Timmerson wrinkled her brow and thought. “No. It’s odd now that you mention it, but no one else was about—though they’re usually quick to complain of any noise. It was very plain to hear. We caught it the moment that we stepped through the front door. I went right down the hall and knocked. When no one answered I tried the door, to let the cat out if she would come. She didn’t come right away. I peeped in and saw—them.” She swallowed, and gripped a button on her dress.

Mayhew scribbled in his book. “What next?”

“I—I guess I——”

“She fainted!” Mr. Timmerson added hastily. “Womanly

weakness, you know. I was right behind her luckily. I caught her when she fell."

"You didn't go into the room?"

"Well, ah—not then."

"Later?"

"Yes; just before the police got here. I stepped in, thinking that they might not be dead as Mr. Leinster had said and that there might be something I could do to help them. But I saw at a glance that Mrs. Sticklemann was beyond human aid, and the elderly lady appeared to be dead also. So I came out and closed the door as we had found it."

"You didn't touch anything?"

Mr. Timmerson wriggled. "Oh, I—I couldn't have endured to touch any—*it!*"

"This Mr. Leinster. He was around, you say?"

"Not just at first. He came up just after Mrs. Timmerson screamed and fainted."

"Which is his apartment?"

"The one next to Mrs. Sticklemann's aunt—I don't know the lady's name. Mr. Leinster is between her and the Scurlocks, who have the front apartment on that side."

"Did he come from his apartment?"

Mr. Timmerson started to speak, stopped, and looked very puzzled.

After a moment's wavering he went on, "I hadn't thought of it before. Not clearly, I mean. But since you mention it, I can't really picture Mr. Leinster coming out of his apartment. Something wrong about that idea—seems not to fit. He just came up suddenly. I can't remember any door opening."

"Still, you were with your wife. You might have missed it."

Mr. Timmerson admitted that he might have.

"You say that you went into the room before the police arrived. Now that's an important point. Later I'll have you take another look round in there to refresh your memory and perhaps remind you of something you considered significant. But just now I want to know if anybody else went into that room before the police arrived, besides yourself."

"Mr. Leinster went in."

"I see. When was that?"

"Just after my wife had fainted. She was lying in the hall and I was bending over her. Mr. Leinster seemed to have heard her cry out. He came kind of trotting up the hall—he's light on his feet for a big young fellow—and he went right on into Mrs. Sticklemann's room. But he came out immediately."

Mayhew hmmm'd deep in his throat. "Did he say anything to you?"

Mr. Timmerson regarded the lieutenant with bright intensity. "Yes, sir. He made what I consider to be a very odd remark under the circumstances. Distinctly odd."

Mayhew waited with large patience.

"It—it sounded very strange with those two poor bloody ladies lying in that terrible room, sir. He came through the door to the hall and kind of stopped, or hesitated there. He wasn't looking at me at all when he spoke. He just talked to the—the air."

"What did he say?" The stubby pencil waited in Mayhew's huge fist.

"Well, sir, just as he stopped there he spoke out loud. He said, 'This is real. It's honest-to-God. And I've been doing it wrong. *Pale stuff.*' Then he went off, Lieutenant, and telephoned for the police."

Chapter Six:
Paper to Burn

The Timmersons waited in a tense and hushed expectancy for the detective to react to this piece of information. Mrs. Timmerson's stout bosom seemed not to rise or fall as her little eyes surveyed Mayhew's face. But that brown mask gave them nothing—neither surprise, satisfaction nor interest by the lift of an eyebrow. Mayhew seemed to be thinking but his thoughts were far deeper than the inscrutable surface of his face.

He looked at the unreadable cipher in his book, chewed the frayed stubby pencil and looked out upon the sea. The silence grew long. Mr. Timmerson felt of his chins and adjusted his glasses. Mrs. Timmerson subsided into disappointment. But Mayhew spoke at last. "Since you and Leinster were together, so to speak, in the discovery of the crime I think that I'll have him in now. And I'd like you to stay and hear his story. Later, if you think there're any omissions or discrepancies in it, I'd like to know about them."

Mrs. Timmerson brightened, and essayed weak humor. "Put a thief to catch a thief, eh, Lieutenant?" But her husband's glaring frown subdued her.

Edson, who lingered at the door, went for Mr. Leinster. Leinster came in tall and big and blond, having red freckles on his wide face and red hair across the backs of his square hands. He smiled at the lieutenant and at the Timmersons very pleasantly and fell into a chair. "It's about the murder, I guess. What can I tell you?"

Mayhew dislikes people who carry off situations with breezy crispness. He gave Mr. Leinster his best stare. Mr. Leinster stared back with much innocence. "I'd like for you to tell me where you spent last evening and how you came to discover the crime at almost the same time that the Timmersons did. Also anything about the scene of the murder that you consider of importance, or unusual."

Mr. Leinster lolled his blond head back upon the wicker chair and stared at the ceiling. "I'll answer your last question first," he told Mayhew. "I must admit that as soon as I saw that a crime had been committed I hurried in to find a—well, a clue. I felt sure that one would be sticking out at me, so to speak, and I wanted to be the first to find it."

Mayhew stopped him. "Why?"

Mr. Leinster rushed blithely on. "Just a hobby of mine. I'm funny that way. You know, amateur detective and all that rot. Well, I got into the room all right. But, God!—those women! I'd never expected anything like that. I guess in all of my theoretical detective work I'd just kind of thought of the corpses as dummies—no mess, no gore—not staring at you out of a head that was beaten to a——"

But Mrs. Timmerson was standing up and making frantic motions. Mr. Timmerson was turning a gentle green. Mayhew put a damper on Mr. Leinster's eloquence. "We know all of that. The corpse was a mess. Go on."

"Well, it floored me. I'd gone into the room to find a clue right off and settle the whole thing before the police were even called, and instead I'd seen a corpse that——Oh, begging your pardon. Anyway, for a minute things looked kind of funny and I felt sick. It was—well, too real. Too— Never mind. I got out and called the police. I wanted no more of that job, I can tell you."

Mayhew picked the kernel from the large nut of narrative. "Then what you're getting at is that you didn't notice anything that might be of value in solving the crime?"

"That's it. That's what you asked me, wasn't it?"

"Yes. And the rest? Where you spent the evening, and where you were when Mrs. Timmerson screamed when she saw the corpse?"

Mr. Leinster made a large gesture with his square hands. "Oh, I was very innocently employed, I can assure you. I was in this room, in fact. I was writing letters on that desk you're sitting at now. I came in here somewhere around seven o'clock. I was just putting my writing materials back into my leather folder when I heard Mrs. Timmerson scream. It was then that I rushed out into the hall to see what was the matter."

Mayhew scribbled in his book. "You heard Mrs. Timmerson scream, all right, did you? But you didn't happen to hear Mrs. Sticklemann scream when she was attacked?"

Mr. Leinster shook his head. "No. Nothing else all evening. Perhaps, though, it wouldn't be possible to hear a woman scream if she were behind that closed door."

Mayhew snapped his book closed. "A very good idea, Mr. Leinster. You amateur detectives have your uses after all. Let's find out if a scream could be heard through the door."

"How can we?" Mrs. Timmerson wondered, and she found

out all too soon. Trembling and wide-eyed, she was taken by Lieutenant Mayhew to the murder room, and its door being unlocked by a key in Mayhew's big hand she was accompanied inside by that dour gentleman. She gazed about her in tortured fascination, saw the dried blood puddles and the gory bed where the corpse had been, and started to faint. She fainted against Lieutenant Mayhew.

Mayhew can be quite merciless with fainted fat ladies. He simply held her with one arm and closed the door with the other. Gloom darkened about them. Mayhew looked through shadow at Mrs. Timmerson's face. "Scream!" he commanded in a voice like a drum.

His abrupt word brought her to herself. She stared upward at dark angry eyes; she screamed, loudly and long, and she kept screaming until someone began pounding on the door from the hall side. Mayhew flung open the door and got Mrs. Timmerson back into the hall. The landlady, Mrs. Turner, confronted him. "What's all this?" Her bony cheeks were flushed with anger; her big jaw jutted at him.

Mayhew locked the door again and went past her without a glance. He shepherded the half-fainting Mrs. Timmerson ahead of him toward the sunroom. But Mrs. Turner followed. "You're making this place into a madhouse!" she accused belligerently. "I won't have it. Do you hear? I'll lose every one of my tenants—I'll go broke completely—if stuff like this has to go on. A murder's bad enough, but when you take other women in there and do things to them to get them to screaming . . ." Her stare went past him to Mrs. Timmerson, who had stopped to lean against the wall. Mrs. Timmerson's look was frozen, and she clutched the fastenings of her bosom in a way that suggested worse than Mayhew had given her. Mrs. Turner pressed her lips into a bitter line. "Just what *were* you doing with her?" she demanded.

Edson had heard it and he burst into laughter. But Mayhew looked at Mrs. Turner with fury. "Go to your apartment and stay in it!" he commanded her. "I'll call you when I want you, and listen to you when I'm ready. Now get out!"

Mrs. Turner stood her ground and gave him stare for stare. "I'm not afraid of you," she said slowly, and Mayhew knew how well she meant it. He could not, in fact, imagine that gaunt harridan as being afraid of anything or anybody. She had the beak and eyes of a bird of prey, and her neck was wrinkled and grayish as a buzzard's. The raucous scorn of her voice followed him to the sunroom.

Mayhew settled himself again at the desk, and only the knitting of his black brows betrayed the anger he felt toward the evil-minded old woman in the hall. "Let's have it." He fished again and got his pencil and notebook.

Mr. Timmerson looked fluttery and sick. He received his wife into his bosom and comforted her weakness. Mr. Leinster answered Mayhew. "We heard her. Plain. She might have been in the next room for the sound she made."

Mrs. Timmerson raised her head from her husband's shirt front and gave Leinster a reproachful look. "I was dreadfully frightened," she cried.

"Then it's pretty plain that Mrs. Sticklemann could have made no sound at the time of the attack, else it would have been heard. Hmmmm. Now, one last thing. I'd like to know what each of you two gentlemen do for your living."

Mr. Timmerson spoke up promptly. "I'm retired," he said. "I used to teach a church choir, and I've been a salesman too. Wide interests, I guess you'd say—the two of them aren't much alike.

Well, about three years ago I had a chance to get in on a stock deal through a nephew of mine. We put every last cent we had, or could beg or borrow, into it. And it turned out better than any of us had hoped. Since then Maria and I have taken things easy. We just live here by the beach and get by on our little income."

Mayhew gave him a nod and turned to the big young man. "And you, Mr. Leinster?"

Mr. Leinster wore the suggestion of a smile. "I'm retired too," he said affably.

Mayhew raised his black eyebrows; his dark eyes looked surprised. "Retired?" he echoed.

Mr. Leinster shifted a little in his chair but remained pleasantly helpful. "That's what I said, Lieutenant. Retired."

Mayhew frowned then and snapped his book shut in a gesture of annoyance. "This isn't going to help you, Leinster. I want to know what you work at for a living."

Leinster elbowed his bulk up out of the chair, stood tall, and stretched. His face was still innocently composed. On his way to the door he turned and spoke. "I said that I'm retired. Take it or leave it. It'll do, anyway, until you find out differently."

Mayhew's tone was sharp. "I haven't given you leave to go yet."

Leinster hesitated at the door. "What else do you want to know?"

"I want to hear what you know about the dead woman. Every last scrap of information that you can give—so come back and start talking."

"Oh, Lord, what little I know—" Mr. Leinster began, but Lieutenant Mayhew inched himself forward in his chair; his big shoulders came up and seemed to increase in size and his face assumed an expression that Mr. Leinster described elsewhere as nasty. Mr. Leinster made haste to come back but he did not sit down.

"What little I know of her is soon told," he said hurriedly. "And the main part of it is—that she was the most incredibly stupid woman that I've ever known. This example will show you what I mean. My only contact with her was in playing bridge with some other tenants here. She and I were partners. She ran a crooked deck into the game sometime during each evening, and the way that she used the cards and the clumsy attempts she made to win with them—well, it was just ghastly. A child could have seen what she was up to. I'm certain that this other couple with whom we played knew what she was doing. They're dumb like a couple of foxes, and I have an idea that they had their own system too. Anyway, this Mrs. Sticklemann insisted that we keep on playing with them until her losses must have been pretty steep. And she was too stupid to understand why she couldn't win."

Mayhew received this information with apparent indifference. He opened his notebook and scribbled in it. "And the name of these other people—was it a man and wife?" he asked.

Mr. Leinster glanced through the doorway of the sunroom to the closed door that faced it across the hall. "Mr. and Mrs. Scurlock," he said in a clear tone. "They're in that front apartment—the one directly across the hall from us."

Lieutenant Mayhew's actions were odd at this point. They verged on the bizarre, but they were both silent and swift. He closed his notebook, stuck it into his pocket and got up from beside the desk. Mrs. Timmerson has claimed that at this point he leaned forward and looked long and lean. He reminded her, she says, of a stalking black panther. Not that she ever saw one.

But she knows that he was out of the sunroom, his big arms swinging free, and across the hall without a sound. And in the twinkling of an eye, his large brown hand closed on the doorknob.

What happened next was blotted out for the three people in the sunroom by the bulk of Lieutenant Mayhew's figure, which filled the doorway. They saw the door swing suddenly inward, they heard a loud furious curse in a man's voice and a muffled scream in a woman's. And then Mayhew's voice came to them, saying plainly and quietly, "I'll have those papers, Mrs. Scurlock. Don't touch the match to them. That wouldn't help you."

Mayhew's figure moved on into the Scurlocks' apartment, and Mr. Scurlock was seen to be sitting on the floor nursing his head. It appeared as though he might have been at the door, bent over and listening, when Mayhew had flung it open against him. Inside, by the cheap table that occupied the center of the floor, stood Mrs. Scurlock. Her dark face was convulsed, her black eyes flaming. "You've no right to burst in here!" she cried. "Get out! Don't dare come near me!" But Mayhew was at her side, attempting to take a sheaf of papers from one of her hands. She fought him with the other hand, plunging her nails into his face. Mayhew caught her wrist, and she shrieked. Then the papers were his.

Mrs. Scurlock flung herself upon him and with poisonous accuracy she raked his face and throat, took the skin off and drew blood. Mayhew endured it for a while and then held Mrs. Scurlock off a bit with his right hand and sent a blow straight to her solar plexus with his left. She caught at her body just over her stomach, and in a breathless convulsion she fell to the floor and took the table with her. There was neither sound nor movement out of her after that.

Mayhew regarded the papers in his fist with evident pleasure. "I.O.U.s," he murmured to Mr. Scurlock, who licked his lips and cringed. "Signed by Mrs. Lily Sticklemann. I thought they would be. You were waiting to hear if I'd get onto them, weren't you—before you'd burn them?" He ruffled the sheaf between his stout brown fingers. "Quite a wad, isn't there? Represents, I'd say—" He read several, glanced at the rest. "About a thousand dollars, roughly. A neat sum. Did you kill her for it?"

Mr. Scurlock was mute; he shook his head.

"No? Well, that remains to be seen. I'll keep these notes for a while, at any rate." He frowned at the big frightened man on the floor. "Get up, and tend to your wife. Can't you see she's fainted?"

Scurlock got to his feet with too much haste; he stumbled and almost sprawled across the fallen table.

Mayhew watched his quivering hurry with distaste. "And don't go burning anything, or tearing it up, or throwing it out," he said sternly, "until I have a chance to talk to you two. Now bring your wife around. I'll want you in a few minutes." Then he came out of the room and the door closed on the rout of the Scurlocks.

Mayhew looked quickly at the three people in the sunroom. Mrs. Timmerson was pale, Mr. Timmerson was red, and both were agitated. But Leinster was stretched in a chair smoking, and behind the blue drift of his cigarette his eyes mocked at Mayhew. "Bullied 'em good, didn't you?" he asked softly of no one in particular. "March in, toss 'em around, come out proud. That's the system of our subtle detective. Another idea of mine, I see, needs revising. Needs it badly. I thought there might be brains used somewhere."

Mayhew came close to Leinster. The younger man viewed

with obvious surprise the presence of several bleeding furrows down Mayhew's face. He sat up straighter, flipped his cigarette to the floor. "Sorry," he said abruptly. "Self-defense. You're absolved."

Mayhew allowed a corner of his mouth to twitch, then looked at Mr. Timmerson. "A while ago I suggested that you come back into the room where the murder was committed, look over the scene and try to think of some fact or circumstance that might be of importance. You live in this place. You knew the murdered woman. What you might have seen there immediately after the crime may have significance. Shall we go there now? You too, Leinster, since you're such a sleuth."

They went, with Mrs. Timmerson fluttering after like a damaged moth. But Mr. Timmerson came back out of the room immediately and was sick in the hall. Mrs. Timmerson held his head and moaned with him.

Within the sallow gloom of Lily's room Leinster and Mayhew poked about. Edson came back from getting a glass of beer and joined them. "How do you figure it?" Leinster wanted to know.

Mayhew went to the window. "This was open," he said. "The pane was raised and the screen forced open. There are marks here where a tool was used to pry the frame. I think the murderer came through this way."

Leinster found fault with the idea. "But the woman would have screamed if somebody had come climbing through the window."

"Not necessarily," Mayhew objected. "She may have been asleep and never known what hit her. Or she may have known who it was and let them come in without question. It's pretty certain—" His voice died at this point and he stood perfectly still with his eyes fixed on the curtain. Leinster was poking at the bed, lifting the mattress and rumpling the bloodstained sheets. Mayhew called Edson. "Go outside," he told his assistant. "I want you to climb through the window for me."

Edson appeared outside the window after a minute. He flung away his cigarette and approached the side of the building. "There's a box out here. Shall I stand on it?"

"Not unless you have to. Come on in."

Mayhew stood back as the round-shouldered form of Edson crawled over the sill. Edson grunted and turned, and was on the floor. Mayhew bent and picked up something very small and very brilliant. He held it up to the light. It was a pin.

Mayhew chuckled. "That's torn it," he said happily.

Edson came close and stared with his large vague eyes. "What is it?" he asked plaintively.

Mayhew turned it between his fingers. "It's a pin."

"Only a pin?" Edson regarded Mayhew with disappointment.

Mayhew permitted his large mouth to smirk. "Only a pin, as you say. But it happens to have been in that curtain."

Leinster came up. "So what?" he asked.

Mayhew demonstrated. "It was in there like this. See? Holding this torn patch into place. The pin had been run through the material into the wood of the sill." He put the pin back as he had seen it first.

Leinster puckered his mouth to whistle a long note. "Knocks the idea of the guy coming through the window, doesn't it? Or wait—does it? Maybe the murderer noticed the pin and replaced it after he had come through."

"And left the screen the way it was and the pane open? No, that wouldn't be sensible. If the murderer came through the window at all, it certainly appears that he didn't care who discovered it. I think, for some reason, that the murderer wanted it to look as if he'd come by the window, though really he hadn't. He must have done this after he had killed the Sticklemann woman." Mayhew reached between the shabby curtains and pushed open the screen. "He tried to make it look as though the window had been used. But he didn't know about the pin, and the pin tripped him up."

"Couldn't have got in without disturbing it," Edson mumbled, bending and squinting at the bright tip of metal.

"I'll say he couldn't. And that lets the window out."

Edson straightened and scratched his sandy hair. "But look, there were toolmarks on the sill. New ones, not weathered. They'd been made from the *outside.* I helped Thomas get a mold of 'em. What about that?"

A certain tight chagrined look came briefly into Mayhew's face. He said one word, said it bitterly. "Screwy."

"It don't fit," Edson said, letting grammar go hang. "Either he came in through the window, or he didn't. The pin says he didn't, the toolmarks say he did, or made a hell of a fine time trying."

Mayhew raked the room with a hot stare as if to wrest from it the secret of Lily Sticklemann's death and this monkey business at the window which had preceded or followed it. Mayhew looked terrifically angry. Leinster and Edson moved away a little, as if to give his wrath plenty of room.

Miss Rachel thinks that it was just then that he began to enjoy himself.

Chapter Seven:
Mr. Malloy Is Missing

Mayhew settled himself at the writing desk, opened his notebook and glanced up at Edson, who was the only other occupant of the room.

"Let's have the Scurlocks," he said briefly and gestured across the hall.

The Scurlocks came, wearing their separate manners: she cold and haughty; he sidling and sly. They sat down, not comfortably, and looked at Mayhew.

He watched them for a minute. "Let's have it," he said then.

Mrs. Scurlock stared back without opening her mouth, but Mr. Scurlock tried to be obliging. "What is it you want to ask us? We'd be glad to help. Don't judge us by——"

Mayhew broke in. "Yes. Begin there. Tell me about those I.O.U.s. They must be pretty important."

Mr. Scurlock looked at his wife with a mild servility, but she gave him the same glittering cold stare that she gave Mayhew. "Shall I speak, dear? For the both of us, I mean." He seemed to read permission in her eyes for he turned to the lieutenant. "Let's not call them important, Officer. They weren't important, for we had little hope of collecting on them. But, in the present circumstances, they are decidedly—well, shall we admit it?—dangerous. That's a good word for them, I think. You'll grant my point?"

"Perhaps." Mayhew was looking at the woman. She was a tiger if he'd ever seen one. Her eyes looked murder at the rest of them.

Mr. Scurlock managed a smile. "They put us in an awkward position, Lieutenant. With Mrs. Sticklemann dead we knew the papers were worthless. But we scarcely knew what to do with them. They might seem very—incriminating, if they were to be found in our possession. So—quite innocently, I assure you—we decided to burn them."

"Just as Mr. Leinster was tipping me off about the gambling you'd done with Mrs. Sticklemann? What a coincidence!" Mayhew indulged in a wry chuckle.

Scurlock tried to read his face. "Coincidences have happened before, Lieutenant," he said, still affably watchful.

"So they have. We'll let it go. Let's discuss this gambling you did with Mrs. Sticklemann and Leinster."

Mr. Scurlock raised a white hand in protest. "Not real gambling. Just a friendly bridge game. We had stakes, of course, but——"

"What were the stakes?"

Mr. Scurlock let his mouth hang open and seemed worried. "We—we started at a half cent a point," he said at last.

"And went to?" Mayhew prodded.

Mr. Scurlock glanced hurriedly at the frigid face of his wife. Her eyes burned him with contempt. "Mrs. Borgia looked like that!" Mayhew told himself, pleased with his excursion into history.

"The stakes finally got to—to ten cents a point," Scurlock admitted, and found his tie too tight and loosened it. "It was Mrs. Sticklemann's suggestion that they be put up higher. Lord knows why she wanted it, either, because she was a horrible player."

"And a crooked one?" Mayhew suggested, leaning forward as if inviting confidences.

Mrs. Scurlock's dark face came alive with scorn, and she spoke. "Most certainly not," she flung out. "She was honest. We all were."

"So?" Mayhew thrust his tongue into one brown cheek and winked at Mr. Scurlock. The blond man fell back into his chair with a look of astonishment and fear. If he had liked Mayhew's truculent questions little, he obviously liked the insinuating wink much less. It betrayed nothing, but implied a wide and dangerous field of knowledge that might contain anything.

With a look of sly good humor Mayhew turned to his little book. "Let's get on then," he suggested. "Tell me how you spent yesterday evening."

Mr. Scurlock put a limp hand to his forehead and seemed confused. Mrs. Scurlock answered for them both. "We were in our apartment all evening. We ate dinner there—our apartment is one with adjoining kitchen—and we remained there until time for bed."

"You didn't once go outside?"

Her voice remained cool and determined. "Not once," she assured him.

Mayhew met her eyes and found them defiant. "I don't doubt you," he said mildly. It is his way with people who are on their guard with him. "Can you tell me anything about Mrs. Sticklemann that you think might bear on this inquiry?"

"Obviously, I would tell you anything which I might know that would deflect suspicion from ourselves. But I know of nothing. Nothing at all."

"Nor you, Mr. Scurlock?"

Mr. Scurlock struggled with himself and appeared to think. "Nothing, I guess," he said after a minute. "No—but wait! Shouldn't he know about Malloy, dear?"

She shrugged in stony indifference. "If you wish to tell him, Herbert."

Scurlock went on to elaborate. "This Malloy was a middle-aged man. He had the apartment right across the hall from Mrs. Sticklemann's, and I think they were—well, at least sweethearts. About three weeks ago, as I remember it, he disappeared from here. None of us have seen him for quite a while. And I know that Mrs. Sticklemann was upset when he dropped out of sight. She was plenty sweet on him. It's a thought, Lieutenant. Maybe Malloy came back and killed her!"

Mayhew appeared to give this idea serious consideration. "And you, Mrs. Scurlock, do you think this man Malloy might have killed Mrs. Sticklemann?"

Mrs. Scurlock smiled narrowly. "Obviously, someone did, didn't they?"

"You've no opinion?"

"None at all."

Mayhew stared into his book when he had ceased scribbling. "One last question," he said suddenly. "What is your business, Mr. Scurlock?"

Mr. Scurlock started nervously; he cast about him in confusion and even glanced out of the window as though in search of a convenient occupation. But Mrs. Scurlock came to his rescue. "He's retired," she told Mayhew in her rich purring voice. "He's been retired—let's see—about six years now. Isn't it, dear? Yes, six years, Lieutenant."

Mayhew closed his book slowly with his brown face getting red. "I'll be damned!" he said.

"Somebody in this cursed house must work for a living!" Mayhew said fiercely, and regarded his floor plan with its names written into squares. "Next—" He ran a thick finger down the left side of the paper till it came to the last square on that side. "Next—I'll see Mrs. Marble. She has the last room on the other side of the building. Get her."

Edson went off, and returned with a small woman in shabby clothes who looked to be about thirty. Drabness and neglect had washed away her youth. Mayhew gave her his cold stare, but when she flinched and trembled he suddenly changed.

"I'm making an investigation into Mrs. Sticklemann's death," he said kindly. "You needn't be afraid. Just tell me what you were doing last evening, where you went, and so on. And, of course, anything that you noticed that might bear on this case. You have the apartment next to Mrs. Sticklemann's, haven't you?"

The shabby small woman came forward and seemed to be less afraid, though she kept her red hands clasped in front of her and her eyes were wide. "I don't know anything," she said in a hurry. "You see, I was gone all evening. I didn't even know that Mrs. Sticklemann had been murdered until I came home long after midnight."

"Where were you?"

"I was at work. I do housework for Mrs. Terry at the Ravenswood Arms. I'm not a maid, exactly, though I do cooking and serving. I go twice a week in the mornings to clean her apartment. I wash and iron on Tuesdays for her. Every evening I go and get dinner, do the day's dishes and straighten the house. Once or twice a week she entertains, and I must stay late and serve the cocktails and sandwiches, or make waffles. Last night she entertained quite a lot of people, and at midnight I served a fried chicken dinner. It must have been close to two o'clock when I got back to my apartment here."

"How did you learn of Mrs. Sticklemann's death?"

"Mrs. Turner told me. She must have heard me getting the key into my door for she peeped out and whispered to me that Mrs. Sticklemann was dead—murdered. I was too tired to pay much attention, even to that. I thought about it a little, but I soon went to sleep."

"What do you know about Mrs. Sticklemann? Anything that might help in this inquiry?"

"I didn't know much about her. She gave me to understand once that she had sufficient income to enable her to live without working. She had no children, and I believe she was divorced from her husband. She told me once that she had two spinster aunts living in Los Angeles. Outside of those few things I can't think of anything else that might be important."

"What about this man Malloy? Weren't he and Mrs. Sticklemann good friends?"

"Well, yes, I guess they were. It seems to me that I understood at the time Mrs. Sticklemann rented her apartment that she had moved here to be near Mr. Malloy. I can't remember how I got that impression—whether someone told me or I just presumed it. Anyhow, it was my belief at the time. It seems odd, doesn't it, that someone with money should live in this rattletrap?"

Mayhew smiled grimly. "We all have money here," he said

with dry humor. "At least, everyone seems to be retired. Except you. It's good to meet an honest workingwoman. Are you a widow?"

"Yes, I am. Mr. Marble has been dead several years. I'm alone with my little girl."

The brown of Mayhew's eyes came alive and he looked eagerly at the pale face in front of him. "Your little girl?" he asked quickly. "Where was she last evening?"

"In the apartment, asleep. I put her to bed when I left here at six-thirty."

"I'd like to see her. Is she in the apartment now?" The woman nodded slowly. "Edson, go after Mrs. Marble's little girl."

Edson returned with Miss Rachel's small highwayman of the writing desk. Clara Marble looked from her mother to Lieutenant Mayhew's brown face. She screwed her features into a fearful frown and addressed the detective. "You're a cop, ain't you? I know. But don't you go hurting my mama. I'll run the ice pick in your belly if you do!"

The mother looked sick with shame and humiliation. "Lieutenant, please don't be angry with her! I have to leave her alone so much while I'm working, and she picks up all sorts of terrible expressions, running around loose on the amusement zone. She—she's not a bad girl, really."

Lieutenant Mayhew gazed down at the narrow face with its prominent cheekbones. His eyes took in, without seeming to, the thin small body, the knobby knees, the skinny arms. He held out a big hand tentatively. "I'm sure that she's not a bad girl, as you say. She does love her mother. Now, Chicken, I'd like to ask you a question."

She was not to be won over at once. "What'd you call me?"

"Chicken. Don't you like it?"

She wrinkled her small nose. "Kinda. It's a funny name. Can I have it for keeps?"

"Sure. Your name is Chicken from now on. Remember that, Mrs. Marble. Your daughter likes the name of Chicken, so Chicken it is. Now, Chicken, answer me this—did you hear any funny noises last night?"

Her blue eyes clouded; she looked toward her mother. "Answer, dear," Mrs. Marble told her.

"I didn't hear nothin'," she said promptly.

"No noises at all? Well, then, did you see anything? I mean something like a person sneaking along outside the window or peeking in at you, anything like that?"

She shook her head decidedly. "I ain't seen nothin' either," she assured Mayhew.

Mayhew fished in his pocket and brought out a nickel. He held it out toward Clara. "Here's something. It's to help you remember that if you should happen to think of anything that happened last night, you must tell it to your mama. Will you do that?"

Clara took the nickel solemnly. "I'll tell her if I remember anything. But I don't think I will."

Mayhew eyed her innocently. "Why won't you?"

Clara took interest in her shoelaces. "I just don't think that I will. I might. But I mostly might not."

"I see. Well, Mrs. Marble, I believe that is all. Ask Clara—oh, pardon, I mean Chicken, here—if she can remember anything at all that happened last night. Do this every once in a while. We might get something though it's doubtful. You may go now."

Mrs. Turner followed Edson into the sunroom and looked

scornfully at Mayhew. It was well into the afternoon. There had been an interval for lunch.

She was a tall sinewy woman. Her face, under its pompadour of frizzed rusty hair, reminded Mayhew of nothing so much as a horse. She neighed at him in her high voice and the illusion was complete. "I have nothing for you. It's useless to ask me questions. Besides, I've got work to do."

"Sit down," Mayhew told her. "There's a lot I want from you. You're the landlady here. You probably know more about each tenant than anyone else does. Start out by telling me all that you know of Mrs. Sticklemann."

Mrs. Turner made a bitter mouth, but she gave way enough to seat herself. "I know very little about the woman, except that she was divorced and didn't have to work for her living. That's all."

"What about her relationship with a man named Malloy?"

"What do you mean—relationship? They knew each other, I guess. She moved here to be with him, but I'm no spy. I don't know what my tenants do when they're together."

"They were together then? Very much?"

"I don't know. And what's more, if they *were* immoral, I don't care."

Mayhew leaned forward to look more closely into the coarse rugged features of the landlady. "That's a serious insinuation, Mrs. Turner. Please elaborate on it. What grounds have you for thinking that Mrs. Sticklemann was immoral?"

"I didn't say that she was. I just said that if she had been, I didn't care. Don't try to twist my words into false meanings."

Mayhew regarded the woman with keen resentment. "I'm not trying to twist your words, Mrs. Turner. I merely want to establish clearly the relationship between Mrs. Sticklemann and this man Malloy. I have reason to believe that they were very much interested in each other. Malloy has disappeared from his lodgings here, according to the other tenants, and Mrs. Sticklemann is dead. Now I'd like for you to tell me all that you know about Malloy."

Mrs. Turner fixed him with her angry stare. "He's a cousin of mine on my mother's side of the family. He's been married and was getting his divorce. About three weeks ago he left this house and didn't come back. That's all that I know about him."

"He is your *cousin*—and yet those few facts are all that you know about him? That seems unreasonable. Surely you know a great deal about this man!"

"Oh, a lot of unimportant stuff. But you needn't take my time getting it. Ask his wife and daughter."

"I shall, when I locate them. Do you have their address?" He propped his little book open and waited.

"They're right in this house—in the apartment next to the Timmersons and across from the little old lady—Miss Murdock. They're in there now, I think, waiting for you to call them."

Mayhew could not quite hide his surprise. He consulted his floor plan and saw that the apartment in question had been marked with a question mark because he had not yet inquired who its tenants were. As he stared at the paper Mrs. Turner rose and made for the door.

"Just a minute, Mrs. Turner. I'd like to have the key to Malloy's apartment. I suppose you have a master key of some sort that will open his door?"

She stiffened in defiance under her ill-fitting clothes. "And what if I have?" she flung back. "I need it, and I won't let you have it."

"Yes, you will," Mayhew said calmly. "Edson, go with Mrs. Turner and bring back the key. And—Mrs. Turner, one last question. What were you doing between seven and ten last night?"

For the first time a look of thought, of concentration, replaced her defiance. "I sewed most of that time. I was hemming some curtains for the house. I must have started about seven-thirty, for I'd been at work some time when the little old lady came to ask for a towel." She told him briefly of Miss Rachel's call at nine. "I was almost done with the last lot when the screaming started. Mrs. Timmerson making her fuss."

"The noise of the machine would have kept you from hearing any unusual sound in the hall?"

She pursed her angular mouth. "I think that it would have. I didn't hear anything."

Mayhew dismissed her, and Edson followed.

As he sat, thoughtful, at the desk Mayhew caught sight of a white capped, blue-caped figure stopped at the front door. He called to the nurse, "What's the little old lady doing? Any change?"

The girl's eyes smiled at Mayhew. "She's coming along fine. Couldn't be better."

"Good," said Mayhew. He had been thinking that the murdered woman's aunt might be of some help, and yet it was unlikely. Elderly people were usually slow; they neither heard nor saw clearly. And this particular old lady had apparently been sound asleep of an overdose of morphine at the time the crime had been committed.

Still, he ruminated, she might be able to help, if only to throw light upon the past life of her niece.

Somewhere in that past lay the seeds of this crime—either in the immediate past, during which Lily had foolishly attempted to cheat the Scurlocks at cards, or in some distant and yet unknown period of the woman's mismanaged life.

Chapter Eight: Enter Mrs. Malloy

THE GIRL came in looking casual and withdrawn and cool, and she studied Mayhew's face a moment before she sat down. She marked its good masculine lines: its heavy brows, its strong chin, and the reserve in the brown eyes. She judged him by other men of his type—big men, gallant and cumbersome—and she behaved accordingly.

One white hand came out toward him and hesitated, gracefully outstretched. "I hope you'll help us, Officer," she said with a frank and perfectly charming smile. "Mother and I are very—well, confused. This terrible crime—we scarcely know what to do." She was very appealing, very feminine, as she sat there in the sunroom facing Mayhew.

Mayhew saw that she was surprisingly beautiful, but he is a wary man, and he has met beautiful women before. Mrs. Michaels, who chopped up her husband and sent him inside his own steamer trunk to San Francisco, had been slender and lovely and frail. Mayhew had heard her sentenced to Women's Prison for life less than a year ago. Remembering her, he looked stolidly back at Miss Malloy without a single flutter of gallantry.

Her mother came in gray and quiet. She sat down and folded her hands.

Mayhew turned to her at once. "Mrs. Charles Malloy?" he asked. She nodded without speaking.

Mayhew thumbed through his little black book and fished awkwardly for his stubby pencil. The girl, watching him being clumsy, sneered a little with her pretty mouth. Then she caught the glitter of Mayhew's eyes under the bushiness of his brows, and knew that he had seen her. Her face went pink.

Mayhew looked at the older woman. "I'm investigating the death of Mrs. Sticklemann," he told her. "As a matter of routine, I'm getting the statements of everyone in the building as to their movements last evening. Let's have yours."

Mrs. Malloy's gaze crept by way of her shoe and the floor to her daughter's face. "I was reading," she said after a moment. "I was inside our apartment all evening."

"And you, Miss Malloy?"

"I was reading too. I believe I sewed a little also. Neither of us went out."

"I see. Both indoors. About what time did you retire?"

The girl answered him, but she watched her mother.

"I think that it must have been about half-past ten or eleven." It seemed to Mayhew that the older woman gave an imperceptible nod of assent but he could not be sure.

"Did you hear the disturbance made by Mrs. Timmerson when she discovered the dead woman?"

"Oh, yes." Mrs. Malloy met his eyes. "I heard it plainly."

"And did you and your daughter go out into the hall?"

"I did. Sara stayed in the apartment."

Mayhew looked curiously at the girl. "Weren't you interested in what was happening?"

She shook her head and replied quickly, too quickly. "Blood always makes me sick," she said.

Mayhew frowned at her. "That's very strange," he said.

"What is?" She seemed momentarily confused, then she glanced toward her mother, saw the look of new terror on the other woman's countenance and realized that she had said something she shouldn't have. "What is strange?" she asked Mayhew again.

"That you should know there was blood about," he said simply. "I have been under the impression that Mrs. Timmerson was the first to discover the crime. She was the first to give an alarm, at least. But now you're saying that you didn't go out when the woman screamed because you knew there was blood there and you were afraid you might be sick."

The girl sat up straighter. She looked at Mayhew with respect and fear. But she wasn't to be trapped. "I guess I'm confusing things. You see, afterward I learned that there had been a murder. At the time, from the way that Mrs. Timmerson was screaming, I just presumed that something very unpleasant was happening. So I didn't go out. But I didn't really know for sure about the blood. I just—well, I had a hunch that someone was hurt, and I was busy inside our apartment . . ."

"Doing what?"

"Just then? Oh, reading or mending—I don't exactly remember."

"But you're sure that you waited inside your apartment for your mother to come back and tell you what had happened? You remember that without any trouble?"

The girl hesitated a second, flushing slightly and staring at her hands. Then: "Yes. That's right."

Mayhew stared at her in impatience and annoyance but he

pressed the point no further. "Let's get on then. Please think carefully about this next point. Did either of you notice anything, during the evening, either sight or sound, that was suspicious or unusual?"

They conferred again with their eyes, and the girl answered him. "I can't remember anything out of the ordinary."

Her mother spoke quietly. "I remember hearing Mrs. Turner's sewing machine. She was using it most of the evening. Not that it's an unusual sound but it's the only one I can remember."

Mayhew thumbed through his book, found another page and studied it. "You're certain of that?" he asked Mrs. Malloy. "About the machine being used, I mean. There weren't any long intervals of silence?"

Mrs. Malloy took a minute to think. She answered with careful precision. "Not longer than were natural, I'm sure. I was sitting by our window, which was open. I think that Mrs. Turner's window must have been open too, for the sound of the machine was very distinct. She seemed very busy at it. I would have noticed any long interruptions, I'm certain, and there weren't any beyond the normal short ones that one has, to change thread or arrange material. Even so, come to think of it, she must have been running long seams. Clothing, you know, must be fitted and adjusted as it is sewn."

"She says that she was hemming curtains," Mayhew explained.

"New curtains?" the girl asked thoughtfully. "Well, this place certainly needs them."

Mayhew, remembering the pin at the window, smiled grimly. "So it does," he agreed. Then, sinking a little in his chair, he let a minute go by in silence while he leafed through his book in an abstract way and swung one foot in a slow arch back and forth.

The girl and her mother gave each other a quick look. Sara Malloy smiled. Her mother drew in a long breath and let it out in a sigh. They appeared relaxed and relieved of some fear. Mayhew scrutinized them out of the corner of his eyes, then he turned on them. His voice was quite low but it carried with startling clearness. "Where is your husband, Mrs. Malloy?"

For a minute she looked as if he had struck her, and Mayhew knew that it was this question she had dreaded. One of her hands jumped to touch her throat; it continued to cling to a brooch in the neck of her dress. "I don't know where he is," she said softly, at last.

"Didn't you come here expecting to be with him?"

"No." Her eyes, moving, had fixed on the sea. "We have been here only a few days. He was gone when we came."

"Did you come to investigate or break up the affair between him and Mrs. Sticklemann?"

She shook her smooth gray head. "Oh, no—not at all! We were being divorced. We have our interlocutory degree, and in four months, in accordance with California law, our decree becomes final. It's a year, you know, between the interlocutory and the final. And as far as I am concerned he's perfectly free to have—friends, if he wishes to, during this time."

"Won't you tell me, then, why you have come here? It's odd—you must admit that—if you and he are divorced and he is no longer anything to you."

"I didn't say that." Her fine face showed reserve and grief.

"I beg your pardon," Mayhew hurried to say.

"I will tell you, though, why I am here. I came to find out about my husband's disappearance."

"His disappearance? Do you consider it—mysterious?"

"Very much so! It's utterly unlike him to go away without some word to us. You must understand that though we no longer lived together as a family he kept in close contact with us. Mostly on Sara's account, I must admit. And he's never done this before. When we learned that he had disappeared we came down at once from Los Angeles."

Mayhew looked at her very thoughtfully. "When did you learn of it, Mrs. Malloy?"

"When M——" But the girl was ahead of her, her eyes alive with some warning to her mother.

"Mrs. Turner notified us of my father's absence," she said quickly.

"Mrs. Turner is your father's cousin?"

For one moment there was a flicker of uncertainty across her young assurance. "I—I believe so." To Mayhew there was an indication of a little frown, not on her brows but in her voice.

"You're not certain?"

"Oh, yes. Well, I mean, we'd never met any of my father's people before. His parents were dead, and he'd never contacted any of the others until lately. Then he mentioned Mrs. Turner. She's some kind of relative. If she told you she's his cousin, I guess that's it."

Mayhew turned back to shrinking Mrs. Malloy. "Have you any theories to account for your husband's disappearance?"

"None," she told him hurriedly. "I cannot imagine where my husband could have gone or why. I'm afraid it means something has happened to him, that he's met with an accident somewhere." Before Mayhew's embarrassed gaze she quietly began shedding tears. Her voice died in the midst of her grief.

Sara Malloy went to her mother and, kneeling, put her arms about her. She gave Mayhew a glance that appealed without pretense. “Couldn’t you help us find him? We’ve looked through hospitals and morgues, and at pictures of people with amnesia, or gone suddenly insane. . . . Mother can’t stand much more of it.”

Mayhew ruffled one bushy brow with a thoughtful thumb. “It seems to me that the disappearance of your husband should be investigated by the police, Mrs. Malloy. Not only to assuage your personal feeling, however. I am here to get at the bottom of the murder of a woman who was his friend. His disappearance, though it preceded her death, may be related to it in some way. I believe he should be found as quickly as possible, or his disappearance at least accounted for.”

Mrs. Malloy crushed a handkerchief against her eyes. “Please find him.” She struggled to regain control of her voice. “I should have asked the help of the police before this.”

“Yes, you should have, if you suspected foul play. However, don’t spend too much time worrying. There may be a perfectly sensible reason why you haven’t heard from your husband.”

Sara Malloy gave Mayhew an anxious look from her blue eyes. “Is there anything else that you wanted of us? If not, could I take Mother to our apartment?”

Mayhew pulled a blank sheet from his notebook. “Take this with you. Write on it the names and addresses of any friends of your father who might be able to give information about him. When you have finished, return it to me.”

The girl took the paper and stared at it. “There’s only Mr. Nicholson,” she murmured. “He lives in San Diego. He might know something, if there is anything to know.”

By seven o'clock in the evening the amusement zone was coming to life. Belated diners filled its cafes, munching fish dinners and drinking beer and watching from their open booths the kaleidoscopic scene on the fairway. Hoarse-voiced men in various booths begged for players of their games. They shouted of opportunity being wasted and practically promised that all one had to do to win a blanket, a ham, or a papier-mâché cupid was to toss an insignificant ring around a very obliging pedestal. There were also a two-headed baby (bottled), a man from Borneo, a snake house, an anatomical museum and a merry-go-round. Farther up the Strand, on the pier, were dance halls and other concessions not yet open.

Mayhew and Edson, in a restaurant that faced the Strand, ate their dinners soberly, with due regard for the beer and a careful attention to the lemon meringue pie. By the time they had reached this last delicacy Edson was probing for information. "Who do you think did it?" he wondered innocently. "Somebody who lives in the old shack, or an outsider?"

Mayhew crushed the top of his pie in thoughtfully, detaching a generous mouthful. He chewed it and looked at Edson. "Right now, I'm inclined to think it was somebody at the house. Of course it's early yet to figure much of anything. But there's one fact that seems to point in that direction."

Edson never tried to think, which was comforting to Mayhew. "Such as?" he asked.

"The fact of the old lady being doped as she was. You see, I think it must have happened something like this. The old lady was supposed to stay in her own room. She had a tonic there—Doc Aaronson gave me the bottle with a drop or so in it—that she was supposed to take at bedtime. Well, the stuff in the bottle had morphine in it. It looks to me as if the murderer intended for her to take her tonic, go to bed and either sleep through the whole thing, or else die—I'm not sure which. But according to my way of thinking, it looks like the work of someone in the building. One of the tenants would have so much better an opportunity of slipping the drug into her tonic than an outsider would. Whatever the doubt about the murderer entering Mrs. Sticklemann's apartment by the window, there can be none about the old lady's. Her window hasn't been moved for years, and I looked at it just this afternoon, when the doctor let me in for a minute. Someone came into her room *by the door*, put morphine into her tonic and went out the same way he came in. You can see what a chance an outsider would be taking. If he met anyone, even in the hall, his presence would be noticed instantly. That line of figuring made me practically sure the murderer is inside the place."

"Hmmmm. Sounds reasonable the way you tell it. Which one among the tenants seems likely?"

"Well, there are two of them sticking out like a couple of sore thumbs. Which may mean something, and may not. The Scurlocks. The dead woman owed them money, and she apparently wasn't paying them. However, I'm holding all opinions open until I can talk to the little old lady. She ought to be a pretty valuable witness."

"Provided she isn't nearsighted and deaf. A lot of the old ones are, you know," Edson reminded helpfully.

"That's true. Well, here's hoping." Mayhew drained his beer and set the mug down with a thump.

"Going to call it a day?" Edson asked, stretching himself.

"Not yet. I want to have a look at Malloy's room." He fished in his pocket for change and slid a quarter under his plate. "Let's go."

After a short walk they came into the musty darkness of the hall. Mayhew glanced into the sunroom as they went past its door. It was empty. They proceeded to Malloy's room and Mayhew opened it. A light hanging from the ceiling in the middle of the room gave a glaring yellow light when Mayhew switched it on. They went to work.

"Everything's a mess in here," Mayhew complained, opening the drawers of the dresser. "Looks as if the place had been rummaged, or else Malloy tumbled it getting out in a hurry. Writing paper's all wrinkled and folded. That's something you seldom find unless the stuff's been gone through a little too quick."

Edson looked under the bed and then dragged out a suitcase. Mayhew looked over the contents. There were collars, ties, underwear.

Mayhew stared about him, puzzled. "Left his clothing, or else he had a lot of it. But it's funny, there isn't a single letter or personal paper here of any kind. He either cleaned them out or someone else has. Let's have a look inside his shoes. It's a chance."

In the toe of one shoe was a ten-dollar bill wrapped in a dirty slip of paper. The paper had been part of a written sheet of some sort. On it was faded tracery. Mayhew held it to the light. "Looks like the word *Caves.*" He studied the scrap a moment longer, then thrust it and the bill into his pocket. "Remind me to give this money to Mrs. Malloy. I've a hunch it's the sum total of her husband's fortune." Mayhew poked into the closet again and from a shelf brought down a rusted length of iron, about a half inch by a foot, which must at some time have been part of a shelf support. This he regarded critically. The surface was red, pitted with decay, the pits filled with dust.

"We might try this on those toolmarks outside the Sticklemann woman's window," he proposed. "It looks a little wide, but we'd best make sure."

They left Malloy's room closed and went down the hall to the back door and out of it and around the house on the other side. Here, while Edson played his flashlight on the window, Mayhew attempted to fit the piece of iron into the scars in the wood. It was obviously wide. Mayhew used it tentatively on a far edge of the sill. The mark it left was uneven, jagged, while the other scars were smooth and workmanlike.

They went back inside the building by the back door. They were almost again at Malloy's closed door, when Mayhew came to a slow halt. He stood still for a moment, listening. Then he went silently to the door and flung it open.

Sara Malloy faced them across the disorderly room. She was at first pale, then she went pink to the roots of her fair hair.

"Well," Mayhew said with cold emphasis. "And what are you doing here?"

She straightened her mouth and made a half-defiant gesture with one hand. "Nothing. I—this is my father's room. I have a right to be here, I think."

"Yes, you have, I'll grant you. But who was it just went out the window?"

Her eyes went unwillingly to the window where the pane was now pushed up, and where the sagging rusted screen swung outward on its hinges. She didn't meet Mayhew's gaze again. "I wouldn't know," she said sullenly.

Big as Mayhew is, he can move with surprising swiftness. He was at the window almost before Sara Malloy answered, sensing her mood before she expressed it. He leaned through the window and looked toward the front of the building. The faint thud of footsteps in the sand came to Edson and the girl. Then Mayhew drew back into the room. He looked very satisfied.

"Leinster," he said shortly, watching Sara Malloy.

She did not deny it. "He was just helping me. I heard someone in this room and I asked him to come with me to investigate. When we got here there was no one, but the light was on."

Mayhew laughed abruptly. "So he hopped through the window and left you to your fate when he heard someone else coming." He watched the angry light come into her eyes, measured her self-control. "Tell me, Miss Malloy—who is Mr. Leinster?"

She flared back at him: "I won't tell you. He's not a criminal, if that's what you mean. But you'll never get his name——"

"Oh. Then he has another name?"

"I didn't say it!"

Mayhew came closer to her, and he suddenly took her wrist in his hand. He cannot remember that he had any rude intentions. It is a gesture he uses to let his opponents feel his strength. But Sara Malloy was tense and angry, and when he touched her she flew at him like a cat.

There is a quality in Mayhew's personality that makes women want to hurt him. Miss Rachel has studied it and labels it sex appeal. Which proves that Miss Jennifer is right when she maintains that Miss Rachel goes to too many moving pictures. But Miss Rachel is quite firm in her belief about Mayhew. She says that the principle is the same when a cave lady of the Late Stone Age put out her head to see if her gentleman friend would club her.

Sara Malloy's fingernails were long, pretty and sharp. She used them—as had Mrs. Scurlock in her time—upon Mayhew's big brown face.

Mayhew responded in a manner much approved in the Late

Stone Age; he held Miss Malloy off gently and shook her until her teeth rattled. He was engaged in this pleasant if vigorous occupation when Leinster burst through Edson's weak-kneed defense and came at Mayhew.

Miss Malloy, flung into a corner, watched the short and bloody battle that followed. Leinster landed a neat one on Mayhew's eye, and Miss Malloy winced and started crying. Which wasn't consistent.

It took Mayhew about five minutes to throw Mr. Leinster out into the hall. Miss Rachel thinks that it was during this time that Miss Malloy fell in love.

Chapter Nine: The Murder Room

Mayhew likes hunches, and he played one that night by remaining alone in the murder room.

It was nearly two o'clock in the morning when the doorknob started to turn. The lock slid back slowly and squeakily as the door was tried. Mayhew had been sitting in the big leather chair. He got silently to his feet and crept to the door, listening. There was rustling movement in the hall. By the time he had the door open there was no one in sight.

At six o'clock the door was tried again. In the gray of dawn, red-eyed and tired, Mayhew again went to the door. This time he didn't stop to listen, he flung it open and went through.

Sara Malloy, in pink nightgown and white woolen robe, stood in the passageway. She looked up at Mayhew calmly, not startled nor confused, and her face seemed thinner and more shadowed than before. "I haven't been asleep," she said quietly. "I knew you were in here. It worried me. Besides, I'm sorry about what happened in my father's room."

Emotion came and went in Mayhew's square brown face as he took in her loveliness and her appeal. He started to put a hand on hers and did not. Instead, he rubbed his weary eyes. "That's all right, Miss Malloy," he said gruffly. "I'm doing well. Missed somebody who came earlier. Was it you?"

She shook her head, and if Mayhew noticed the way her yellow shining hair cupped her face as she did so, he gave no sign. "I've stayed in bed till now," she told him.

He watched the lifted face, and he must have been blind not to have read the timid feeling that mirrored itself there. He came to himself with a snap, for he is first of all a police officer and ready to turn everything to his own ends. Sara Malloy was in a softened and humble mood. Mayhew questioned her carefully, keeping his voice low. "Miss Malloy, where were you at the time the murder was discovered?"

The blue eyes widened, looking into his own. The young breast lifted in a long breath. "You don't think that I was in my own room?" she asked.

Mayhew smiled briefly. "I'm afraid I don't."

She glanced about at the narrowness of the dusty hall in apparent confusion. "Well, I——" She stopped, not meeting his look. "I was in my father's room," she said suddenly.

"Doing what?"

"I was going through his belongings. There are some souvenirs and trinkets that he took that Mother wants. I went in about seven o'clock, out our window and into his, to find them for her."

Mayhew showed evidences of satisfaction. "You were in there, then, when the murder took place. You were right across the hall from where it was happening. Surely you heard something?"

She nodded her admission. "I've been trying to think of a way to tell you without admitting that I had lied before. Anyway—well, I guess it isn't much—but I did hear someone going and coming from that room across the hall. Someone went in about eight-thirty. The little old lady, that was. I heard her speak before she closed the door. Then—I can't remember just how much later, but not very long—someone else went in and closed the door. A few minutes later they came out."

Mayhew's glance narrowed. "The murderer. That was murder you heard—going in."

"And then—it seems about five minutes later or so, as I remember it now—someone went into the room again. They were there just a moment and came out again."

Mayhew looked incredulous. "You're saying that the room was gone into twice after the little old lady went in?"

"Yes, that's it. I listened pretty carefully, for I felt guilty, somehow, breaking into my father's room as I had done. I was afraid that it might be illegal or something. And I'm sure of how many times the room across the hall was entered."

"And from what direction did the steps come in the hall?"

"I don't know. Whoever it was—two different people or one—they came both times very silently."

"You can't remember anything else?"

"No, I'm afraid not."

Mayhew's thoughts swung off into another channel. "About Mr. Leinster. I'd like to hear what you know of that young man."

She turned half away, with an expression of sudden worry and reserve and a stiffening of her shoulders. "I'm sorry," she said in a low voice, "but it wouldn't be fair for me to tell you his affairs. He has helped us in a great many ways, and I am grateful. I can't betray a trust that he impressed upon me as being very important."

"He is putting himself in a very awkward position. Suspicion naturally attaches itself to a person who will not explain his occupation nor give his correct name."

She looked round in open surprise. "Oh, but that is his right name!" she said quickly.

"But you said that he had another name."

She bit a delicately colored lip, not looking at Mayhew. "So I did, I guess. But I can't explain it. Please don't ask me to."

"I shan't," he said easily. "It'll all come out in the wash, anyway. Let's get back to our first subject—your being in the room across the hall from the murder. Today they're holding the inquest. I'd like you to do something for me."

"Surely. Anything," she agreed simply.

"It may involve some risk to yourself. I can't be sure of that, but I feel that I must warn you."

"It's all right. I want to help, and I think I'm well able to look after myself."

"Very well. Now, at the inquest, I'd like for you to admit that you were in your father's room. But I'd like you to embroider on that statement a little."

"But I'll be under oath!"

"It won't be an outright lie. All that I want you to say is that you believe you can identify the murderer if you're given time to think things over; that there's a vague impression somewhere in your mind that links the sounds you heard with someone you know. Just say that. Then we'll see what happens."

Into her shadowed face there crept a look of bewildered fear. "I'll very likely be murdered also," she said slowly.

Mayhew's hand brushed her shoulder. It was a gesture at once eager and reserved. "I'll be watching," he told her.

The inquest was brief and to the point. Two witnesses identified the body: Mrs. Turner and Mr. Leinster. Sara Malloy gave quietly convincing testimony concerning the opening of the door. The jury brought in a verdict of wilful murder by person or persons unknown.

That afternoon Miss Rachel received Lieutenant Mayhew.

She looked shrunken and small in the midst of the pillows, with the lace of her nightgown a snowy foam under her sharp little chin and her big eyes the only live thing about her. She regarded the immense bulk of Lieutenant Mayhew with awe, and when he settled upon a rickety chair she held her breath for a moment.

Whatever his treatment of the Mrs. Scurlocks of this world, Mayhew is gentle with little old ladies. He asked pleasantly after Miss Rachel's health and led her tenderly on to the subject of the murder.

"Begin at the beginning," he requested. "Tell me how you happened to be down here with your niece, and all that occurred before her death."

Miss Rachel's voice was weak but earnest. "Lily telephoned me," she began. "She said that she was in some sort of trouble and needed help. So I came down to see her."

"Did she explain what her trouble was?"

"No. I think that she had other plans by the time I got here. You see, she had remembered the cat. The first night I was here she tried to kill it."

The black line of Mayhew's brows went up to reveal the incredulity in his eyes. "Did you say that she tried to kill your cat?" he asked. "Or is it her cat?" He glanced at the black satiny figure of Samantha, who opened one golden eye at him scornfully.

"It doesn't properly belong to anyone," Miss Rachel explained. "I don't really know how to put it. You see, Samantha is an heiress."

Mayhew had a moment of looking angry, for he thought that Miss Rachel was making sport of him.

She went quickly on. "Samantha belonged to my sister, Miss Agatha Murdock, who has been dead for more than five years. Agatha was very fond of her, in fact—" Here Miss Rachel's pale face became mildly pink. "My sister was very strange before her death, Lieutenant. I might as well make it plain. We all thought that her mind was affected. She had made a lot of money with the small inheritance which was her share of my father's wealth, and she took a notion that all of us were waiting for her to die so that we could have it. She—she became very difficult. After she died, though, we learned the strangest thing of all. She had left her money to her cat."

A thoughtful expression came across Mayhew's square face. "I believe I remember something of the case, now that you have explained it. Wasn't it written up in some of the Los Angeles papers?"

"It was. Much to our embarrassment."

"I understand the part about the cat having a fortune. But how did it affect Mrs. Sticklemann?"

"Well, the cat couldn't live forever. Even my poor sister must have known that. So her will went on to say that at the cat's demise, if it had been a normal death, the money was to be equally divided between my sister Jennifer, myself and my brother's stepdaughter, who was Lily Sticklemann and my brother's only heir. If any of us should die before the cat did our share was to go to our heirs, whoever they were. But if the cat had died in a manner not entirely normal—and her going must be certified by three registered veterinarians—the entire fortune was to be set aside to found a home for stray cats. You see, Agatha never liked Mrs. Sticklemann, and I have a firm conviction that she was sure in her own mind that Lily would attempt to kill Samantha to get her share of the money. That was Agatha's idea of a joke—to have Lily irrevocably lose the money in trying to get it prematurely."

"Odd kind of humor," Mayhew said cryptically. "And you say that Mrs. Sticklemann did indeed make an attempt to kill the cat, just as your sister had thought?"

"She did, I'm sorry to say. Lily was—well, not shrewd, in some ways. The night after I'd arrived here I let the cat out in the backyard for a moment to—to—" Miss Rachel faltered, again turning pink and at a loss for words.

Mayhew was undisturbed. "Cats have to go out occasionally," he said calmly. "Go on."

"Well, as I stood there I suddenly smelled an odor of stale Turkish tobacco. It was an odor that I'd always associated with Lily, and I somehow knew all at once that she was there hidden in the dark yard. I called the cat. When she came she had a piece of meat in her mouth, and the meat had been cut with a knife in several places and some whitish stuff rubbed into the slashes. I'm sure that it was poison and that Lily had given it to her."

"Your niece needed money then?"

"Yes, I'm sure that she did. She admitted to me that she had been gambling and had lost heavily."

Mayhew considered for a moment, and then, sensing Miss Rachel's hopeful attention, he told her what he had discovered concerning her niece's relations with the Scurlocks.

"I was sure that it was they," Miss Rachel informed him

when he had finished. "They made an attempt to frighten me as well as Lily." She went on to tell him of Mrs. Scurlock's accompanying her on her walk. "I think that they believed that I would somehow get the money for her if I were afraid of them. Perhaps Lily consented to the scheme. I'll never know now."

Mayhew shifted his weight in the groaning chair. "Thinking of the money side of it, as a motive—who benefits by your niece's death?"

"Only Jennifer and I. On the morning of the day she died my niece made a will. I think that it was her last. It was a holographic will, unwitnessed, which as you doubtless know is perfectly legal in this state. She gave the will to me in a sealed envelope with instructions to open it only in case she died."

"That would seem to indicate that she expected trouble of some kind."

"Yes, I think that she did. You see, she had been attacked and choked senseless the night before and I think she was at last genuinely frightened of the Scurlocks."

This was a new piece of information to Lieutenant Mayhew and he had Miss Rachel elaborate upon it.

"And the will?" he asked her at last. "Where is it?"

"I put it into a new envelope after I'd read it—it seemed best to know at once what the letter contained—and sent it to myself at my home in Los Angeles. It's doubtless there now. It is quite short and simple and merely states that all of her estate is to go to Jennifer and me."

"It was when you went out to mail this will that Mrs. Scurlock went with you, as you have told me?" he asked her.

"It was."

"And now to get down to the actual crime. Will you tell me just what happened during the course of the evening?"

"I—I took my tonic. I suppose the doctor has told you about it before now. He says that it contained the morphine that almost killed me. After I had taken it I went to ask Mrs. Turner for a clean towel, and then went into Lily's room to say good night. Lily was lying down because she had a headache. For a few minutes we talked about her worries. At least, she talked. I kept getting drowsier and drowsier. I wanted to tell her how strange I felt and yet I could not."

Miss Rachel was silent a few seconds, remembering that queer terrifying lethargy that had crept through her in Lily's room.

"Then—I must have been almost unconscious—I felt a draft on my neck and knew the door was being opened behind me. I was afraid and yet too sleepy to move. I wanted to see who was coming in so quietly, and yet because my head was sinking forward all that I could see was Lily and the clock. The clock's hands pointed almost exactly to nine, and I believe that it must have been about right. Nine."

Over the covers Mayhew glimpsed Miss Rachel's remembered horror.

"Lily had let the cloth slip down over her eyes," Miss Rachel went on softly. "She wasn't watching and didn't seem to hear. Oh, I so wanted to tell her to look up, to see what was happening, and I couldn't. Just at the last, just as everything was sliding off into darkness, I had a terribly clear moment. I heard and saw things so plainly. . . . Someone was rocking on a squeaky board in the room across the hall. Mrs. Turner's machine was running. The room looked stark and queer. Then everything went out, as if the light were off."

Miss Rachel's eyes got bigger and filled brilliantly with tears.

"Then it was the end, and I'd never got to tell her that I understood and forgave her for her foolish attempt to kill the cat. I did understand, really. Lily was so shortsighted in everything, so hasty and unthinking. She couldn't help it if she forgot that killing Samantha would only cheat her out of a fortune."

Mayhew nodded with sober reserve. "I understand. It's usually unfortunate when somebody gets in a hurry about a killing. Ten to one the thing won't come off right. That's why I think this crime was done a little too quickly. Parts of it don't jibe." He told her about the toolmarks on the window and the pin in the curtain.

He listened with surprise as Miss Rachel told him of putting the pin where he had found it. It was at that moment that he had an inkling of what a really valuable aid this small elderly woman might be. He began to sense that keen insight into people and situations that he now thinks was given to Miss Rachel as a special dispensation of the gods. While she listened he began to reconstruct the crime as he saw it: the murderer standing outside the window, perhaps attempting an entrance, to watch his quarry and to see Miss Rachel subside into slumber; then coming in through the back door—for Mr. Leinster had been in the sunroom which commanded a view of the front entrance—and entering the apartment and killing Mrs. Sticklemann. Going out, and then for some reason coming back, for Sara Malloy had heard the room entered twice, and unless the second entrance was by someone who had kept from giving an alarm it followed that the murderer had returned for reasons of his own. "It's the likeliest theory," Mayhew concluded. "He remembered some tag end of the thing that he'd forgotten and he came back to fix it. It's an opportunity that few of them have, and I only wish that I could have beaten him to that second chance."

The white lids drooped over Miss Rachel's dark eyes in a gesture of pain. "And all the while I was there, sleeping," she said softly. "Sleeping soundly—and Lily was being killed."

"You nearly were, yourself," Mayhew said bluntly. "But I guess you know that."

"Yes. It was terrible coming out. I wanted to sleep so badly, and they wouldn't let me. I had fits of being awake, and then I'd doze off feeling that the doctor and the nurses were angry at me for doing it. Once, during that time, I remember so clearly that the cat jumped on my bed and purred and I reached out and touched her . . ." Miss Rachel's voice trailed away on an odd unfinished tone. She stared at the cat with abruptly aroused interest.

Mayhew was watching her closely; he marked the disturbance in her manner.

"I can't remember what it was now . . ." The cat opened one quizzical eye as Miss Rachel's fingers crept across her fur. "But there was something about the cat that wasn't right. I knew what it was then. But it's like coming out of a fog. I can't quite place what it was I wanted to remember."

Mayhew got up from his chair and came close to the bed. He bent, picked up the cat and stared at its immobile haughty face with much interest. He held the animal, who was attempting to claw him, toward Miss Rachel.

"Is this your cat?" he asked suddenly. "The original one, I mean. The cat who owns a fortune?"

Miss Rachel's small form came erect against the pillows. She took the cat from Mayhew's big hands and held it, standing on its hind legs, in her lap and looked it over from nose to tail. Then there was a moment when she looked out the window. At last she answered Mayhew.

"I think this is the same cat that I've always had. It looks exactly like her."

"Do you mean that you're sure?"

She frowned with one eyebrow and stroked the black silken fur.

"No," she told him slowly. "I'm not sure."

Chapter Ten: We'll Be Murdered in Our Beds

That night Mayhew again tried to find comfort in the leather chair in the murder room, and he interrupted the attack upon Sara Malloy.

It was deep in the hush of early morning hours that he sat up suddenly, looked about him in the darkness and listened. Something had telegraphed alarm to the tired brain that, worn with vigil, had lapsed into sleep. He tried to remember, to force his mind back into that half-waking state where he had known, somehow, that something was wrong. He got stiffly to his feet and felt through blackness to the doorknob.

The hall was silent, dimly lit and smelling faintly of dust as it always did. He went forward one door on the opposite side, tapped gently and asked, "Is everything all right?"

The utter silence that answered him might have indicated the innocent slumber of two women, but to Mayhew it was unaccountably sinister. He tried the door, thumped it loudly. "Open up!" he said sharply.

There was a stumbling movement inside the apartment; a key turned in the lock at the same moment that a light showed beneath the door. Mrs. Malloy was revealed, shivering and rubbing her eyes. "What is it?" she asked. "Why are you knocking?"

He looked beyond her into the room; his arm swung out to crush her, protesting, backward. He went immediately and bent over the figure on the bed. Mrs. Malloy came close, and then she screamed. Her daughter's body was oddly arched and straining, her eyes were glassy. There was a look of stark fear on the unconscious face. Knotted about the white column of her throat was a necktie, drawn tight so that it strangled.

Mayhew tore at the necktie while Mrs. Malloy hovered and sobbed. "She's dead!"

"Shut up," Mayhew said brutally. "Call Doctor Southart on the phone."

Dr. Southart came, looking alert and pleasant though he was dressed in an overcoat over pajamas. He went to work on Miss Malloy without delay. "Aren't we having fun down here?" he asked Mayhew dryly. "Who'll be next? Don't go sticking your neck out, Mayhew."

Mayhew was watching the dark lashes of Sara Malloy. They lay in a dusky arc across her cheeks and showed no sign of lifting. Her face had the precise waxen beauty of a cameo under the glare of the overhead bulb, and her yellow hair gave back light for light. Miss Rachel, teetering a little from weakness, slipped into the room at that moment, and she has claimed that she understood much of what went before when she saw Mayhew looking at Miss Malloy. His blunt brown face, hardened by seven years of work with criminals, is not yet quite a mask.

He had told Miss Rachel of his plan to use Sara Malloy as a decoy, so that she grasped in a moment what had happened. She looked at the window. It was closed securely and in a manner which could not have been done from outside.

Sara Malloy began to come awake. She stared up at the doctor, who grinned at her in a comforting manner, and then, as if seeking someone who should be there, her eyes went round the room. They fixed on Mayhew; her lips moved. "Who was in here?"

A minute ticked by, and everyone in the room noted the sudden dull boom of the surf that preceded Mayhew's words. "Only yourself and your mother—when I got here."

Mrs. Malloy trembled inside her blue wrapper. "They must have got away," she whispered, and looked at no one.

Sara sat up, pushing away the doctor's hands. "Didn't you hear them?" she demanded of her mother.

"No." It was a small word, weak in its denial and washed over by the sound of the sea. The woman's eyes were tormented but she went on. "All at once, while I was sound asleep in bed, I heard someone beating on our door. I opened it and the lieutenant was outside. He came in and I—I hadn't realized what had happened until then."

The girl did not look again at Mayhew. She fell abruptly back against the pillow, but when the doctor bent to hold an unstoppered bottle beneath her nostrils she said soberly, "I'm all right."

There was an awkward silence. The girl's face looked stunned with some shattering inward revelation. Her mother stood quivering—rigid—then quivering again. "I've been taking sleeping powders," she got out. "If they were quiet, as they must have been, I wouldn't have wakened."

Mayhew jerked a look at her as though he were thinking something he couldn't quite believe. . . .

That morning, with Miss Rachel's help, he went through Mrs. Sticklemann's belongings thoroughly. In the middle of an old packet of letters Mayhew found an oddly folded note. It cryptically informed the reader that one must pay honest debts or suffer the consequences.

The Scurlocks were made to write notes, and Mr. Scurlock's handwriting was found to match that of the note found in Lily's room. Shown the two sets of papers, with points of correspondence succinctly traced, Mr. Scurlock turned green and drooled.

Lieutenant Mayhew searched their belongings and came forth from the depths of a bureau in triumph. Under the starched brightness of Mr. Scurlock's shirts he had found a screwdriver.

"That isn't mine," Mr. Scurlock said promptly, and no one believed him.

Mayhew made experiments. This screwdriver, without a doubt, had made the scars on the outside of Lily's window.

"Tried it from outside first, didn't you?" asked the lieutenant, back in the room with the Scurlocks. Mrs. Scurlock stared back with the fixity of a cat. Mr. Scurlock was wild.

"Off to jail with you then," said Mayhew.

Miss Rachel thinks that for the rest of the morning the lieutenant was happy, and mercifully she let him be. But later in the day, when he told her that now he supposed she would go back home, she disturbed him by telling him that she most certainly would not.

"Do you like this place?" he demanded incredulously.

They had met in the hall. Miss Rachel looked about her in scorn at the dust, the cobwebs in easy reach of a broom and the scuffed places in the colorless carpet. "I don't indeed like it at all," she assured him. "I think, in fact, that this is the most completely undesirable place that I've been in."

"Well." He bunched his eyebrows at her. "You said you weren't leaving."

A little pink stained each white cheek. "I rather like being a detective," she said with modesty. "You see, I've been to see so many murder mysteries, in the movies, but I've never had a—er—chance at the real thing. It's gruesome"—she refrained from looking at Mayhew—"but fascinating. Fascinating."

Lieutenant Mayhew assumed an expression that kind people wear when they are dealing with stupid children. Miss Rachel has described it, after thought, as maternal. "But there's no need for a detective here any longer," he said, and patted her small hand. "The Scurlocks are under arrest. They killed your niece and we got them for it. Aren't you satisfied?"

"No. Not quite."

His smile was a little difficult. It tried to be affable and reproving at the same time. "The police are satisfied, at any rate. The district attorney says that there's no chance for anything but a conviction, with what we've given him. I just came back here to tell everybody they can go if they want to. I won't be back again."

Miss Rachel's brows made small arches of surprise. "Won't you?"

Mayhew was getting impatient. "No. Why should I?"

"Because a lot of us are going to be murdered in our beds, if you leave us alone," she told him in a matter-of-fact manner.

Her answer obviously shook his mind out of the complacent trench of thought it had settled into. He let out a deep breath and drew another, staring at her from beneath his black eyebrows. Miss Rachel thought he looked like a trained bear lost from its circus. He seemed bewildered and suddenly younger than thirty-three, which is his age.

"Look," he demanded. "Do you know something you haven't told me?"

She shook her white head. "Oh, no. I've told you everything

that could bear on this case from my point of view. I think we have the same set of facts in mind. We've arrived at different conclusions, however."

He stepped beyond her and thrust open the door of her room. "Let's talk," he said, motioning her in ahead of him.

They seated themselves—Miss Rachel on the bed and Mayhew in a rocker from which the veneer was curling in saw-toothed rolls.

"You don't think that the Scurlocks killed your niece?"

The black cat jumped into Miss Rachel's lap and she stroked the satin fur absently. "No. I can't think that they did."

He moved impatiently; the rocker emitted ominous creakings. "But it's an open-and-shut case against them—against him, at any rate. And a charge of being an accessory should stand against her. Look at the evidence against them: the screwdriver, with which an attempt had been made to enter the window, the threatening note in his handwriting, the I.O.U.s. that Mrs. Sticklemann wasn't paying on. If that doesn't spell conviction for murder I'll eat the I.O.U.s personally."

"You could very likely convict them of the murder. I don't doubt it for a moment." She drew purrs like the ruffle of a tiny drum from the cat and a look of relief from Mayhew. "But, you see, I still don't believe them guilty."

The look of relief was replaced by one of bafflement. "Do you *like* the Scurlocks?" Mayhew leaned forward; there was a loud screech from the rear part of the chair.

"No, I don't like them at all. Certainly not. They're just about the most unpleasant, the most cruel people I can remember meeting."

"Then why are you saying they didn't murder your niece?"

"Because they had no motive."

He fell back at this, and the chair started actually to give way beneath him, with its rockers inching forlornly in different directions. Mayhew looked down in large annoyance. His thought processes were interrupted by the knowledge that he was being let gently to the floor, and he changed to the other rocker in the room. *"No motive?"* he boomed above the shrieks of his new habitation.

"No," said Miss Rachel firmly, and met his eye. "You've got to accustom yourself to the idea that all the Scurlocks wanted was for my niece to obtain enough money so that they could collect what she owed them. They weren't getting any blood, so to speak, because Lily was financially a turnip—her small fortune had been left in trust. She couldn't touch its principal, and the interest barely kept her in living expenses. I think, that in the friendly period which must have begun the bridge games, that she told them of the inheritance she would receive on the death of the cat. Lily *would* tell a thing like that. Then later, when her own attempts to cheat the Scurlocks at cards had failed so disastrously, it would be the Scurlocks who first suggested the cat ought to die so that they could collect. Lily was regretful after the first poisoning attempt failed. It was Mr. Scurlock who had a second try at killing Samantha." Miss Rachel went on to describe the fall of rocks.

She stopped then, waiting for Mayhew to make some comment on what she had told him, but he remained silent, frowning.

"Don't you see?" She fixed him with her brilliant pleading gaze. "If the Scurlocks had entered a room where I was asleep, drugged, and the cat at their mercy, they would have immediately killed it?"

"Perhaps." He made a wry mouth. "But it doesn't let them

out. Perhaps Mrs. Sticklemann argued with them about killing it and they killed her instead. And, anyway, there's Scurlock's screwdriver. It made the marks on your niece's window—a plain attempt at unlawful entry."

Scratching Samantha's ears, Miss Rachel grew very thoughtful. "Tell me about the screwdriver. What sort was it?"

"A common enough kind. The handle's been repainted to black over a varnish finish, and that's all that's different about it. Edson's working the hardware stores today, trying to trace the sale."

"Hmmmm." Miss Rachel seemed very far away.

Lieutenant Mayhew grew suddenly impatient as though realizing that he was spending official time trying to convince a stubborn little old lady of an obvious truth. He rose, pinched his hat into shape and muttered good-bys. Miss Rachel ushered him out.

Looking very trim, very determined, Miss Rachel followed the lieutenant some fifteen minutes after. She was in her best taffeta, with Samantha's basket on her arm and a slightly foxy expression about the eyes.

She went first to the public library and requested to see back files of the local paper, being especially interested in numbers about the time of Malloy's disappearance. "Either his being away is connected with this thing or it isn't," she said quietly into the paper. An elderly man at the same table gave her an ogling of rheumatic surprise. Miss Rachel read quickly, seriously.

When she found what she was looking for she made notes on a bit of paper. The advertisement read: FIRE SALE, *good bargains in stock slightly damaged in our recent conflagration. Some not to be told from new.* And more, including the address.

Miss Rachel went out of the library in a hurry.

On West Fifth Street, amid a jumble of warehouses, machine shops and wholesale butcherers, she found a squeezed-in tool shop whose front showed new paint over the scars of a fire. "Same technique," she muttered, pushing open the door. A sallow-faced man with limp black hair looked up from behind the counter. No least flicker of curiosity showed in his glance. "Yes?" he said.

"Ahhh," murmured Miss Rachel, stalling. She took in the stock on the shelves. "Have you any good screwdrivers, cheap? Something left from your fire, perhaps?"

He shook his head, not coming closer. "All of them's sold. We've got new stock now."

"I'd like to see one, please."

He angled up out of his chair and found a screwdriver and brought it to Miss Rachel. She examined it critically.

"It's for my nephew, you see. He wanted one just like the one he bought here. He's lost it."

"This one's O.K.," said the lackadaisical man.

Miss Rachel forced a persimmon acidity into her tone. "I'd have to be sure. Haven't you a single one of those repainted tools? Even a used one—something to compare this with?"

The man sighed, then scratched the side of his face. "Believe there's one next door. I'll be gone a minute." He gave a quick glance round the shop as though to tabulate its contents mentally before leaving it in the doubtful hands of Miss Rachel, then went out with the door slamming behind him.

Coming back, he held an ordinary screwdriver with a black-painted handle. Miss Rachel took it, squinted at it. Close to the steel careless work had left bare a bit of the original varnish. Miss Rachel gave the tool back to the sallow-faced man.

"And this is the same?" she said, looking at the new tool.

"Yeah."

"I'll take it then," said Miss Rachel. She opened her purse. "I'll bet you remember my nephew." She attempted now a simpering fondness, which was hard, for she had at the same time to think of Mr. Scurlock. "He's a blond fellow, very pleasant." She added details to this which would have surprised even Lieutenant Mayhew.

The man shook his head, watching her take out her money. "I ain't sold him one that I remember. Most of my stuff goes out into the shops hereabouts. I ain't advertised, except for the fire sale."

"But you'd remember my nephew," persisted Miss Rachel. She clutched the money tight so that the waiting man was forced by his own impatience to listen to her. "I'm sure if you'll think, you'll recall him. He's a nice blond man, and he——"

"Look," said the sallow-faced man, "I had forty of them burned screwdrivers and I give five to the dope that painted them. That left thirty-five. I sold twenty in a lot, cheap, to the garage on the corner. The Metal craft people took ten. The carpenter shop across the street bought three. Ol' Andy next door has one, and that leaves——"

"One," said Miss Rachel briskly, watching the man.

He scratched the side of his face again. "Well, it wasn't no blond feller," he said at last.

"Yes?" said Miss Rachel on a small breath.

"As I remember——" The door slammed suddenly behind Miss Rachel. She saw the man's eyes widen, then settle into a look of defensive boredom. Miss Rachel looked round. Lieutenant Mayhew had come into the shop.

"How do you do?" he grumbled in Miss Rachel's direction. "Hello, Jipp," he said to the sallow man.

"I ain't done nothin'," said the other lounging toward his chair.

"It's not bicycle parts today, Jipp. I'm tracing this." The lieutenant held out a duplicate of the screwdriver that Jipp had brought from next door.

Jipp shrugged. "So what?" he sneered. "I sold a lot of 'em."

The interview went from bad to worse, with Miss Rachel a pained and exasperated listener. Jipp was bored; he yawned; he professed a bad memory about his screwdrivers. The lieutenant went out boiling.

Miss Rachel paid for her new screwdriver. The sallow-faced man, still looking dull, rang up the charge on a battered cash register.

"About my nephew——" Miss Rachel began again.

The sallow-faced man gave her a stare of angry suspicion. "To hell with your nephew," he said distinctly.

Miss Rachel went out very quietly, very much rebuffed.

Chapter Eleven:
Human Hands, Detachable

Miss Rachel refrained from giving the lieutenant an outright scolding. She did, in the later course of the afternoon, point out to him the inopportuneness of his entrance into the tool shop.

The lieutenant carried a frustrated expression even so late as the next morning, when he went early to police headquarters. The police of Breakers Beach occupy a wing of the new City Hall, A.D. 1938 and as modern as possible. Edson stepped suddenly from the office of the chief of police and Mayhew almost ran into him. He put out a big hand but Edson ducked. He has seen Mayhew's way with obstacles.

"Screwy nut," said Edson crossly.

Mayhew's face changed and Edson saw that it was wise to explain himself. "Guy in the chief's office. Drunk all night and wound up sometime this morning on the beach. Some kind of nightmare down there. If somebody doesn't get him out of there the chief's going to kill him."

Mayhew slowed his step. "What does he think he saw?"

"The guy? Oh, he thinks he was lyin' there half asleep and a guy *down under the sand* reached up and tried to grab him."

Edson grinned at the remembrance of the drunk's misery. "You should have seen the chief when he heard it. McGarvey, at the desk this morning, thought there might be something in it and waltzed him in. If he doesn't get demoted for it I'll eat my hat."

Mayhew showed interest in the account. Some inner sense—Mayhew simply calls it smelling a rat—makes him feel the significance of things that don't fit. "Guess I'll have a look," he said and went in to meet the raging eyes of his superior.

Opposite him, on the other side of his broad polished desk, cowered a slight young man in gaudy clothes, much rumpled and very soiled. Above a purple tie his face was sick. "'Tain't no use sayin' I didn't see 'im. I saw 'im, all right." He swung bloodshot eyes toward Mayhew and waggled his head in a slow rhythm. "'E was in the sand, 'e was." With rabbit teeth he nibbled his lower lip. "Don't tell me 'e wasn't. I saw 'im."

The chief beat on the desk and roared, "Get out! Get out—damn you! How many times do I have to tell you? McGarvey! McGarVEY! Oh, Lord. Mayhew, why'd I want this damned job, anyhow? Look at this bird—as drunk as a fool, and sassier. If McGarvey sends me in another delirium tremens I'll have his badge, and damned if I don't. What did you want?"

Mayhew nodded his head in the direction of the drunken young man. "I want him," he said briefly. "Come along with me, man."

They went into the cubbyhole that Mayhew calls his office. The young man huddled himself quickly into a chair again and sat hunched as if he were cold, with his hands hugged down between his knees. His voice was running down like a phonograph that needs winding. "I saw 'im. Really saw 'im," he whispered and closed his eyes.

Mayhew, attending an auction once, found a chair that

would not groan under his weight, and he bought it after a trial sitting and did not inquire into its history. The fact that it had been built for Bertha the Fat Lady, for her sojourn on the Strand one summer, might or might not have interested him. The big chair dwarfs the little office.

Mayhew sat himself in it now and fixed the bleary-eyed one with a ruthless look. "Come on and tell me about it. You're sure you saw a man on the beach?"

The hunched miserable figure shook its head. "Didn't see 'im," it mourned. "Just felt 'im."

"But you've been saying that you *saw* him. I heard you say it in the chief's office and you've said it here. Now. Did you see a man buried in the sand?"

The reddened eyes came open and gazed watery woe at Mayhew. "I just saw some of 'im."

Mayhew's face tightened with exasperation. "Well, tell me what you actually did see." He waited, silent, for the other to speak.

"I saw some 'uman 'ands," the hoarse voice said at last on a falsetto note.

Mayhew was beginning to understand the chief's anger at this befuddled crackpot, but some vague urge would not permit him to give up. "Start at the beginning. Where were you last night?"

The head went loosely from side to side like a weary doll's. "My girl ran out on me. She's a blonde—and too damn good-looking too. The sailors won't leave her alone."

Mayhew's broad shoulders bunched beneath his coat and he stood up slowly, gripping the edges of the desk with whitening fingers. The weary youth opposite him watched without fear, being in that state of after-drunkenness when nothing seems to matter. As Mayhew stood there, looking to be on the verge of an explosion, the singsong voice took up its chant:

"My girl ran out on me. I said that, di'n't I? So I went to a party. Bad party." He waggled a naughty finger. "Too much to drink. When I woke up this mornin', not really awake—but—" He struggled with words. "Drowsy. That's it. Drow—Ah. I was on the beach. Down at the east end, where there aren't any houses."

He watched Mayhew subside into the timbered vastness of his chair. Mayhew, making an effort, managed to quit gritting his teeth long enough to get out: "Go on from there."

At this point some measure of lucidity seemed to flicker in the eyes of the gaudy young man. "I was just layin' there—I kind of wanted to get up—when all at once this guy reaches up outa the sand and touches me with 'is 'and. On my face too. It give me a start. And then when I got to sittin' up, the funny beggar 'ad 'is other 'and stickin' up beside my shoe. I never met nobody before like that. None of 'im showin' but 'is 'ands." A look of anxiety came into the parchment-colored features. "What I kept thinkin'—'ow could 'e breathe down in the sand like that?"

Mayhew was beginning to get hold of the thing in his mind. "What did you do next?" he prodded.

"Oh, I thought I'd 'elp the cluck, whoever 'e was. It di'n't seem right to leave 'im down there. 'E might have been drunk like me. Never know. . . . So I took 'old of 'is 'and and tried to lift 'im out."

"And you pulled him out of the sand?"

The young man wavered in his chair, looking confused. "No. I couldn't. 'E wouldn't let me. 'E let go."

"He let go of your hand?" Mayhew was standing again, incredulous and annoyed.

"Not my 'and. 'E let go of *'is own 'and.*"

Mayhew had a suddenly humorous vision of this befuddled drunk standing on the lonely beach in the dawn holding a detached human hand in his own. For a moment, so pathetic was the drunk, and so worriedly sure, that Mayhew was almost convinced. Then the idea left him and he became frankly angry. "Look here," he snapped. "That's a lot of rot. Nobody can let go of his own hand."

"'E did. 'E let go of both of 'is. And well 'e orght, I guess. They sure stunk plenty."

The truth came at Mayhew like a blow between the eyes. He went after Edson, and the two of them, in a headquarters car, took the sad young man to the spot on the beach where he was sure he had lain. "He's stumbled on a corpse down here," Mayhew muttered to Edson as they tossed sand about. "The body was so badly decomposed that it came apart when he touched it. Go easy where you're walking around. I don't want the face squashed in."

"Any ideas?" Edson asked him.

"Yes—one. There's a man missing from the rooming house where the Sticklemann woman was killed. I've had him on the teletype for several days now and nothing's come in. This could possibly be him on the beach."

"Long enough to be as rotten as that?" Edson wondered.

"I don't think so. But if he's been in the water the fish might have worked on him and loosened the wrists somehow. Come on. Look around."

But though they scouted the eastern beach in all directions they found no corpse, nor any depression where one might have been buried. It was sometime later that Mayhew thought to consult the tide tables and realized that the drunken young man could have been lying on sand that was under water when he and Edson were there. They went back again when the tide was out and got wet to the knees in the eddying foam, but there was still no corpse.

"The chief was right," Edson comforted. "The guy had the D.T.s, and he dreamed it."

But Mayhew shook his head.

He mentioned it to Miss Rachel later in the day.

In the face of Miss Rachel's polite curiosity he tried to be adamant, but she had wheedling though ladylike ways with her and he usually ended by telling her things that were, strictly speaking, police business. He found her now in her room, reading a murder novel and with the cat asleep in her lap. Before he quite understood how she did it she had obtained the story of his morning's adventure.

She looked at him with her wide dark eyes, putting down her book. "You think it has something to do with this case?" she asked him.

"I can't know," he admitted, "but I'm inclined to think that it's possible. You see, here at Breakers Beach we haven't a great deal of crime. A murder once in a long while, and most of them are not mysteries. There's practically no underworld here, or rackets either. The place simply isn't big enough to make them pay. During the height of the summer season, when the tourists are in, we usually pick up a few confidence men who are out looking for suckers. That's about all of it. For that reason, when I hear of a dead body at the same time that I know a man is missing I'm inclined to connect the two. Of course I'm frankly playing a hunch. There mightn't be anything in it."

She smoothed her taffeta skirt with a small hand, looking

very sober. "It seems logical to think that there might be a connection. Was he sure that it was a man's hands he saw?"

"Oh, he was sure enough. It's true he was drunk, and that you couldn't swear by what he says. And the body must have been much decomposed, or injured, to separate as it did so that a drunk person might not be able to know whether it was the hand of a man or a woman. The point that puzzles me is that we couldn't find the thing afterward, if he were telling the truth."

"There were no signs of it—no hole in the sand?"

"None. Of course the tide had been in. It's possible that it could have washed out to sea again."

She puzzled over the thing in silence for several minutes. There was no sound in the narrow dingy room save the purring of the cat and the deep breathing of Lieutenant Mayhew.

"Are bodies often found on the beach—bodies of people who drown accidentally, I mean?" she asked.

"We don't often get them, unless they've gone swimming near by. The breakwater, which was built about ten years ago, has changed the currents along this stretch of the coast. If people are drowned at sea, or up or down the coast, we almost never see them. A harbor engineer explained it during a trial I was interested in that concerned a murder by drowning. Something to do with the tides."

"I see. Then if a body were found on the beach it might be supposed that it had been a person who had entered the water near here?"

"It would be most likely, though not absolutely certain. That's the thing that made me interested in this drunk's story. Otherwise it could have been a body washed in from God knows where, and no likelihood of a connection with the murder of your niece."

"You're thinking, then, that it might be Malloy."

"Yes. That was my idea."

"Have you tried to locate him otherwise?"

"Yes, I have. I put his description on the teletype immediately, and so far I've had no results whatever. Edson interviewed several of Malloy's acquaintances, here and in Los Angeles, and none of them had seen him lately or had any idea of his whereabouts. He's dropped completely from sight, and it seems to me there are two reasonable explanations for it: he is either the murderer of your niece and in hiding; or he has been killed, in which case his death would seem logically connected in some way with that of your niece."

"That seems a natural explanation."

Mayhew ruffled his dark thatch in a puzzled gesture. "Which brings us back to the question of motive. Why should Malloy want to kill her?"

"He might have had several perfectly good motives."

"Such as?"

Miss Rachel's delicate face saddened at the memory of Lily's persistent dissembling. "I think that he and my niece were more than friends. They were, I think, either married or—lovers. Somewhere in their relationship there might have been difficulties that would provide motive for murder."

"But, see here! They couldn't have been married! Malloy isn't legally divorced for some time yet. He and his wife have only an interlocutory decree."

Miss Rachel frowned. "That's so, isn't it? I rather thought, from Lily's manner, that they might have been married. She seemed kind of worried and shy, as though she had a romantic secret of some sort. And I've never figured her as the sort to—to—" Miss Rachel coughed delicately and lifted her brows a little, which was the most polite way of expressing what she meant that Mayhew could imagine. "She was foolish, and I guess you must know that by now, but I can't quite believe that she was immoral."

"Well, they couldn't have been married in California without Malloy perjuring himself and technically committing bigamy. So it looks as if it might have been—the other."

Miss Rachel leaned toward him from where she sat, her face lighted with the blow of some new idea. "Do you read movie magazines very often?" she asked suddenly, and when Mayhew looked slightly insulted and shook his head she rushed on in embarrassment. "I mean—well, I do. And ever so often I've read about some of these movie people getting into scrapes about their marriages. You see, they get their first decree here in California and then rush off into Mexico—Tia Juana—and marry some new person. Of course California doesn't recognize such marriages, but it does seem more respectable than—well. Now remember that Malloy had been an actor. Perhaps people on the stage are something like those on the screen. Maybe he got Lily to go with him into Mexico and get married!"

Mayhew started to say something in a hurry, bit it off and looked shrewdly at the little old lady before him. "Would your niece have done that?" he asked.

Miss Rachel said slowly, "She'd love it from the romantic, the daring side. There's just one thing—Lily was married somewhat that way before and it turned out poorly." Miss Rachel related Lily's unfortunate and costly adventure with the bigamous Mr. Sticklemann and Mr. Sticklemann's thoroughly successful efforts to milk Lily for money. The lieutenant was interested until Miss Rachel told him that Sticklemann was now dead.

The talk drifted, came round again to the hands on the beach. "It was hands, you know," she reminded the lieutenant.

"And not a body, as you say," he muttered, his mind following hers into this new line of thought. "If they'd been detached from the body previously—that would account for them. It doesn't account for their being removed in the first place."

"Why are hands removed from bodies, Lieutenant?"

He considered some of his previous cases. "To prevent identification of the corpse, usually."

"But—presuming that these are Malloy's hands—there's no object there. His corpse, if there is one, has never been discovered."

"That's not saying that it won't turn up in time."

"There's something careless about this part of it," said Miss Rachel thoughtfully. "It's almost as if the hands, if they're connected with this, were thrown away as useless."

The lieutenant sat silent for a while, obviously deep in thought. "There's one thing," he said at last, "that they would be perfectly useless for, and that would be to plant fingerprints with. If anyone had a mad idea—"

"Hmmmm," said Miss Rachel to her cat.

Mayhew pulled the skin of his throat in a gesture of worry. "This case is absolutely and completely a mess," he pronounced. "It isn't getting anywhere."

"Vague. Yes," Miss Rachel consoled him. . . .

Mayhew had not heard the last of the hands on the beach.

Late that day a little boy brought proudly home to his mother what he considered to be an unusually fine fat starfish. His mother gave one look into his little bucket, screamed loudly enough and long enough to bring neighbors running and fainted. The neighbors took the little boy's bucket to the police.

In it, unpleasantly decomposed, lay a human hand.

Mayhew put Dr. Southart upon it at once. Southart complained moodily, and invited Mayhew to smell of the damned thing, and wondered why corpses couldn't be buried decently entire and stay put. But he did his job well enough. After Mayhew returned from having dinner Southart was ready with a brief report.

"Hand was severed at the wrist, not skillfully, by the use of some sharp instrument. Maybe a hatchet," he outlined to Mayhew. "It's a man's hand. He was well nourished, well groomed, and hadn't done any work to get calluses. I can't determine age without further work." He looked frowningly about him at the immaculate little room full of apparatus and gleaming glassware. "There are times," he said quite distinctly, "in which I positively hate this work, Mayhew."

Mayhew shrugged; he considers Dr. Southart, with his sensitive nose, not well fitted for police work. "I'm sorry. I knew it was far gone."

"I'm not still griping about the smell," Dr. Southart flung at him. "This damned hand's got far worse than that wrong with it."

Mayhew was interested. "What's that?" he asked.

"Just come have a look at what's under the fingernails." The doctor led him to a table where an oversized microscope was focused onto a brilliantly lighted slide. Something wrapped in a cloth rested partly on the slide. Mayhew put his eye to the machine and the doctor manipulated things with tweezer and scalpel.

"Good God," Mayhew muttered, and a little of his tan left him. He caught at the edge of the table and lifted his face to Dr. Southart's. "Where did they get a damnable idea like that?"

Southart made an impatient motion with one hand. "Oh, the idea's pretty common property by now, I think. Remember that motion picture: *The Frontiers of India?* It was carefully explained during the course of the film, in case one hadn't previously heard of it. And the picture was pretty popular. Remember the scene where the maharajah has the hero tied down and has those little slivers driven under his nails and then set afire? Nice thought."

Mayhew touched the skin of his upper lip and brought away the sudden perspiration that had gathered there. "But, damn it, this is the United States!"

"Dear little Breakers Beach, in fact," the doctor mocked him. "And the year of Our Lord 1938. And we have ingenious people with us who play at being maharajahs and poke slivers under people's fingers to set afire. It must feel good, that kind of torture."

Mayhew caught at a straw. "Maybe they did it after his hands were cut off," he said lamely.

The doctor's grin was sardonic. "Likely?" he asked Mayhew.

Chapter Twelve: The Weapon

Mayhew was disturbed by the evidence of the severed hand more than he liked to admit. He had been in contact with violent death many times, death both planned and accidental and most often hideous, but outright, cold-blooded torture was rare to him. He found himself wondering about the hand and about the man who had owned it: what frozen superhuman control or babbling frenzy had possessed him in his hour of agony, and above all, what the purpose of the torture might have been.

And was it, by some wild chance, Malloy's hand?

Southart gave Mayhew his promise to work further on the thing that night; to study the hair on it, and if possible to get prints from the fingers, though these last would of necessity not be perfect. Mayhew made a flying trip to Surf House, grim and sinister and still in the midst of a sea of fog, and obtained from Malloy's room hair samples that were certain to be his. By comparing such hair with that found upon the severed hand it might be possible to make identification complete. Mayhew also hunted for fingerprints, and brought away with him Malloy's hairbrush and a shaving mug that showed evidences of handling.

Prints were developed from the articles from Malloy's room and from the fingers of the dead hand, and in a few minutes Mayhew had a report on them. They were almost certainly the same, though further examination was necessary for the prints from the decomposed fingers were somewhat distorted. Dr. Southart also gave as his opinion that the hair from the hand and from Malloy's room was enough alike in color and structure to presume that it had come from the same body.

Mayhew sat in his office with a hanging lamp burning above his desk. He had a blank piece of paper in front of him on which he occasionally drew meaningless triangles and circles. His small notebook lay open beside the paper, and twice he leafed through it in an aimless manner.

It occurred to him that he had allotted to each person in the old house at the beach a page in his book—except Malloy.

He chose a clean page and began to sketch in such facts as he knew about the man. Malloy was somewhere near fifty years old; he had been married for almost half that time to Mrs. Malloy, and had one child: Sara. Writing that last name Mayhew hesitated. It was a pretty name, he thought; and almost without seeming to think what he was about, he wrote it on his scratch sheet in among the circles and triangles and drew a heart neatly around it. It was such a thing as small boys or very young men are fond of carving on trees. Mayhew studied it abstractly as one would a work of art, and then rumpled the sheet and cast it into his waste-basket and went on with Malloy.

Malloy had moved into Surf House at the time of his separation from Mrs. Malloy, which had been almost a year ago. He had moved there at almost the same time that the establishment had been taken over by his cousin, Mrs. Turner, with whom he was newly in contact, and because its location on the amusement zone must have appealed to a man just freed from matrimony which had become irksome. At the house, Malloy had had close contact with but two people: Mrs. Turner and Mrs. Sticklemann; and he had played cards with the Scurlocks.

Mrs. Sticklemann was dead; the Scurlocks very much under suspicion. What about Mrs. Turner, the acidulous landlady?

Her alibi for the time that the murder had been committed was at once the most casual and the best corroborated of any of them. She had been sewing. Miss Rachel herself, in last moments of fogged consciousness, had heard the machine at the end of the hall. Mrs. Malloy, sitting at her open window to keep guard on Sara, who had gone out their window and into the one of Malloy's room, had also heard Mrs. Turner sewing. Mayhew reasoned why she had so especially noted the sound—also why, when Miss Rachel heard the machine stop, the rocker stopped too. Mrs. Malloy had been afraid that Mrs. Turner might hear Sara's movements and go to investigate.

And Sara—little as he liked to consider this point—had she *really* been in her father's room and *nowhere else?* Sara would have no motive, and senseless as the case appeared to be there must be motive in it somewhere.

The Scurlocks, to his mind, had an excellent motive for murder: a gambler's vengeance upon a welcher. But Miss Rachel had pointed out the weak points in the case against them and had practically proved that Mr. Scurlock was not the purchaser of the screwdriver—points which an adroit defense counsel would be sure to stress—so that the Scurlocks had been released, though still not in the clear. They had been warned against leaving town and had returned to the old house, not stirring out of the door since, so far as he knew.

Mrs. Turner, whose only connection with the case was her

relation to the missing man, had, for all that he could see, no motive of any kind.

But other people connected with Malloy may have had reasonable motives. Jealousy of Mrs. Sticklemann might have caused Mrs. Malloy, or conceivably Sara, to murder the other woman. Leinster, whom Mayhew now knew to have been a college friend of the Malloy girl though not known to her mother and father, had, Mayhew suspected, come down to Surf House as a favor to Sara, to see what her father was up to. It was far-fetched, and yet not impossible, that some complication of their acquaintanceship had caused him to kill the woman.

Mayhew stared moodily at the notebook and tried to force his mind through the fog of contradictions that surrounded the case. He considered the character of the Sticklemann woman as he knew it—vain, stupid, given to secrecy and small intrigue—and he told himself that her personality set the pace for all of it. The thing was like that in its entirety: as stupid, as ill thought, as involved in clumsy manipulations as the victim herself.

It was, on the whole, a clumsy crime, and yet its very grotesqueness eluded him.

The senselessness of cutting off a man's hands, of letting them be discovered, no matter how accidentally, was stupendous when he came to think about it.

Uneasily, he shifted in his chair. He wondered what was afoot, even now, in the old house by the beach. . . .

At nine o'clock, as he was leaving his office, Mayhew received a call from Surf House. Miss Rachel's precise clear voice came over the wire. "We've discovered something," she told him. "A short-handled ax. It was sewn into the mattress in Mrs. Malloy's room."

"I'll be right down." He hesitated for a moment, thinking. "How did you come to find it?"

"Mrs. Malloy says that she turned the mattress today. A few minutes ago she went to bed and Sara felt it at once. It was near the ticking and near the edge of the mattress."

"Don't handle it," cautioned Mayhew, and put away the phone.

He found Sara Malloy, her mother and Miss Rachel in the Malloy apartment. Sara and her mother in gowns and robes, and Sara's hair, in a long sheath down her back, incredibly golden. Miss Rachel was fully dressed in her usual neat taffeta. All of them were standing uncomfortable and silent. Mayhew greeted Mrs. Malloy, let his gaze linger for a moment on the lovely but troubled face of her daughter and turned to Miss Rachel for an explanation. She led him to the bed where a gaping ripped place bulged stuffing from the mattress.

"It's in there," she said quickly. "None of us have touched it. As soon as Mrs. Malloy and Sara had the mattress open—they had only to loosen these big stitches here, you see, where someone's sewn it—and as soon as they saw what was inside, they called me. And I called you."

Lifting the mattress covering, Mayhew saw inside it a short-handled ax. The blade of the thing was stained and crusted with a dark, brownish substance—blood, long dried—but Mayhew saw at once that there were no corresponding stains upon the mattress filling. This ax, then, had been placed in the mattress after it had dried. He removed the ax and questioned the Malloys closely as to how it might have got into the mattress. They assured him that they had no idea how it might have come there. They were out of their apartment part of every day, as a usual thing. Yes, the ax could have been put inside the mattress that very day. Mayhew sighed. Why had Mrs. Malloy decided to turn the mattress? She just thought of it? So . . .

Mayhew took samples of the thread—though these wouldn't help him, barring a miracle, for it was common stuff—and wrapped the ax in newspaper to take it with him. He warned all of the women to stay inside their apartments, unless necessary to go out, and to keep their doors locked at night and their windows secured in some way so that they could not be opened enough to admit a human body. He demonstrated a simple way to secure a window by putting a nail through the upper sash. The nail would keep the other pane from being raised also, because it would bar the channel that the frame rose in.

It was also clear to Mayhew that he should prepare Mrs. Malloy for news of her husband's death, for he had no doubt in his mind but that the severed hand indicated such a contingency. He broached the subject carefully, asking her if she had had any recent news of her husband and if she were prepared to receive some which was not pleasant. It wasn't exactly an original approach but Mayhew could think of no other.

Mrs. Malloy started to tremble, as she had done on the night of Sara's misfortune, and her eyes widened to pools of fearful pain. "It's true then—the thing I couldn't quite believe!" she whispered, reading Mayhew's sympathetic face. "He's dead!" The brief words drifted to silence under the distant boom of the sea.

Mayhew nodded, wishing that he was of the glib type of man who can readily express sympathy in words. "I'm afraid that that is the conclusion we must draw from the evidence we have. It's practically a certainty, Mrs. Malloy. I wouldn't tell you, otherwise."

Above her mother's bowed and shaking head Sara's eyes met those of the big detective, and anger, hotly blue, grew in them. A deep pink rose into her face to drown the paleness that had been there. "You shouldn't have told her!" Sara cried, with her chin lifted in defiance. "It was a cruel, a tactless thing to do. Why couldn't you have waited? You admit that you aren't sure!"

Miss Rachel spoke slowly, as though she were thinking aloud. "You've found the hands again, then? And they were Malloy's, as you thought they might be?"

Mayhew had started to agree, and to tell her of what the boy had found on the beach, when he saw Mrs. Malloy lift her head stiffly and uncertainly, and he realized what horror must be hers if she were to know all of the truth. Quickly he excused himself to the mother and daughter, leaving one in questioning grief, the other in anger.

Miss Rachel followed him into the hall. "Come into my room for a minute?" she asked eagerly. "Please tell me what you have learned about Malloy."

He went into her apartment, where the fragrance of lavender struggled against the musty smell of the old house. Mayhew looked at the chairs, selected a straight-backed one that he had not previously weakened by sitting in it and sat down. "The hands are almost certainly Malloy's," he told the little old lady, who reminded him at once of a mouse and a ferret. "We've matched prints from them with prints taken from his belongings here and with hair from his room. There's not a chance in a thousand that the hand we have didn't belong to the missing man."

"You have only one of them?"

"Just the one. The other's probably kicking around the beach somewhere. The doctor says that the hand we have was severed by a sharp instrument, but not carefully, or with any skill. Chopped off, he thinks; and with an ax or hatchet."

Miss Rachel's eyes strayed suggestively to the bulging package that protruded from Mayhew's pocket. "That means," she said thoughtfully, "that your drunken man did not see a body, as I had a hunch he hadn't. He saw these hands, took it for granted that they were thrust up out of the sand with the body concealed below, and he took hold of them. When they came away freely in his grip he thought that the man had let go of his own hands."

Mayhew nodded grimly. "Shows what drink can do to your senses," he agreed.

Miss Rachel spent a silent minute thinking. "There's someone awfully fond of working with an ax," she remarked.

"Axes—and other things," Mayhew said bitterly. He went on to describe the evidences of torture—the bits of charred wood under the nails of the severed hand.

Miss Rachel shivered, her eyes gone big. "That's monstrous," she said after a moment. There was an uneven note in her voice and a white line about her lips.

"The whole thing is monstrous," Mayhew said shortly. "That's why I am going to make the request that I am. I want you and the Malloys to go home. There's no sense in your sort of people being here. You may be in terrible danger, and if anything happened to one of you I'd never forgive myself."

Miss Rachel managed a smile. "Oh, but you're here to watch us."

Mayhew sneered at himself. "I'm wonderful protection. Really. A little slow, however," he mocked. "Remember what happened to Miss Malloy? She was going to help me by pretending she might be able to remember who had entered Mrs. Sticklemann's room the night of the murder. Then what? She nearly got murdered for it, and I came in barely in time to save her and without seeing hair or hide of who had done it."

"An odd thing—wasn't it? The window was closed tight, locked, and you were in the hall. Yet only Mrs. Malloy was in the room with Sara."

Again a look, half disbelief, half angry certainty, came into Mayhew's face. But Miss Rachel burst in upon his thought. "No. Don't think it," she cautioned him. "Mrs. Malloy isn't capable of a thing like that."

"If she killed the Sticklemann woman—pardon me, your niece—she would be capable of killing Sara. You know she would."

But Miss Rachel stubbornly shook her head. "She isn't a killer, Lieutenant. Don't ask me how I know. She just isn't."

He stared at her in gloomy uncertainty for a while. When Miss Rachel spoke again it was upon another subject. "Have you thought of investigating the Mexican marriage possibility?"

"It's a wild chance. I haven't any faith in it."

"You didn't know Lily Sticklemann," she said quietly. "It's the kind of thing she would have loved."

"It's pretty certain that they weren't married in California, at any rate," he told her. "We've had reports from all county registries, and even from some places close to the border in Arizona. I'm inclined to discount the marriage idea anyhow," he went on. "What's the point of it?"

"What's the point of the murder?" demanded Miss Rachel waspishly. He ruffled his thick dark hair with an angry movement. "Damned if I know," he said frankly.

Miss Rachel straightened and looked at him in an intensity

of emotion. "I think that I know why my niece was murdered," she said in an eager tone. Mayhew looked at her, his orderly and methodical brain half annoyed at the way she took fliers off into theory. "I think that the whole thing revolves around money—around the hope of an inheritance."

He shrugged that one off with obvious incredulity. "Couldn't have been. You and your sister inherit her money. Unless, of course"—he smiled without humor—"you killed her."

Miss Rachel looked almost insulted at this bit of brutal nonsense. "Listen." She shook a finger at him twice. "And don't make fun. It's true that my sister and I inherit my niece's money; her will disposes of it in that way. But supposing that she hadn't made that will on the morning of the day she died? Who would have inherited her money then? The person who expects to get it now, I think. The person who does not know that Lily made that last-minute document."

Mayhew's attention was caught by the logical thought. "All right. To whom do you think your niece left her money?"

"Obviously, not to my sister and me. Otherwise there would have been no need for a new will. I think—and that has been my main basis for the marriage theory—that Lily left her money to Charles Malloy. I think that after she made that will and he disappeared that she waited here for him until her death, gradually suspecting more and more that something serious was wrong."

"But see, you're her aunt. If she were married to this man wouldn't she have told you about it?"

"I don't think that she would have. If it were not a strictly legal marriage—whether she knew so from the beginning or learned so after the ceremony—I believe she would have kept quiet about it to me. In fact, when I hinted that she and Mr. Malloy might be more than friends she seemed positively frightened. So afraid, in fact, that in thinking the thing over since, I am sure that she and Malloy were intimate in some way and that she had cause to conceal it. Let's presume—"

Here a baffled look came over Mayhew's face and he stretched his big legs impatiently. He claims that at this stage of the thing Miss Rachel's dizzy imaginings were aggravating. But she went on nevertheless, though she sensed the incredulity in his official mind.

"Let's presume that Lily didn't know that her marriage to Malloy wasn't all that it should be; that she learned it *after* she had made a will giving him her money in case she died. Then, learning somehow—perhaps from Malloy himself: it would give him sort of a hold over her—that his divorce was incompleted, she saw what a mess she was in and decided to keep quict until things could be straightened out and a legal marriage performed. And that somehow, during the course of Malloy's strange absence, she became frightened for herself. That theory, I know, must seem farfetched to you, as if I'd picked it out of thin air. But I didn't get it that way—I got it by piecing together a whole series of tiny apparently unimportant things that happened while I was here and before Lily came to her death."

Mayhew shrugged. "We haven't any proof that they were married," he pointed out.

"Aren't you going to try Mexico?"

He got up, pulling his coat into place over his big shoulders where it had been pulled to one side by the weight of the ax in his pocket. "Yes, I'll try Mexico," he said with sudden agreeableness. "You are the woman's aunt and you should know more of her than anyone else. I'll make the trip to Tia Juana tomorrow. There's another reason I want to go south—a man lives in San Diego who was a good friend of Malloy's, a lawyer that he knew from boyhood. So far, from the list of people that Mrs. Malloy gave us, we've drawn blank. Tomorrow I'll talk to Nicholson and also cross the border and have a look at the marriage register in Tia Juana."

"Good," said Miss Rachel.

Mayhew rose to go.

"Now we're getting somewhere," she finished, and ushered him out.

Chapter Thirteen:
The Rented Car

The day was cool and without sun. A fog had crept in upon the little beach city, dampening it and blurring the outlines of its buildings. In the business section traffic was careful and slow. Mayhew waited in his light sedan for a truck ahead to make up its mind about crossing the street. The truck hesitated like a giant bug caught in a mist, with its headlights beaming like yellow feelers, blindly, and bunched with its high tarpaulined load like a grasshopper ready to jump. Mayhew, taken with this absent fancy, almost missed the bell, and a fellow officer handling traffic gave him a hail.

His way took him through the tortuous maze of traffic and into more open streets to the south, until he at last was on the coast highway to San Diego. The road is wide, paved beautifully and invites speed. The speedometer needle in Mayhew's car crept from 40 to 50 to 60, and when the fog disappeared at San Juan Capistrano it shot to 65. Here it hovered, pulsing once in a while to 70. Mayhew relaxed behind the wheel. The morning had that bright glittering clarity that is common to the beaches of southern California and could be a condition of the atmosphere reflected from the blue splendor of the sea. Mayhew felt a vague sense of happiness stir in him as he looked across beaches to the windy surf, or shot his car over hills brown as a camel's back to drop again to the sea. He thought suddenly and unaccountably of Sara Malloy.

She was new and sound as the world is, on mornings like that one, and her hair had the yellow beauty of sunshine. It occurred to Mayhew that girls like that do not usually marry blunt and unpolished detectives, men who know death and crime better than how to please a woman. No, she belonged to another sort of man, a tactful and sensitive fellow who would know with better instinct than Mayhew's how to make her happy. This thought discomforted him, so that he watched the road with but half his mind and chided himself for a fool with the remainder.

Love and death, Mayhew decided, are uncongenial companions.

His car swept through the small communities that dot the coast between Breakers Beach and San Diego, and just beyond one of these there was a branching road, a high archway and a sign. The sign said: *To San Dimas Caves.* Some ripple of memory stirred in Mayhew's mind and he turned to glance frowning back at the archway as it drifted past. A truck came into view ahead, lumbering along in the middle of the road. Mayhew caught sight of it and gave it his whole attention. The Caves, famed over the world for their subterranean wonders, left his mind and he gave them no further thought.

In San Diego he debated whether to go see the man Nicholson first, or to go to Tia Juana. At last he decided, with a tinge of irritation, to lay Miss Rachel's wild fancy before doing any solid business on his own. He had a substantial lunch of Mexican cookery, of which he is extremely fond, and went on to the border.

Tia Juana was never a pretty town. It is baked colorless by the sun, and the apathy of its inhabitants has permitted a remarkable architectural disarray among its buildings; they lean, they sigh on the breeze, and their sagging doors allow the wind and the gaze of the passerby to enter alike unhindered. Till prohibition was repealed it was at least nervously alive, self-consciously wicked, full of drunken Americans, drowsy Mexicans and shrewd profit-takers of other divers nationalities. Now it is sunken in lethargy and has become a gateway to more luxuriant Agua Caliente, which is at times permitted by local authorities to become a racing capital.

Tia Juana has, however, one remaining claim for the attention of the world: it is used at times for a marriage place by sundry screen notables. The common herd, which has trailed the motion-picture stars to this Gretna Green, doesn't count. Mayhew found the marriage license register bulging with names of persons whom the urge to marry had overtaken in haste, so that they could not wait the required three days in California. A little yellow Mexican clerk helped him in his search, and to Mayhew's stupefaction they found what he was looking for. A Lily Sticklemann and a Charles Malloy had been married in Tia Juana some three and a half months ago.

Mayhew made careful note of the page, the date and the time, tipped the black-eyed clerk and drove back to San Diego.

He did not attempt to consider this information in all of its potentialities during this time, except that he began to remember seriously what Miss Rachel had postulated about the existence of a will previous to the one that Lily had given her. He had proved that the Sticklemann woman and Malloy had entered into a marriage, a semibigamous one on Malloy's part; and Miss Rachel had somehow sensed a deeper connection between Malloy and her niece than what had appeared on the surface. She had also thought that there might be another will in existence which gave Lily's money to Malloy in case of her death. Mayhew wondered how he might prove or disprove this last supposition and saw no obvious way to do it.

He let this problem rest and drove to the home of Jasper Nicholson. The man lived in an older section of San Diego in an immense white house, well kept and with spacious grounds looking out from the side of a hill above the bay. Mayhew was let in by a butler, and after a few moments Nicholson joined Mayhew in the library.

Mayhew studied the man, struck instantly by his odd appearance. He was big, spare-fleshed, with a great bony face and perfectly white hair. He wore a Vandyke beard which was not quite straight on his chin, a mustache of the drooping variety, and his eyebrows slanted strongly upward, giving him a slightly diabolical expression. Mayhew had the impression that the man shaved himself and that neither his eye nor his hand was steady. Two hounds entered the room with him, and when he settled himself into a chair opposite the one that held Mayhew they lay down beside him, putting their heads upon their front paws and surveying the visitor with mournful calm.

Mayhew had had a letter from Nicholson at the time when inquiries were first sent out about Malloy, so that the object of his visit was known. Nicholson had written that he had seen Malloy on a certain date, and by comparing that date with others remembered by tenants in Surf House Mayhew was sure that Nicholson had seen Malloy at almost the exact time of his disappearance.

Nicholson began talking about his old friend in a deep hoarse voice. He again named the date upon which he had seen Malloy. Mayhew asked him how he so clearly remembered the date. The old man's eyes flashed: "I have it written down," he said sharply. "I keep track of such things. I am a lawyer, and though I do not practice much any more, beyond taking care of legal matters for my friends, I keep my old habits still. I have made it a point to write down all appointments, even to the hour."

"And at what hour did Malloy come?" Mayhew asked.

"At about four o'clock in the afternoon. He stayed not more than fifteen minutes and then went away to keep another appointment."

"Mr. Nicholson," Mayhew said soberly, trying to impress upon the old man the seriousness of the situation, "I am convinced that you were one of the last people to see Malloy alive. He disappeared from Breakers Beach upon the day that you saw him here. Now I would like to know what his business was with you."

Mr. Nicholson made an impatient gesture with one bony blue-veined hand, and when he spoke his voice was rough as the sound of a saw. "He came here on a fool's mission, I consider. He wanted my opinion on the validity of a Mexican marriage, presuming that one party to such a marriage were not legally divorced in California. Of course I told him straight off that such a marriage was no more than a farce, and that if the marriage relationship were entered into in such a case it would be immoral conduct in the eyes of the law." Nicholson went on shaking his head after he had finished speaking, and drew his white brows into a frown.

Mayhew could not quite conceal the eagerness with which

he went on speaking. "Did he tell you that he himself was party to such a marriage?" he asked.

"He did not—though I suspected that he was personally interested in such a case from his manner."

"Was that all he wanted of you?"

"Not quite all. He also asked me to look over a will and to tell him if it were drawn up properly so that it would stand in a court of law."

"A will? His own?"

Mr. Nicholson shook his head, so that his poorly placed white whiskers waggled. "No, not his own. It was a will which left money to him from someone else's estate—signed by a woman, I believe. I do not recall the name."

"Was the will in good order?"

"It was—perfectly so. It was a holographic will, written entirely by hand, that is, and therefore required no witnesses according to California law. It left all of the person's possessions to Mr. Malloy."

"You have no recollection whatever of the name? Could it have been such a name as Sticklemann—Lily Sticklemann?"

The old man sat sunk in silence, his long fingers stroking the silken ear of a grateful hound in a meditative manner. He seemed to be trying to concentrate upon the events of the day that Charles Malloy had been to see him. At last, however, still seeming puzzled, he shook his head. "No, I couldn't say. The name has entirely escaped me."

"We'll have to let that point go then. If during the next few days you should happen to recall the name signed to the will, please call me at Breakers Beach and let me know. Now I'd like you to go further into another detail. You said that Malloy mentioned to you that he had another engagement to keep after he left your house. Do you remember where, and with whom, the appointment was?"

"I don't remember, because he didn't tell me. He was distinctly vague about it, I recall; and when he left, he seemed in a hurry."

"How did he arrive then—in a taxi, or by foot?"

"Neither. I noticed a car at the curb when I showed him to the door, and I asked him about it. It's very clear to me what he told me—that the car was a rented one and that he had taken it from an agency in San Diego."

Mayhew made careful mental note of this last fact, for such things are easily checked. He continued talking to Nicholson for several minutes longer but the old man was unable to add anything to what he had already told Mayhew.

It was nearly evening when Mayhew left Nicholson's home. Across the placid waters of San Diego bay the sun was sinking in red glory into the sea, and the sky above had the peculiarly faded hue that precedes the night. The sea winds had a salt smell in them, crisp and chill. Mayhew drove into town, found a restaurant and had dinner, and then began the round of car-rental agencies.

At nearly nine o'clock, after having looked fruitlessly through three previous sets of books, he found the record of Malloy's rental of a car. The office of the agency was neither large nor prominent; their stock of cars was small and not select—it was the kind of place to be patronized by a man who wanted to remain inconspicuous and to keep a rendezvous without too much attention. A conviction was growing in Mayhew's mind that Malloy's appointment, after his visit to Nicholson, had been with his murderer.

It must have been in the vicinity of San Diego, else there

was no point in renting a car there. But if such were the case, and Malloy had met death at the appointed place, where was his body?

The record of the car rental had no details for Mayhew beyond the date, and the charge, which had been according to the mileage. The manager of the agency, figuring from the amount Malloy had paid them, thought that the distance traveled by the rented car had been between 40 and 50 miles. He had not been on duty when the car had been returned but he asked Mayhew to wait until 9:30 when the night man would come on duty—the same man who had received the returned car when Malloy or some other person had returned it.

The night man appeared promptly at the proper time. He was a slender man, red-haired and good-natured in appearance, and he seemed intelligent. In answer to Mayhew's question, and after studying the entries in the book as to date and amount charged, he said that he believed that he remembered the return of the car.

He recalled it, he said, because of the damaged condition of one rear tire, for which he had had to charge a dollar for repairs. A piece of broken clam shell had imbedded itself in the tire, puncturing the tube and allowing a slow leak that had kept the tire from going entirely flat. The man—here Mayhew jerked to eager attention—had willingly paid the charge.

Yes, it had been a man. A man in the uniform of a chauffeur, with a beaked cap well down over his face so that his features were almost entirely hidden.

It was Mayhew's first sight of his quarry, the person whom he felt sure was the killer at Surf House—a man in a chauffeur's uniform with his face half hidden by a cap! Mayhew saw at once the use of such a garb: it permitted the wearing of a wide-beaked cap as a matter of course.

The point of the clam shell caught his attention. It suggested the beach, or a road on filled or uplifted land near the sea. A grove of trees, or a cave somewhere on the coast near by, some isolated beach cabin—one of these, Mayhew was positive, had witnessed the torturing and killing of Malloy.

He began to piece some of the puzzle that related to the man who was missing. Malloy had come to San Diego for two reasons—to sound out Lawyer Nicholson on the Mexican marriage and to make sure that Mrs. Sticklemann's will was valid—and to meet some other person in or near San Diego. After Malloy had visited Nicholson he had gone to meet this other person. The next trace to be had of him was the discovery of his hands on the beach at Breakers Beach, with the hands showing evidence of terrible torture.

Malloy's death was a reasonable presumption. Since the body was not found in connection with the hands, the next most likely place for it to be was at the scene of the crime.

The purpose of cutting off the hands had been made clear to Mayhew only that morning, when the report of what was found on the ax handle had been put on his desk. There had been attempts made to implant fingerprints on the handle. The police expert had at once recognized the prints as made by the hand of a corpse, for upon death the fingers shrivel and prints show characteristic long crevices.

Only a stupid murderer would have left the useless prints on the weapon, for they so patently betrayed that the hand which made them was incapable of crime or of anything else. Mayhew cursed inwardly. He had called the murderer stupid, and much of the murderer's actions were stupid—and yet the fact remained that at bottom the crime was a shrewd one, ably planned and plotted far ahead, and lacking only expert technical knowledge to make it work.

Mayhew left the car rental agency with thanks for the help he had been given, and in his own car swung off onto the busy highway that led toward home.

As the car swerved and dipped, passing La Jolla, Oceanside, coming up to San Clemente and San Juan Capistrano, he teased out bits of the puzzle in his mind. He was getting a much clearer picture of the two unfortunates in this business: Lily Sticklemann and Charles Malloy. He saw that to the woman's characteristics of stupidity and secretiveness he must add now romantic rashness, for she had married Malloy without evidently knowing much about him. Malloy was coming into view as not too honorable, willing to stoop to shady doings if it promised a profit, willing to marry a woman without the legal right to do so, if the woman had money.

Malloy must have been interested in that money!

So, as Miss Rachel had said, must that other person be!

Would Malloy have signed a will, knowing that other person as he must have? Could Malloy have been forced to sign it, through exposure as a bigamist, *or by torture?*

The lights of San Clemente dropped behind him. Laguna shed light into the dark night sky far ahead.

Had Malloy gone to Nicholson on his own, or had he been sent? It was conceivable that Malloy was not the moving force behind the entanglement of Lily Sticklemann; that he had been used as a tool; that even the marriage had been arranged.

Mayhew tried to picture Mrs. Malloy sending her husband out upon a fortune-hunting expedition. The shrinking character of the woman made it seem unlikely, and yet, in crime, it had been Mayhew's experience that nothing was impossible.

There were two logical heirs to any estate which Malloy might have had through inheritance from Lily Sticklemann. They were Mrs. Malloy and her daughter Sara.

Chapter Fourteen:
Miss Rachel Sits in Fear

There was no moon that night in Breakers Beach, though it shone fitfully upon Mayhew's speeding little car, far down the coast. The fog had remained, lightening a little at noon as though it might almost be leaving, and then settling down thicker and damper throughout the afternoon, until by six o'clock its thickening stuffiness was thoroughly depressing. Miss Rachel watched it gathering beyond the pane of her window, watched it slow and settle, and watched the wall of the building next door fade and disappear. Then at 6:30, feeling the need of dinner, she went out.

She supposed, as she picked her way down the subdued and gloomy amusement zone where nobody seemed much amused tonight, that a thick fog would always remind her of the murder of her niece. The rolling in of those eerie billows of white seemed a proper prelude to violent and mysterious death. They positively invited crime, Miss Rachel thought; and she was glad to finish her dinner quickly and go back to the house.

She unlocked her door, reached inside to switch on the light and went in. She found Samantha standing in the center of the floor, her golden eyes spitting annoyance and her plump tail aswing. Miss Rachel stopped in her tracks and regarded the cat carefully. She sensed at once that something had disturbed the animal, usually so quiet and willing to stay curled in her basket while Miss Rachel was away.

"Kitty?" Miss Rachel said tentatively, holding out her hand. The tail described a wider arc, the eyes blazed, and the yowl that Samantha emitted was filled with anguish.

An idea flitted into Miss Rachel's mind and it seemed to have some connection with her knees, for those parts of her immediately went to the consistency of jelly. But Miss Rachel, though elderly and small, has stern stuff in her. She forced herself to go to the closet, fling open the door and search the recesses of the place thoroughly, and after that, to go to the tiny lavatory next the closet and do the same to it. There was no one in either place.

She came back and sat on the edge of her bed and watched the cat. Once the animal's eyes seemed to stare with especial malevolence to a spot beneath the bed, and Miss Rachel went through a breathless spell of fear before she examined the floor thoroughly and made sure that nowhere in the room was anyone hiding.

Still the cat was angry, still she prowled the room and switched her tail, and still her eyes insulted Miss Rachel for that lady's lack of intelligence.

At last it occurred to Miss Rachel though no one was now in her room, someone could have been there during her absence at dinner; and that another person's intrusion would account for Samantha's behavior. Perhaps, if someone had entered the room, he had treated the cat roughly and antagonized her. Miss Rachel made hasty examination, but upon Samantha was no mark of violence. Miss Rachel also knew the cat's fondness for following people—it had caused the animal's presence in the room during the time of Lily's murder—and she wondered if her visitor (if indeed there had been one) had been brutal in his methods of keeping the cat from going out with him. That, to her mind, was a very probable theory.

It seemed likely, too, that if someone had been in her room he had been there for a purpose. Thinking thus, Miss Rachel wandered about her room, investigating things. Everything was exactly as it should be—until she looked at the window. Absently she touched the nails which she had driven into the window frame to keep the lower pane from being lifted more than the two inches she required for ventilation, and one of them dropped at the slight contact into her hand.

It startled her; the inexplicable looseness of that nail at once assumed immense and frightening proportions. She stood quite still by the fogged pane, staring in turn from the nail in her hand to the hole in the window frame where it belonged. Then she raised carefully on tiptoe and looked closely at the place from which it had fallen, and at the other nail still on the opposite side of the window, and she at once saw obvious signs of tampering. The nails had been loosened by wiggling them back and forth, and then setting them gently back into place, but precariously. Slowly, Miss Rachel raised the sash. The lower pane went up until it touched the remaining nail; a little more pushing and the nail was dislodged, flipping outward and landing in almost complete silence on the carpet. The pane was then free to go as high as anyone cared to push it.

It had been Lieutenant Mayhew's idea to put the nails into the window. But whose had it been to dislodge them? Miss Rachel had no idea of the answer to this last question, but the knowledge that the loosening had actually taken place—that someone had made careful preparation to open her window when the fancy seized him—this made Miss Rachel very breathless and fluttery indeed.

At first thought, too, it seemed a rather unnecessary thing to do. If someone wished a way of entering her room, why not tamper with the lock upon the door? Out of the chaos of Miss Rachel's thoughts emerged the practical notion that the door had not been considered because of the chance of being seen in the hall (a chance, however, that the murderer had taken!) and also, and more likely, that the person responsible for this tampering had learned in some way, and perhaps by trying the door at night, that when Miss Rachel was sleeping her door was securely braced by a chair pushed under the doorknob.

This, then, brought her to the premise that there was a person who wished to enter her room, and obviously while she was either absent or asleep; and since she was absent for such few minutes during the day, if the errand was one which took any time, he must be planning to enter the room during the night.

Miss Rachel, reaching this terrifying conclusion, sat numbly upon her bed and stared at those two sinister little pieces of metal: the nails from her window. An urge for flight was growing within her bosom. With a sudden burst of nervous action she jumped from the bed and began throwing things into her suitcase. But Miss Rachel, besides being a little bit timid, is also as curious as Alice in Wonderland, and she began to wonder, as she packed her things, who it was who wished to come into her room in such a surreptitious manner. This puzzlement gradually took hold of her mind, so that her hands moved more and more slowly at their task and finally she stopped and looked long and absently at the window. She came out of her abstraction with a jerk, looked down at the article in her hand, put it into the suitcase, took it out again and finally left the enterprise entirely and began snooping about the room again.

She showed the most interest at the closet. There was a built-in set of drawers across the end of the closet; these she removed from their places, arranged a sheet in the manner of a curtain across the framework and got inside it. It was an excellent hiding place: roomy and easy of access. But there were two unalterable drawbacks to its use. These were that it was a trifle conspicuous, and that there was no storage place for the removed drawers. Regretfully, Miss Rachel got out and put the drawers back into place.

She scorned the underneath-the-bed idea. She pictured herself being drawn out by one foot or the scruff of the neck, if she should choose any such obvious hiding place.

She continued her survey of the room. The lavatory she had dismissed without even going into it, for it contained, besides the elementary equipment of such places, only a cement-lined shower stall that did not even boast a curtain. She wandered about thoughtfully, and, at last, seeing absolutely no place where she might hide and spy upon her midnight visitor, she went back into the closet and, quite accidentally, she happened to glance upward to the ceiling.

There was a scuttle opening overhead.

Now in southern California, where houses are not the serious affairs that they are elsewhere in the country, the formal attic is practically unknown except in very large establishments or in houses built by unconverted Easterners. What might be termed the casual attic is, however, quite common; an attic that is there simply because there must of necessity be a space between a flat ceiling and a peaked roof. Such attics come in handy when there are repairs to make upon the roof, or when odds and ends need storage out of the way; but no such notice is paid them such as building a pair of stairs to get into them. Instead there is usually an opening left in the ceilings of closets, which is closed merely by a loose wooden square laid into place over the hole.

There was such an opening in the ceiling of Miss Rachel's closet, and when she saw it her heart gave a bound of pure sleuthly joy. She saw at once that in such a retreat she might hide, peep down, and with luck get a view of her visitor.

To get into this place without leaving an obvious stack of chairs, or similar means of mounting, seemed at first quite a problem, and then it became exceptionally easy. Miss Rachel simply pulled each drawer of the built-in chest slightly outward, so that its edge gave a firm foothold, and then upon this arrangement she mounted daringly upward. When she stood upon the top of the chest she found that she was unable to stand upright until she moved aside the covering of the scuttle opening, and that after she had done this her head and shoulders were well above the attic floor.

It was as black in the attic as the uppermost depths of Hades might be presumed to be. There was a dank musty smell like molded wood, and the cold of the place crept against Miss Rachel's skin. It seemed such an unpleasant place to put oneself that for a moment Miss Rachel's heart failed her, and she climbed back down to continue packing. She put a toothbrush and a nightgown into her suitcase before it occurred to her that it would not be exactly exciting to go back home to Jennifer this evening, but that to stay in that chill black attic would have more thrills per minute (provided her room were invaded!) than all of the movies she had seen, rolled into one.

Little prickles of gooseflesh came out on Miss Rachel; she

looked at them, as they swept up her arm, with her eyes wide and bright. Then, with an air of sober determination, she replaced all of her belongings in the big shabby dresser.

But how to account for herself, if her visitor came tonight? Wouldn't he look for her if her absence weren't expected?

Miss Rachel puzzled over this for a while. Then she put on a wrap and nipped out to a lunch counter in the next block, where a buck-toothed waitress had been kind about breakfast. Coin passed from Miss Rachel's hand into the waitress's anxious one. There were whispered words which left the buck-toothed one puzzled but willing, and Miss Rachel came back to Surf House.

In a half-hour there was a telephone summons for Miss Rachel.

At the phone in the front part of the hall Miss Rachel showed surprising lack of refinement in her speech. She was loud. She argued offensively about the dangers of night air. She said that two o'clock in the morning was too late for her to be out. Yes, she appreciated the invitation. Still . . .

The phone squeaked into Miss Rachel's ear. "But, ma'am, I was just sayin' what you ast me to. About the correct time, I mean. I don't quite get this other . . ." The voice had a buck-toothed lisp.

Miss Rachel became suddenly amendable. "Well, if you're sure you can bring me home in the car, I'll come. When was the last séance? Two weeks ago? Did you get anything from Papa?"

She seemed to listen while details of Papa were related.

The waitress said patiently, "I'm doin' my part, ma'am. It's nine-fifteen to the dot. Now, I've told you."

"And is this woman good?" Miss Rachel said waspishly. "She really *gets* things? I'd know if it weren't really Papa, you know."

A minute of silence; the waitress had given up.

"Well, I'll come then, Mrs. Sims. I'll start right away." Miss Rachel swung sidewise, let a wary eye rove the hall. Mrs. Sims, she told herself, was deaf. "I'll start right away," she said even more loudly. "And you must promise to bring me home in the car at two."

She hung up the receiver and went back to her room. At 9:30 she departed with unusual clatter, with Samantha's basket on her arm.

Ten minutes later—how afraid she was of her room now!—she crept back into the hall without a sound, got into the room without the scrape of a lock or the clatter of a key, braced her frightened mind against the dark and went into the closet.

Dizzy upward climbings. Samantha mewed. The attic cold crept beneath Miss Rachel's clothing.

Miss Rachel, feeling with her delicate hands, arranged a crack at the edge of the opening through which she could peer downward. The room below was as silent as a tomb.

Miss Rachel, now having time for thought, began to wonder about the motives behind this business. After due process of reason she decided that there were two possible motives: either this person had business with herself, or with something in her possession. If the motive concerned herself she felt that most likely some harm was intended, possibly death—a death that was meant to overtake her in sleep, before she could make an outcry.

This, then, would settle that. If the intruder came in thinking that she was gone, it would prove that actual bodily harm was not the first motive.

If her room were entered tonight while she was presumably

at a spiritualists' meeting, it could only be because there was something in the room, or in her belongings, that the intruder wanted.

Eons of time seemed to troop through the darkness. Miss Rachel squirmed upon the hardness of the scuttle entry.

How should she know when it was two o'clock and time for her supposed return from the meeting? Best, she decided, to stay all night in the attic and be safe.

She shifted about in the darkness. The cat meowed an indignant protest to her wrigglings.

More eons passed, trooping through Miss Rachel's tired head with maddening slowness, and at last Miss Rachel positively fell asleep. The raising of the window in her room below did not wake her, nor did the first cautious stumble of footsteps; but a reflected beam of light, shooting up through the narrow opening she had left at the closet entry, caught her delicate eyelid and telegraphed alarm to her brain.

For a moment she was confused, not realizing where she was. Then everything clicked into place. She knew what the lighted crack in front of her meant and leaned over to peep down into it. She saw a flashlight poking its yellow beam leisurely round the closet, spotlighting shoes, dresses, the cat's basket, and her suitcase set in a corner. A hand could be seen, very faintly, holding the light; but the body and face of the person below were hidden beyond the edge of the closet door. Miss Rachel waited, holding her breath, for the intruder to step within the closet so that she could see his face, but this act of considerate revealment he failed to do.

Instead the light suddenly snapped out, and below a dragging noise could be heard. It sounded to Miss Rachel as if her suitcase were being taken out of the closet.

The invader was careful about showing light. Only once or twice more did Miss Rachel catch a glimpse of the flashlight in action. Her visitor was obviously working in the dark, but working he was indeed. An uninterrupted series of small sounds reached her: rippings and sly taps, and the rustle of careful movement. It sounded very efficient, unhurried and quite thorough.

In the midst of her excitement there came upon Miss Rachel an uncontrollable desire to sneeze.

She did various frantic things to herself: held her nose, breathed deeply through her mouth, pinched the back of her neck, and finally put two fingers firmly into her ears as though to shame the sneeze away by not listening to it. All of these things were vain; the sneeze grew inwardly, as it were, until Miss Rachel felt that it was to be the biggest and loudest sneeze that she had ever performed. But at the last moment, with her head back and her mouth unbeautifully open, she had presence of mind enough to take her hands away from her ears and to muffle her nose with them. The result was quite painful; the sneeze backfired convulsively and seemed to explode inside her. Tears burst from her eyes and she snuffled into her taffeta sleeve, moaning softly.

The darkness that had wrapped and disembodied her, so palpable it was, now became sinister and full of a life of its own. It gathered over her, she felt, and frowned down upon the disturbing creature who had sneezed. She was also terrified for fear that the person in her room had heard her, so that, when her nose stopped running, and the darkness quit seeming so tense, she peeped downward again and listened.

She held her breath and became nothing but ears. For a little while there was frightening silence; a minute ticked away—perhaps two. Then the whispering rustle below went on and Miss Rachel breathed again.

The cat had been disturbed by the quiverings of Miss Rachel, and now she writhed about and opened her mouth with a small wet sound. A second's terror again flooded Miss Rachel's heart. Would the cat yowl—or only yawn? She waited. The cat made a small dissatisfied snort—a purr in reverse—and curled down again to go on sleeping.

The search went on below; went on, it seemed, for hours and hours. The excitement that had played a rippling hopscotch through her nervous system dribbled away. Miss Rachel got frankly tired, and then uncontrollably sleepy. She curled herself upon the lid of the closet opening, for safety's sake, and drifted into a land of troubled dreams.

Daylight, early and thin, shone through the narrow windows of the attic when she awoke. This time there was no start of surprise. Her protesting body warned her, long before she was completely awake, just where she had been sleeping.

She listened. There was no sound at all in her room, but she let the silence reassure her for many minutes before she descended from her refuge. Descending, she came into chaos.

Her belongings, and the articles of furniture in the room, had been reduced to their original materials. That is, her suitcase was now hacked-out squares of leather, several piece of fiberboard and a length of moiré lining; her shoes were kid and cloth and odd wooden things that had been covered heels; the mattress was an unsavory-looking bundle of loose cotton and a torn tick; and all other similarly reducible articles in the room were back where they had been before their makers had assembled them. It was as if a malevolent magician had snapped his fingers and by some hocus-pocus *unmade* everything within the four walls of the room.

The wallpaper had shown crevices before, now it showed the rotten plaster beneath, and was itself most undecoratively upon the floor.

Miss Rachel was quite tired from her sojourn in the upper regions and so she made no futile attempt at reorganization, but sat dismally upon the wrecked mattress and closed her eyes. Sitting thus she heard a knock at the door. With elaborate cunning she went and peeped through the keyhole, and thus beheld an unusually large hand ready to take hold of the doorknob. She unlocked the door and opened it. Mayhew looked in.

"Hell's fire!" he cried with feeling. "Who's been murdered now?"

Chapter Fifteen:
Miss Rachel Listens In

It was several minutes before Miss Rachel could convince Mayhew that no more homicides had occurred.

Once his mind was laid to rest upon that point, however, he became intensely interested in the purpose of wrecking the room. He poked about in the rubbish and picked up the harried-looking piece of leather that had covered her suitcase. "What was this?" he asked.

"My bag."

"What did you have in it?"

"Nothing."

He waggled the leather impatiently. "Then why this? Why torn up, if it was empty?"

"I rather think they were interested in what might have been put between the lining and the cover."

"They?"

"The—person who came here last night."

"Hmmmm. Anything missing? What did they want?"

"The will, I think. No, nothing's gone. Just torn up. I'll have to get some new things." Miss Rachel looked not displeased. It may be that she relished the thought of a shopping spree.

"You've told someone, then, that your niece made a new will?"

"Oh, no. Why should I? Lily expressly made it a secret. I think our murderer is getting afraid. Nothing has come out, no move is being made to settle the estate. He must be beginning to wonder why. He might have thought he could find a will, if there should be one, and destroy it."

Mayhew gave up his aimless potterings and fell into a chair. From somewhere within the chair's recesses there caroled forth a harsh and chattering scream; two screws popped out with considerable force and the bottom fell with a smash. Mayhew picked himself off the floor and dusted himself off.

Miss Rachel regarded the wreckage of what had been the chair without any particular concern. "It doesn't matter," she replied to his muttered apologies. "The room was a mess already." But she watched him cautiously from the corner of an eye as he found a more secure perch upon one corner of the bed frame. She herself found a sitting place upon a fold of the mattress; there she drooped like a small wet hen.

Mayhew told her then that he had found that her niece and Malloy had been married in Tia Juana almost four months ago. She tried to look happy and interested in this confirmation of her theory, but weariness was blurring her thoughts. Mayhew talked for a short while longer, and then, seeing how tired she was, he advised her to go somewhere else and get some sleep.

This last she did not do. Mayhew went across the hall and spoke for a few minutes with Mrs. Malloy. He wanted some definite date upon which to fix Malloy's departure from Surf House. Mrs. Malloy thought that Mr. Leinster might be better able to give him such information. Mr. Leinster had been here at the time and—though she did not say so—had apparently been keeping a fairly close watch upon her husband.

Mayhew stepped into the hall from the interview with Sara's mother and found Miss Rachel and Mrs. Turner carrying a new mattress between them into Miss Rachel's room.

"I bought this one to replace that bloody one next door," the gaunt and rusty-haired landlady was saying, loudly and without tact. "Now I will have to buy another new one. These mattresses cost four and a half apiece. The profit's gone out of this business, I tell you."

Miss Rachel did not answer. Through the open door of her apartment Mayhew watched the woman fall to work upon the clutter of the room. Mrs. Turner expressed neither curiosity nor surprise. She simply got busy in an angry determined way, gathering up the heterogeneous mess and taking it by way of the hall to the dust barrel at the back door. Miss Rachel made rather ineffectual efforts to help, but the larger woman put her to shame in the matter of energy and strength, and Miss Rachel turned to making up the bed.

Mayhew interviewed a surly and suspicious Leinster. The younger man had made no bones about his dislike for the detective ever since the night of their scrap in Malloy's room. He did, however, definitely fix the date upon which he was sure Malloy had left Surf House for the last time. . . .

When Miss Rachel awoke, late in the afternoon, she felt much better. The stiffness had largely gone out of her limbs, and her back had quit aching from lying upon the hard attic floor for so many hours. She lay still for a few minutes, looking at the bare unbeautiful room flooded now with the afternoon sunlight.

Her thoughts turned to the other people in this house and she wondered what each of them was doing at this moment. She dwelt upon each in succession: upon Mrs. Marble, Mrs. Turner, the Malloys, Mr. Leinster, the Timmersons, and Scurlocks. A small sigh escaped her. "We don't know enough about any of them," she complained inwardly. "If we did, this murder would be no mystery."

Rising and getting into her dress she kept thinking of her companions at Surf House. There ought to be some method of getting more information about these people than what they had volunteered to tell. If one could just listen in on their conversations when they thought that they were unheard—or spy upon them in secret. A month ago Miss Rachel's cheeks would have burned scarlet at such a low thought, but since then she had become a detective and nothing was beyond her. She remembered wistfully that there was a thing called a dictaphone, which you planted in people's rooms when they were away, and listened to their talk when you pleased, later. But she had no idea in the world where she would get such a contrivance, nor how to use it if she had one.

In this state of half-discouraged puzzlement she thought of the attic, and at once knew that she had a ready-made solution to her problem. If her closet had an opening into the attic, wasn't it reasonable to suppose that the others did? And that if you wanted to take the trouble to listen at these openings you might hear some very remarkable things? A kind of slow happy dazzlement came over her and she visualized the possibilities of the attic. At six o'clock she ate dinner with subdued joy. At seven o'clock she was mounting her set of drawers in the closet, and at 7:05 she had discovered the first of the other entries to the attic. It was toward the front of the building from her apartment, and a moment's listening convinced her that it led into Mr. Leinster's room.

She slipped the covering of the entry a little to one side and saw the closet door open a crack and a band of light entering it from the room beyond. Voices reached her ears: the voices of Mr. Leinster and of Sara Malloy.

Mr. Leinster was reading something aloud in a rapid expressionless tone. Once in a while Sara interjected a comment, such as "That's good," or "You're hurrying it."

All at once Mr. Leinster broke off his reading. "I'm going to murder Miss Rachel too," he remarked in a perfectly normal voice.

There followed a few seconds of what Miss Rachel hoped was shocked surprise on the part of Miss Malloy. But when the girl answered Leinster her tone betrayed no such feeling; it held a kind of regretful remonstrance.

"Oh, I wouldn't," Sara said.

Leinster's voice became firmer. "Yes, I must. The thing needs it."

"But you've already killed my father."

"No matter. Miss Rachel must go too."

"But she is such a dear little lady, Gerald."

Mr. Leinster made a scornful noise deep in his throat. "Listen, Sara," he said patiently. "I've killed a dozen like her, if I've killed one. It's nothing—nothing at all. I'm going to kill her."

Sara yielded the point much too easily, Miss Rachel thought. "How are you going to do it?" she asked with mild curiosity. "Poison her?"

"No." Mr. Leinster was prompt in his decision. "I'm going to shoot this one. It'll give a little variety to the thing."

"Then you'll have a gun in your hands," Miss Malloy pointed out helpfully.

Miss Rachel had started to shiver, thinking that never in her life had she heard such cold-blooded planning, or dreamed that such nonchalance in the face of crime could be. At the same time there was something queer about the whole thing; it didn't match the character of these two young people as she knew them. Leinster the murderer, and Sara Malloy his accomplice . . . ? It couldn't be. But Miss Rachel went on listening.

They disposed of the gun quite neatly by leaving it beside Miss Rachel's body with her fingerprints on it. "Then that dumb cluck of a detective will decide she is the murderer and quit looking any further," Leinster decided. "He'll think she committed suicide from remorse."

Miss Malloy answered with some heat. "He will not," she flung back. "He's not as dumb as you think."

There was more silence after that; a kind of thoughtful silence on Mr. Leinster's part, Miss Rachel decided. Then: "Sara, are you stuck on that guy?"

"Oh, piffle!" Sara exclaimed carelessly. "Get on with your murders."

At this callous urging Miss Rachel's white hair rose along her neck. Could there be any doubt, after such talk?

But Mr. Leinster was not to be turned aside from the object of his hatred. "He is dumb, Sara. Don't fall for a guy like that."

"Some of these days," Miss Malloy replied evenly but with feeling, "he's going to find out that you write murder mysteries under the name of Beverly Barstow, and I haven't a doubt but that he'll let the newspapers in on it. Then where'll you be? Can't you just see the headlines? *Murder Expert Piddles Futilely in Beach Case*—or *Barstow Blubbers in Bafflement,* or——"

"Don't go on," Mr. Leinster said, somewhat subdued.

"You've got to let him solve this case," Sara demanded.

"Like hell I will," Mr. Leinster cried, forgetting himself.

"Then I'll let on who you are," she threatened.

More silence—the angry kind, Miss Rachel thought. Then, even more subdued than ever, Mr. Leinster replied, "All right. He can solve the thing in this story I'm writing about it, but I'll bet you dollars to doughnuts that actually he can't do it."

"And who will then?" she taunted.

"Me," Mr. Leinster said flatly.

Miss Rachel listened a while longer to their conversation. A sweet relief possessed her. She knew now the answer to the riddle of Mr. Leinster's murderous intentions, and she had no fear of really being killed by him. His murders were only paper ones, dished out lavishly for the entertainment of his public. Miss Rachel herself had read Beverly Barstow's *Cunningly Killed* and had considered it really good. In it seven people, no less, met hideous death. Miss Rachel still remembers, on dark nights, the place in the book where the little boy finds his cold and bloody grandmother stuffed into the pen with his pet rabbits. She had unwisely read that section aloud to Jennifer. Jennifer had had to sleep with her for nearly a month afterward, with Miss Rachel on the side of the bed next the door. . . .

There was no opening to the Scurlocks' closet, and this fact gave Miss Rachel much thought.

The Timmersons, however, were easily listened in upon. Their closet door was standing wide when Miss Rachel peered down through a crack at the entry, and she even caught a glimpse of Mrs. Timmerson's shoe and a corner of the gas heater that she sat beside.

They didn't do a great deal of talking during the half-hour that Miss Rachel listened to them. Each apparently had a book or a magazine. Miss Rachel plainly caught the rustle of paper as they regularly turned pages. There was only one bit of conversation that was in any way mysterious or interesting. That occurred after Mr. Timmerson had gone to the kitchenette for a drink of water and had brought a glass back for his wife.

"Thanks, dear," Mrs. Timmerson said pleasantly. There was a faint swiggling sound. "I *was* thirsty. Guess this dry book is to blame." A full laugh from both of them at this excursion into humor, then Mrs. Timmerson turned abruptly serious. "Dear, you ought really to tell him where you got it."

It was evidently a remark coming from a topic that was familiar to Mr. Timmerson for he seemed to know at once to what it referred. He was quite sober in his answer. "No, I don't think I should. It might rouse suspicion—more than you think." Miss Rachel could picture the short plump little man shaking his head and indulging in his habit of feeling of one of his chins.

Mrs. Timmerson's voice matched her husband's in seriousness. "But he's very apt to find out about it anyway. And with Malloy missing this way it won't look well for you to have kept it back. You should really tell him the whole thing. I have a dreadful feeling that it will cause trouble if you don't."

"Nonsense." Mr. Timmerson's voice tried hard but it failed to carry conviction.

"And you quarreled about it. Perhaps someone else heard that quarrel, dear. Counterfeit money is——"

Whatever Mrs. Timmerson thought counterfeit money was, Miss Rachel was not destined to learn. Mr. Timmerson broke in upon his wife's talk and forbade her to mention the subject again. He spoke with some considerable anger, and Miss Rachel sensed that the man had heard much from his wife on this topic and that he himself was quite worried about it. Mrs. Timmerson was obedient; she abandoned her request for her husband to tell someone—Mayhew?—about some incident that concerned counterfeit money and a quarrel and that evidently related somehow to the missing Malloy. The two Timmersons went back to their reading and Miss Rachel gathered no further bits of mysterious talk from them.

It was boring, listening to nothing but the rustle of pages being turned, so Miss Rachel slid the entry cover back into place and made further exploration in the attic.

Mrs. Malloy's closet also possessed an entry to the attic. This fact offered considerable illumination to Miss Rachel. She had always wondered how Sara Malloy's assailant had skipped out of the room without opening a window or being caught by Mayhew in the hall. She had never shared Mayhew's suspicions of Mrs. Malloy, and she saw now that she was correct in not doing so. In Mrs. Malloy's closet there was the same arrangement of built-in drawers that she had found in her own; and even if Sara's attacker had not taken the time to open the drawers to make steps, as Miss Rachel had found it necessary to do, the problem of climbing to the top of the chest and getting into the attic was not one to worry an active person or a strong one.

Mrs. Malloy was evidently alone in the apartment, for Miss Rachel heard no sound of voices. It took her a while to identify the sound that she did hear: a soft sibilant clicking, and a rustle not quite like that of paper. At last, opening the closet entry quite wide and leaning head downward through it, she made out the figure of Mrs. Malloy in the room beyond. The closet door was hardly ajar. All that she could see was a leg of the table and portions of Mrs. Malloy's dress on either side of it, but the meaning of the sounds was suddenly clear. Mrs. Malloy was shuffling and dealing a deck of cards, apparently playing a game of solitaire.

The floor of the attic was not entirely boarded in. At places the timbers of the ceiling had been left exposed, and on these sections Miss Rachel had to go carefully to keep from stumbling and falling in the dark. In spite of the cold and the dust she persisted in her scouting expedition until she was sure that she had found every entry that led into the attic. Not every apartment had an entry, and what openings there were appeared to have been built in haphazardly. In all, there were five: in her own room, in Mr. Leinster's, in the Timmersons', in Mrs. Malloy's, and in Mrs. Marble's.

At Mrs. Marble's apartment she drew a complete blank. The closet door was apparently closed and no light showed beneath it. It was the time when Mrs. Marble was ordinarily at work and her little girl asleep, so that the absence of light was to be expected.

Back in her own room Miss Rachel constructed a floor plan of Surf House much like the one that Mayhew had drawn in his black notebook. She wrote in names to correspond with the tenants in the various apartments, and then by means of little crosses designated the apartments which had access to the attic.

Afterward she studied this plan for a considerable time. It seemed to her that there should be some sort of significance in the fact that some apartments had attic entries and some did not; but beyond the knowledge that Sara Malloy's attacker could have fled her room through such an entry, Miss Rachel could think of no other. And yet—some vague idea nagged at her consciousness, demanded to be brought into the light of day. What the thought was, she could not quite fathom, and at last she gave the problem up and went to bed.

Tomorrow, she decided, she would do some really intense thinking. Didn't all good detectives think intensely, cudgel their brains and wrangle with facts until the solution of the crime burst brilliantly upon them out of nowhere?

Miss Rachel thought she could do no less.

Chapter Sixteen:
Suicide

Miss Rachel woke to a gloomy morning. Her window showed the sky obscured with heavy clouds, and a stiff wind whistled by outside. By leaning far to the right with her face pressed against the pane she could glimpse a narrow view of the sea. This morning it looked sullen and dirty and reflected the anger of the sky.

She felt a little forlorn and not quite in the mood for the weighty thinking she had planned to do. Before going to breakfast she wrote a note to Jennifer and spent ten minutes in brushing Samantha's fur, by way of passing time. While she was at this last occupation she tried to throw off the depressive influence of the gloomy weather by a little play with the cat. Tickling Samantha's ears brought many purrs of feline comfort but little lightening of Miss Rachel's mood. At last, feeling actively hungry, she put the cat into her basket and took the brush which was the cat's to the window to clean it.

She had replaced the nails that kept her window from being raised more than a few inches. Unhooking the screen, she thrust her hands through the narrow space and ruffled the bristles of the brush to dislodge the cat's hairs. Many of them floated away on the wind. At last, caught by an eddy of air, a whole tuft of them floated inward and lodged upon the pane not more than two inches from the tip of Miss Rachel's nose. She looked at them absently for a moment; the wind caught them again and they were gone. But just as they swept out of sight it occurred to Miss Rachel that perhaps those hairs hadn't looked exactly as they should have. Weren't they a trifle faded—sort of an off-color gray instead of the coal black they were supposed to be?

Or were they?

Miss Rachel thought that she must be imagining things. And still—she had a distinct memory of a lighter shade in that tuft of blowing fur. She looked carefully at the brush but most of the hair was gone, and what remained seemed normal enough. In the midst of her perplexity came the half memory that had so often tantalized her: the feeling that she had experienced when, on coming briefly out of her morphine-induced unconsciousness, she had touched the cat and thought something about it strange.

She had never been able to identify that impression. It was lost somewhere in her mind, just a little out of reach of her memory. She was positive that the cat had been different, had been altered in some way; but exactly how it had been different, she could not quite remember.

She went slowly now to the bed and sat down upon it and tried to force her mind back through the days to the time of Lily's death and her own near dying. She had been in bed; the doctor and the nurses had been near; someone had helped her to sit up. And then the cat had come and she had reached out to touch it, to feel of something familiar in the whirling fog of her thoughts. And then . . .

Her fingers were sliding now, unconsciously, in the same gesture as that she had used the night of her niece's murder. They crept across the counterpane, and without watching them she had her brilliant eyes focused in an intent look straight ahead. She did not even see the cat jump up and approach her hand with amiable playfulness. But when her fingers contacted the silken fur, and she drew them backward momentarily so that they pulled the surface of the fur aside—then, in that split second, Miss Rachel knew what it was that had been strange about the cat.

How odd—how ridiculously easy—not to have remembered it before! For, of course, next her skin that night, the cat had been *wet!*

She got immediately off the bed, and when she went to breakfast a few minutes later the cat went along in her basket.

Mayhew, coming into his office about an hour afterward, found her sitting there waiting for him. He gave her one of his rare smiles and seated himself in the immense chair behind the desk. "Good morning," he said pleasantly. He was surprised to discover that he had come to like this little old lady very well indeed. It was a positive pleasure seeing her sitting there like a small gray owl, looking very wise. "Anything new?" he queried hopefully.

"I think so," she told him. She took a minute then to arrange things in her mind, and told him each detail of the morning's happenings: the tuft of faded fur blowing by, the attempt to remember what had been different about the cat on the night of the murder and her sudden realization that the cat's fur had been damp.

Mayhew looked very thoughtful for a moment. "What do you make of it?" he asked her.

She wrinkled her brow a little. "I think that perhaps, for

some reason, this cat's fur has been dyed—was dyed on the night of the murder."

"The obvious conclusion," he said slowly. "If the cat is dyed it means that it's not your cat, not the one with the money, I mean. Another animal's been substituted for the real one. Now the fur is growing out and shows its real color. That's it, isn't it?"

She nodded quickly and opened the cat's basket which sat beside her on the floor. A black head emerged, two yellow eyes looked on Lieutenant Mayhew with wrath and a red mouth yowled. When Mayhew thrust out a brown square hand the cat spat at it. Miss Rachel promptly shut down the lid again. "Isn't there some way of testing fur for dye?" she asked. "Then we'd know for sure."

Mayhew nodded.

He went on to explain that the police department laboratory, though having a good equipment for ordinary criminal investigations, would scarcely be able to carry out the complicated tests for dyestuffs. Work of this difficult type, which now and then had to be done, was performed for them by a commercial laboratory in the Foxx Building in the next block.

Here Mayhew and Miss Rachel waited in a tiny reception room for the tests to be completed. Mayhew nursed badly scratched hands, for he had had to pull hairs from the indignant and active animal and she had retaliated by removing some of his skin.

The chemical report was long in coming, but it came. It came embodied in the person of a remote young man in a white smock, who delivered the opinion that there was not a trace of any dye whatever in the fur.

Mayhew and Miss Rachel conferred hurriedly and brought forth the thought that perhaps it had been a spotted cat and dyed only upon the necessary portions. Mayhew again pulled fur, and again was scratched, and they waited for more silent minutes. But the word was still the same, when it came: there was no dye in the fur.

Mayhew argued unreasonably with the young man in the white smock. He took the cat and pulled aside portions of its top hair, risking more scratches, to show the fellow that the fur actually was faded underneath. The young man raised his eyebrows and shrugged. He was, he told Mayhew, only a chemist and not at all a cat expert.

In what amounted almost to rage, Mayhew took himself and Miss Rachel and the cat off to a veterinary establishment on the outskirts of the town and demanded to be told what was wrong with an animal when its fur turned off colors. The tall old bespectacled veterinarian studied Samantha respectfully and gave as his opinion that the fur was faded for two reasons: the cat was old and she was shedding.

"Fur that is shed is usually pale and dull in appearance, for the life has been gone from it for some time. This cat has an enormous amount of loose hair in her fur." He caught gently at the black coat and brought away several tufts of fur. Mayhew wondered grimly to himself why it had been his luck to choose for extraction those that had been so firmly embedded in her hide. "In addition," the older man continued, "this animal is well up in years for a cat. See her teeth?" He pried open a pair of unwilling jaws to reveal the tiny molars. "Often, as a cat grows older, if its fur is very dark, the animal will look faded. It's the same thing, really, as a person growing gray." He touched his own pepper-and-salt head quickly.

They went away subdued, with their fine theory knocked into oblivion.

Sitting beside Mayhew in his car Miss Rachel stubbornly clung to her discovery of that morning. "The cat *was* wet," she said. "I'm positive that she was. Her fur was quite damp when I touched it underneath, next her skin."

But Mayhew was tired of the subject now that it had apparently lost its significance. He did not answer Miss Rachel's musing. . . .

In the hall she found Sara Malloy tapping at her own door and softly saying, "Mother!"

The girl looked round as Miss Rachel approached her. There was a small frown etched between her brows but she gave Miss Rachel a fleeting smile. "Mother's evidently gone out," she said in a half-worried manner. "I wish she had let me know where she was going. She has our only key, and now I can't get in."

Miss Rachel opened her own door. "You can come into my room and wait for her," she offered.

"No, I couldn't do that. Thanks just the same. There are some things in Los Angeles at home that Mother sent me after. I've already gone once. I was waiting in the street-car depot when I remembered a list that I'd made out and stupidly left lying on the dresser. That was about an hour ago—you know how infrequently the trains run. I've missed one by having to come back, too. It's funny that Mother didn't mention—"

She turned the knob and tapped again, but there was no answer.

"It doesn't matter," she said at last. "I suppose if I must trust my memory to bring back everything, I must." She gave the door an annoyed and puzzled look and went down the hall to the front door.

After she had gone Miss Rachel remained in the hall. She, also, was looking at the door, but not in the manner that Sara had looked at it. Sara had stared at the knob; Miss Rachel's eyes had fixed themselves on the floor, and an expression of terror was coming into her face.

She knelt and touched the thing that she had glimpsed beneath the door. It was a piece of cloth wadded into the crack at the doorstill. Miss Rachel plucked at it but it was wedged firmly and did not move. Quickly, then, she peered into the keyhole. There was nothing to see; something plugged the other end.

Miss Rachel felt hurriedly under her hat and got a hairpin. With it she poked at the keyhole until she dislodged whatever it was that filled the other side. And then, instead of trying to see through the aperture, she put her nose to it and sniffed.

The stinging fumes of illuminating gas entered her nostrils and she sneezed.

The door was quite beyond her, and she wasted no time trying to open it. Within a few moments she had both Mr. Leinster and Mr. Timmerson into the hall; together they burst in the door.

Mrs. Malloy was slumped on the floor in front of the gas heater with a hood of white cloth—evidently a folded sheet—across her head and across the top of the heater. She leaned against the legs of a chair and made no move at the crash of the door. The room was filled with the choking fumes of gas. Mr. Leinster turned his head to take a deep clean breath in the hall, then he went into the room, turned off the tap and brought Mrs. Malloy out like a bundle of rags. Her body was slack, nerveless; her face, turned up, was like death.

Miss Rachel knew that they must have a doctor at once, but she was acquainted with no private physician in Breakers Beach. The thought nagged her that what she was to do would very likely bring some unpleasant attention to the Malloys, but she knew of no alternative than to call Mayhew and tell him to bring Dr. Southart in a hurry.

The two men arrived within a few minutes. Mr. Leinster had carried Mrs. Malloy into his own room, the door of which was immediately closed as efforts to revive Mrs. Malloy got under way.

There was nothing further for Miss Rachel to do. She was, in fact, absolutely ignored by everyone once Mrs. Malloy was being cared for. A nurse was summoned by telephone by Leinster, who then sat himself down by the front door to intercept Sara when she should come in. He sat stiffly in a straight-backed chair and showed no inclination to talk. Mrs. Malloy's open door emitted unpleasant gas fumes into the hall. Feeling slightly let down from the excitement, Miss Rachel went into her own room.

It was long past lunch time but she did not feel hungry. She let the cat out of her basket, and that brought back to her mind the problem of the morning. The memory was perfectly clear to her now that the cat's fur had been wet the night that Lily had died. *But why?* Her conclusion, brought about by her notice of a faded bunch of fur, had been that the cat had been dyed; that it was a substitute animal, for some reason colored to resemble her own. But she knew now that it was not a dyed animal; therefore, the moisture which she had noticed as being in the cat's fur had not been the result of a dyeing.

But there was undoubtedly a reason for the presence of that moisture. And the reason depended in a measure upon what the moisture was. It had not been dye. The next most reasonable idea was that it had been water.

But if it were water, again why?

Why put water upon a perfectly clean cat? And Mayhew had

told her that the cat had indeed been clean, even in that room of streaked and spattered blood. Somehow she had escaped being soiled, though every other object in the room had been bloodied. Miss Rachel's thoughts toyed with this enigma.

If the cat had been *washed*—her thoughts took a little skip off into theory—it would mean that she had not been clean as the officers had found her. It might, perhaps, mean that the cat had been an extremely bloody and unpleasant animal, before.

But why should the soiling of a mere cat mean anything to the kind of person who had beaten Lily to death with a hatchet?

Her thoughts strayed. She began to puzzle over just what kind of person this murderer must be. Let's sum up his actions as we know them, she agreed with herself. If we reconstruct the crime as we see it now, perhaps we can guess why the cat was wet, she decided.

To begin with, she thought: this person is in close contact with all of the people in Surf House; he may, in fact, be presumed to live there. He most certainly knew of Lily's semibigamous marriage to Charles Malloy and—here an enormous amount of presumption on Miss Rachel's part—he must also know that Lily had made a will in favor of her new husband.

Approximately three weeks before Lily's death Malloy disappears. He disappears in or near San Diego, and the only further trace of him that is found is a severed hand that shows evidence of intense torture. From this last fact his death may be concluded as practically a certainty. The murderer attempted to use Malloy's hands (the drunken man had seen two of them) to plant Malloy's fingerprints upon the weapon used to kill Lily. Not, Miss Rachel thought, an especially bright thing to do.

Of course it was only the merest accident that had allowed the police to find the hands on the beach, but it was an unnecessary accident from the point of view of the murderer. Untidy, Miss Rachel told herself. If you were going to attempt an unsuccessful coup like that, you ought to at least do a little reading in the public library and learn whether a corpse made different fingerprints from a normal person.

Miss Rachel felt frustrated. Here was a stupid, a ponderously ignorant murderer—and still she couldn't catch him!

She tried, in her mind, to reconstruct the crime from such facts as she knew of it.

She remembered that moment of intense clarity when, with the blue fog ready to gobble her, she had looked out upon Lily's room, had felt the draft cool on her neck from the opening door, had heard Mrs. Malloy's squeaking chair and Mrs. Turner's sewing machine, had known that someone had come into the room behind her.

The cloth that Lily had put on her aching head had slipped down over her eyes.

There had been a moment of stark fearful silence, when the machine and the creaking chair had both stopped. The door had been open then. Was there any significance in the fact of the machine stopping, the chair being quiet, while the door had been open, while the murderer had been slipping up behind her chair?

Beyond the fact that the two sounds respectively cleared Mrs. Malloy and Mrs. Turner of any part in the crime, Miss Rachel could think of no other.

There had then—after the murder—been a clumsy attempt to throw suspicion on the Scurlocks by throwing open the window upon which the toolmarks had previously been made.

All of this fact, all of it true—all of it planned and carried out by the person who had killed her niece. And yet it failed to account for two facts: the fact of the cat being wet and the fact of the room being entered twice, as Sara had heard it being entered.

Miss Rachel now cudgeled her brains in the best detective tradition.

Let's suppose, she told her stubborn conservative other-self, that Samantha was dreadfully bloodied when Lily's blood was let. And let's suppose that our murderer is the kind of person who simply cannot endure to see a little kitty all soiled. *So he bathed her.*

Miss Rachel had stumbled upon a startling point. If the murderer had washed the cat, *where had it been done?* Certainly not in Lily's sink, which had been full of dishes that would have caught traces of blood. Nor in her washbasin in the lavatory in which stockings and underwear had been soaking.

But where?

Miss Rachel suddenly quit puzzling over this point, for something much more important had come into her mind. It was a picture out of her imaginings: a scene based on what she knew of her cat and what she knew of the crime. Because Miss Rachel was so movie-minded the thing unrolled much as a film might have.

A figure came carefully out of Lily's room into the hall. It was a figure without form or sex, or any distinguishing features that Miss Rachel could imagine. At its feet, unnoticed, followed a hideous small animal, a cat that should have been black and was instead red, whose green-gold eyes looked out through streaks of gore, whose fur dripped blood. The obscure human figure darted to another door, opened it and went through. It stood for a moment, then, panting from exertion and excitement, but safe—*safe!* And then, noting some movement from the corner of its eye, it looked down and saw the cat! Saw the bloody and disgusting creature whose unlooked-for presence irrevocably connected that human creature with the crime.

What to do? Miss Rachel visualized that moment of panic, that first split second of despair, and then the frantic endeavor.

What to do? Miss Rachel forced herself into the position of that murderer. Her thoughts hummed.

Kill the animal? Its absence would be noticed; it would be searched for, hunted down. The room might be searched before those fatal little tracks, now here, now there, could be washed up.

Miss Rachel could fairly see her little cat, walking about, sniffing and investigating that strange room.

Then the simplest, the easiest, the most obvious thing was to bathe the cat!

If she weren't bloody, who would dream that she might have left a trail into the murderer's room? If she were back inside that murder room, cleaned of blood, there could be no thought in anyone's mind that she had either left it or that, if she might have done so, she had marked her way. And so the cat had been washed and returned immediately to the scene of the crime.

That gave the murderer time to clean up his own premises as well as to remove the clothing that he had worn and get rid of it.

Miss Rachel felt that her theory was a good one. It had the advantage of explaining more than one puzzling point of evidence. And it was based upon facts: upon the cat's inclination to follow people from a room, upon the fact of the cat being wet after the murder, and upon the fact of Lily's door being opened twice at the time she was dead.

Chapter Seventeen:
Miss Rachel Breaks and Enters

Mrs. Malloy did not die, but it may be presumed that she came to in time to wish that she might have. For Mayhew made no secret of the fact that he regarded her attempt at suicide as tantamount to a confession. Only the doctor's rigid orders prevented him from subjecting her to a prolonged questioning.

Miss Rachel recognized his mood as one of bafflement and anger, and she likewise understood the motive of that mood: his unspoken attachment to Sara, his previous suspicion of her mother, and now a distasteful denouement that practically sealed her guilt.

Miss Rachel did not attempt to hold conversation with him at this time. She knew that her last theory concerning the murder did not coincide with what he was thinking now, and the course that she had mapped for herself from her conclusions would scarcely meet with his approval. For Miss Rachel had decided that if her cat had followed the murderer to his room that there would very likely be traces of thorough cleaning in that room.

The supposition of the cat's being washed depended upon the

need for such washing, and the only apparent need would be to disconnect the animal from some traces of blood left in another apartment. Miss Rachel reasoned that the cat's fur had dripped blood. She knew that some time would be needed to successfully remove blood from wood or rug to such an extent that a chemical test would reveal no presence of human blood. The murderer had not had that much time the night of the crime. He had, she thought, washed the cat instead, so that no one would be likely to notice traces in the hall or to look for evidences in another room. And such lack of suspicion would allow him to clean his own room with plenty of time to do it thoroughly.

However, a thorough cleaning upon such old floors as those of Surf House would most certainly leave noticeable patches of cleanliness. And Miss Rachel had decided that she would look for such patches.

At first her problem had seemed much simpler than that. She had thought that she could examine the floor of the hall and discover traces of a trail from Lily's door to the door of the murderer. A close survey of the hall had discouraged her. It was an ill-lit place; the rug was in an incredibly advanced state of stained and grimy decay, and people persisted in passing along it just when Miss Rachel thought that the coast was clear. Miss Rachel had a very clear idea that if she were to be noticed examining the rug closely she might expect a quick and brutal demise.

So she had set herself to examine the rooms of the various tenants of Surf House, and not having the authority of the police, who could have ordered every one of them to vacate while such search was made, she had to pursue her labors in secrecy.

The first labor was to purchase a length of very stout rope, to smuggle it into her room inside a new suitcase and to tie it around the stool in her bathroom. This stool, let down by means of the rope through an attic entry, would enable her to reach the top of the built-in chest of drawers. These built-in drawers were uniform to the closets of Surf House; and while Miss Rachel had found it possible, by means of unusual exertions, to reach the attic from the top of her built-in arrangement, she knew that she could not hope to continue doing it without serious results. Nor could she do it quickly—as she might have to in an emergency! Hence the necessity for the stool, to help her.

She took her stool with her into the dusty silence of the attic. It was hard to keep it from bumping or thumping; only infinite care permitted Miss Rachel to continue in silence.

Mr. Leinster was at home. The tick of his typewriter reached Miss Rachel's ears through the closed door of his closet.

The Timmersons, however, were on the point of going out. Peeping down through the entry space (and having a horrible moment of thinking the top of a white hat was the upturned inquiring face of Mrs. Timmerson) Miss Rachel made out the figure of Mr. Timmerson standing in the door of the closet and shrugging himself into his coat.

"Hurry, Rodney," his wife's voice urged him from the room beyond. "That mystery picture starts in ten minutes and I want to see it from the beginning. Get your hat and come on."

"I'm all ready," he assured her. "Have you the key?"

Metal rattled against metal as the key was fitted into the lock from the hallway. The lights clicked out, the door shut, the key was turned. The Timmersons were gone to the show.

Miss Rachel waited for some moments to be sure they hadn't forgotten something and were coming back for it, then she edged the stool down into the darkness. Its legs scraped the top of the built-in chest. Miss Rachel angled it until it rested firm, secure below. Getting down, even so, was a ticklish business. Standing on the floor of the Timmersons' closet, with their clothes touching her in the dark, gave Miss Rachel a sudden feeling of deep guilt. Scruples against breaking and entering were deep in her; she found this ever so much worse than simply listening.

She was nervous, too, fearful of the Timmersons' sudden and unexpected return—but at last she forced herself out into the larger room. After a second of listening at the door, to make sure that the hall was silent, she switched on the lights.

The room reflected the personalities of its tenants. It showed traces of fussiness and a kind of lame comfort. Padded doilies adorned the chair backs and embroidered pillows decorated the floor. A few plaster cupids, befeathered and coy, testified to Mr. Timmerson's skill with a ring game on the Strand. The room contained several chairs, a bed made up into a couch and two tables. This furniture Miss Rachel made haste to move about as she examined the floor.

There was no large rug in the room. Two small ones gave what protection was to be had from the bare boards: a small rug in front of the gas heater and a larger imitation Persian before the couch bed. These also Miss Rachel moved. Almost at once she found what she had been looking for.

In a far corner of the room, half under the edge of the biggest table, showed a patch of floor much whiter and cleaner than the rest. It apparently had quite recently been scrubbed with vigor and persistence. Miss Rachel bent to look more closely with her heart strangely thudding from excitement. And as she bent a cold disappointment came over her, for at the side of the table stood a small bottle of ink, about it still the faint remains of a spilled puddle; and the marks upon the floor, that the scrubbing had not quite removed, were not blood colored but black.

The Timmerson apartment remained determinedly innocent. In no other spot was there evidence of much cleaning. Miss Rachel mounted her climbing stool with a lowered opinion of Mrs. Timmerson's housekeeping.

She went at once to Mrs. Marble's room. The mother was at work and the child asleep. No better time could be had than now.

Miss Rachel had provided herself with a small flashlight to use in rooms where putting on the lights would be inadvisable. With this in her hand she crept quietly about the floor, collecting much dust but no evidence.

Out of darkness, Clara spoke to her. "What are you doing?" she asked suddenly.

For a moment Miss Rachel's heart did flip-flops inside her and she was frozen in an attitude of astonishment. Then she rose, not without shaking a little, and turned on the lights in the room. Clara was sitting up in the center of the double bed watching her.

Miss Rachel managed to make her voice quite calm. "Your door was open a little bit and my kitty ran in here. I'm hunting for her."

"Can I help?" Clara asked hopefully, crawling from the bed.

"Yes, you may. You search under the dresser. I'll look under the bed."

With Clara's willing help she went over the room in the better light. The floor was uniformly dusty and stained from years of careless use. There was no sign of unusual cleaning upon any part of it.

"Shall I look in the closet?" Clara offered.

Miss Rachel managed a shake of her head that she hoped was casual. "I looked in there before," she told Clara.

"Well, your kitty must have run outside again," the child surmised. "It isn't in here. I wish that it was. I'd like to play with it."

"Would you?" Miss Rachel looked down into the peaked sallow face with its big earnest eyes. "Would you like a kitty of your own?"

The little girl nodded, looking abashed. "Were you thinking of giving me one?" she asked after a moment's hesitation.

Miss Rachel tried to keep her eyes off the pitiful threadbare garment that served as Clara's nightgown. It was short as well as thin, and showed the sharp angle of elbow and knee. "I might," she told Clara, answering her hope about owning a kitten. "You'd want a little cat—not an old one like mine. They're no fun. But a kitten's darling to play with."

Clara's eyes lit up. "Maybe your cat will have kittens!"

Miss Rachel, remembering the long years of Samantha's proud maidenhood, thought not. "We'll find a kitten somewhere, though," she promised. A small hand, thin as a claw, caught at her own.

"Right away soon?" Clara wondered.

Miss Rachel paused on her way to the door to smooth the tangled pale hair. "Very soon," she agreed, loosening the hold of the tight fingers.

"You gotta go now?"

"Yes. And you must get back into bed and go to sleep."

She turned out the lights, going into the hall. Back in her own room she made haste to get into the attic and retrieve her stool. She felt in no mood to pursue her search further that night, even providing that it were possible. She sat in her room instead, toasting her toes by the gas heater and thinking of the little girl in the last apartment. . . .

Miss Rachel had a positive dread of going into the Scurlocks' apartment. Not only were the people most unpleasant to her, but their room would have to be entered by way of the door. Miss Rachel had no confidence in her window-climbing abilities.

Of late the Scurlocks had been making a show of being normal and unafraid. They were recovering from the fright occasioned by their arrest and they wanted the world to see it. It was a matter of bravado that took them early each morning for a dip in the surf. Miss Rachel, spying from a tiny crack at her door, saw them leave next morning, clad in bathing suits and beach robes and carrying towels.

It was the only time she had been able to think of that their door might be left unlocked. Keys are easily lost in the sand; and it was entirely possible that they left theirs in the door.

Like a gray taffeta mouse she slipped down the hall when the front door had closed behind them. With her eyes big she glanced up and down, and then the door opened at her touch.

It was a dreadfully cluttered room. The Scurlocks' ideas of decoration leaned toward the bizarre: yearned in the direction of Chinese pottery and wall hangings, Mexican serapes to cover couch and chairs, and seashell atrocities in a row across the dresser. There were four small tables in the room, all of them full of bric-a-brac, in addition to the large table in the center. Miss Rachel had to work carefully in moving things to avoid spilling the stuff on the floor, and she was therefore too slow for her purpose. At almost the same moment that she decided that there had been no extensive cleaning within the space of a generation upon the floors of Mrs. Scurlock, the Scurlocks came spluttering and coughing through the front door.

If they had entered at once they must have caught Miss Rachel standing wide-eyed and helpless in the middle of the room, but an argument about a dropped towel ensued between the front door and the door of their room. Mrs. Scurlock was sure that the towel had been lost. Mr. Scurlock was as positive that he had never taken it with him, but at her urging he went back to the front door to look. This moment's grace gave Miss Rachel time to come out of her stricken pose and to wriggle through an incredibly small opening to a haven beneath the couch.

The Scurlocks presently entered; they showered, and Mrs. Scurlock cooked breakfast. It was a wonderfully sweet-smelling breakfast as far as Miss Rachel was concerned, for she had not had any. After breakfast was finished the two settled themselves to examine the morning's paper, and when the news was had Mrs. Scurlock made a half-hearted attempt to dust. In the middle of her labors at one of the little catch-all tables she halted abruptly. Miss Rachel, peeping through a worn place in the couch cover, marked the startled intensity of her pose.

"Someone's been in here while we were gone," Mrs. Scurlock said in an ominously quiet voice.

"Uuuh?" Mr. Scurlock grunted from the sporting section.

"Here's a thumbprint in the dust on this table. I didn't put it there." Her large handsome figure straightened and she pointed to a spot upon the table.

Mr. Scurlock lifted his greasily blond head to look at her.

"You've forgotten," he told her insolently. "Who'd come in here?"

She matched his insolence with scorn. "How should I know who wants to get in here? Somebody has. I tell you, it isn't my fingerprint. I haven't dusted this piece in a week, nor touched it either."

Mr. Scurlock refused to take the thing seriously. "Well, what if somebody did come in? There's nothing to be had in here, God knows."

Mrs. Scurlock's dark face reminded Miss Rachel of something out of Dante's *Inferno.* "If I catch anybody meddling in this place," she said in a voice like muted thunder, "I'll cut the heart right out of them."

"And eat it, I suppose," Mr. Scurlock finished flatly, reading the racing results.

Under her couch Miss Rachel started to tremble. There was a Saint-somebody-or-other who was supposed to look after thieves, she had read somewhere, and she considered that he might perhaps also be interested in people who were guilty of unlawful entry. She prayed a little in the vague general direction of this gentleman. "Dear Saint—well, you know whom I mean . . ." She wondered if he did. "Please get me out of this."

There was no answer.

At noontime the Scurlocks went out for lunch, Mrs. Scurlock deciding that she didn't feel like cooking. They locked the door very determinedly after them and took away the key. Not that it mattered to Miss Rachel. As soon as they were safely gone she was out and had the window open and was getting through it. The drop to the sand jarred every bone in her small body.

She stood panting for a moment, nursing a torn place in the palm of one hand. It was then that something touched her, tugged at her skirt. Without looking around Miss Rachel felt her heart go dead. The Scurlocks . . .?

Mayhew's deep voice rumbled through the chaos in her mind. "You're taking chances, monkeying with people like the Scurlocks," he told her. She didn't reply, simply swallowed and looked tired.

"What were you after in there?" he asked, getting curious.

Miss Rachel looked a dusty woebegone picture of guilt. "No—nothing," she managed.

Mayhew brought his thick brows together in a frightful frown. "Now, see here," he scolded gently, "we can't have you poking into places that might be dangerous. The Scurlocks aren't kittens, you know—they play for blood. If they were to catch you in their apartment——"

"They almost did," Miss Rachel admitted breathlessly.

"And they aren't entirely in the clear on that murder charge," he reminded her. "Tell me what you were looking for and I'll perhaps tend to it."

His word "perhaps" sounded very indefinite to Miss Rachel, and in addition she had not a very clear explanation as to why she was hunting for scrubbed places in Surf House. The whole thing would sound highly ridiculous to the sensible ears of Lieutenant Mayhew. Miss Rachel put him off with a vague explanation about missing documents. The look he gave her was stern in the extreme and set Miss Rachel into the place of an unreasonable and naughty child.

He was on his way to talk to Mrs. Malloy. He and Miss Rachel parted in the hall to the accompaniment of Miss Rachel's false promises not to pursue any more dangerous and silly leads that might occur to her. Behind her door she heard Mr. Leinster come out of his room, beat on Mrs. Malloy's door and demand to be admitted to the conference. Miss Rachel was torn between a desire to listen in upon possible fireworks and the thought that now was the time to look over Mr. Leinster's dwelling. Duty won, and after Leinster had pushed into the room across the hall Miss Rachel went, via the attic and her roped stool, to his apartment.

It was bare in the extreme—bare and dirty.

Miss Rachel believes that if a mop had been applied to Mr. Leinster's floor its path would have been as plain as the swath cut by Sherman's march to the sea.

She retreated to her own room, not exactly in disappointment but with some of the fine fresh enthusiasm she had felt for her theory gone. It began to appear likely that nowhere in this ancient building was she to find a floor that was clean, much less one that had been scrubbed. If the broom and the mop were unknown, why expect to make the acquaintance of a scrub-brush? She sighed, feeling misled by her own fancies.

A tap at her door brought her to attention. Clara's rumpled head stuck itself into view.

"Come in," Miss Rachel invited.

Clara came, twisting her faded dress round a finger. "I was thinking about the kitten you promised me," she said shyly. "Have you bought it yet?"

"Not yet," Miss Rachel admitted to Clara's instant and apparent disappointment.

The little girl shuffled about the room, examining Miss Rachel's scant belongings. At last, with a sharp look, she said hurriedly, "If you'll get me the kitty right away I might tell you something."

"Would you? What about?"

Clara ducked her head and put her tongue in her cheek. Miss Rachel was conscious of a wary scrutiny. A minute ticked by as the childish eyes surveyed her. Then: "Something what happened the night the lady died."

Miss Rachel's slight body tensed and she half rose from her chair. But like a moth Clara was at the door ready to fly. "I won't tell," she said with finality. "Not unless I get the kitty."

"Clara—listen!" Miss Rachel cried, getting up.

But Clara was gone.

Chapter Eighteen:
A Kind of Mewing Sound

Inquiries which Mayhew had set going in San Diego had borne no fruit. Officers there, in their routine duties, had kept eyes open for out-of-the-way places in which Malloy's body might have been concealed. They had tried to discover traces of the car he had rented from outlying service stations where it might have stopped for gas, but to no avail. No one remembered seeing the car on that particular day, and no hiding place yielded up Malloy's body.

Mayhew felt himself at an impasse. But he is like a bulldog who gets his teeth into a chunk of meat. Letting go is out of the question. Mayhew decided to chew at the thing from another angle. He ordered all tenants of Surf House to gather in the sunroom that evening at seven.

Six forty-five found him at the writing desk studying his notebook, with Edson lounging at the door. At five minutes before the hour Sara Malloy came quietly into the room. Mayhew minded his manners enough to half rise at her entrance, which gesture brought a look of keen attention into Edson's usually vacuous face.

She was dressed in a blue knitted suit that curved to a thick ruffle at her neck and met the golden wash of her hair. Under her level brows her eyes met Mayhew's straight; his dropped before hers did. She kept looking at him without seeming to notice his discomfiture. She watched as though she saw for the first time the good stout lines of him: his solid honesty, his forth-rightness and the determined look of his brown face. If she resented the stiff questioning he had given her mother a short while before, there was no sign of it. Her mouth looked troubled, half ready for crying, but her eyes held something the opposite of anger.

Leinster flung into the room next, and then Miss Rachel, softly. She was in time to catch the half-incredulous look with which Leinster took in Sara's regard of the big detective. His eyes opened wide for an instant, watching the still figure of the girl, and when he sat down he did so slowly. Miss Rachel could guess the hurt that gnawed him; the certain knowledge of something that he had only surmised, scoffing, before.

The Scurlocks brought a frozen tension into the atmosphere of the room. They spoke to no one. Mr. Scurlock helped his wife to find a comfortable chair in a far corner, and thus retired, she looked murder out upon them all. Mr. Scurlock was not at ease; he played with his face, with his hair and with his tie, and seemed not to know one from another. He put most of his attention upon the ceiling.

Mrs. Malloy slipped in, very white of face and not looking at Mayhew. She found a place beside her daughter and sat down quickly. She was followed immediately by Mrs. Turner, who had for each of the others a stare of personal enmity. The Timmersons came at the same time that Mrs. Marble and Clara did; and all of them straggled in together, not smiling but managing to look pleasant.

They filled the sunroom: a thoroughly uncomfortable and uncongenial group of people. Mayhew surveyed them in a moment of silence before he spoke. He marked the expression on each of them: saw Leinster's hurt, which he did not understand, and Mrs. Scurlock's rage, which he did. Then he got down to business.

"I'm checking alibis," he told them bluntly. "So far we haven't got together in our accounts of the evening Mrs. Sticklemann was murdered. We're going to do it now. I'm going to have each of you tell me again exactly how you spent the hours of that day from six until ten o'clock. And if any of the rest of you can corroborate such statements, I'd like for you to do it. If, on the other hand, you know of some omission or discrepancy in any statement given, I must warn you that it is your duty to inform me of the truth, and that to neglect to do so lays you open to a criminal charge. All set?" He studied the faces that circled the room. Mr. Timmerson was wavering in the throes of some sort of indecision. Mayhew could see a beading of sweat on his forehead and his eyes rolling woefully in the direction of his wife. The rest of them took the announcement calmly enough.

Mayhew turned to the Scurlocks. Mrs. Scurlock gave him the same glare of cold ferocity with which she regarded everyone else. Mr. Scurlock made an effort to keep his hands still and look intelligent. "Let's have your stories first," Mayhew told them.

Mr. Scurlock emitted a dry cackle that would have been a laugh if it could. "Why, we've told you, Lieutenant. We were at home." He glanced at his wife and quit laughing rather too suddenly. She had given him one venomous stab with her eyes and gone on watching Mayhew.

"At home," Mayhew repeated, and looked round the circle of

listeners. He stopped at Leinster, but that young man was too busy with his own thoughts to give heed. "Mr. Leinster!" The blond head lifted. "Did Mr. and Mrs. Scurlock go out during the evening of the murder?"

Leinster looked blank for a minute, then, catching himself: "Oh—I see what you mean. When I was in the sunroom across from them—no, they didn't go out. Not out of the door, at any rate."

Mrs. Scurlock gave him what amounted to a smile.

"And you, Mr. Scurlock—can you verify Mr. Leinster's statement that he was in the sunroom?"

"Ahh—well, I'm afraid not. You see, I didn't even so much as look out. Did you glance out, dear?"

Mrs. Scurlock had not glanced out.

"Can anyone here verify Mr. Leinster's statement?"

No one, it appeared, could do this. Mr. Leinster had been seen by no one, in the sunroom.

Mayhew dropped the subject of Leinster's whereabouts to question the Timmersons. Mrs. Timmerson again got off on the discovery of the murdered woman's body, but her husband stopped her and began manfully to reveal the subject of a quarrel he had had with Malloy.

"The man's been missing so long it's beginning to look odd, and we think it might have something do with the death of Mrs. Sticklemann. Anyway, here it is for what it amounts to. I'd rather be the one to tell you, than someone else who might not know the whole of it." He got out a handkerchief and mopped his face quickly.

"Go on," Mayhew encouraged him.

"Well, this man Malloy asked me to change a bill for him

one day. It was a twenty-dollar bill, and it just happened that I had that much money with me. I changed his bill for him all right, and then later a storekeeper told me it was counterfeit. I tried to make Malloy give me back my money but he denied that his bill had been a fake. He pretended that I was trying to put something over on him, and it ended up in a big fuss. I guess plenty of people heard us going to it." He glanced about with his eyes round and fearful.

Mayhew leaned toward the fat nervous little man. "Is that the same bill that you offered at the theater the night of the murder?"

Mr. Timmerson started, and his face went as slack as though he had heard the crack of doom. "Yes," he got out quickly. "But how did you know——?"

Mayhew shook his head in resignation at Mr. Timmerson's forgetfulness. "You told me," he reminded him. "Or rather your wife did, that you had created a fuss at the theater over a counterfeit bill."

Timmerson looked thoroughly frightened. "It was wrong, I know," he admitted. "But it meant quite a bit to me—twenty dollars. I thought if I could pass it on, and get my money back, it wouldn't do any terrible harm. Not to a big business like a theater, at any rate."

Mayhew ignored his explanation of his act. "Have you this bill now?"

Mr. Timmerson, quite pink of face, fished in his pockets. A limp bill came to light and was handed to Mayhew, who looked at it in impatient scorn. "This thing wouldn't fool anybody," he growled. "Why do you pretend that it fooled you?"

Mr. Timmerson started to rise with each of his chins doing a separate quiver of its own. "Oh, but I was fooled with it! I was!" He glanced about him at the pained indifference of the others. The silence was ominous.

It was Mrs. Malloy who came to his rescue. "Perhaps I can help," she said timidly. "My husband once got hold of quite an amount of counterfeit money. As long as he was on the stage he used it as stage money, but afterward it occurred to him that it might be passable. I always understood that he used it merely as a joke—that he returned the actual money he got in exchange when he had had some fun out of the situation." She was obviously ashamed to have to explain such an act on her husband's part. "It was his idea of humor," she finished lamely.

Mayhew studied Mrs. Malloy and Timmerson as though he suspected them of a conspiracy to defeat the purposes of justice. "Let's get on," he said at last, to Timmerson's open relief. "You and Mrs. Timmerson were at the theater the night of the murder. I'll accept that until I can check with the theater people. Now—Mrs. Marble?"

Mrs. Marble had been plucking at a mended place in her cotton skirt. At Mayhew's mention of her name she collected her thoughts quickly. "I was at work all evening. It will be very easy for you to check my statement. Mrs. Terry at the Ravenswood Arms will tell you that I was working."

Mayhew swung his slow stare to Clara, who hung upon the arm of her mother's chair. "And now—Clara, is it?—what about you?"

"My name's Chicken," she corrected succinctly.

Mayhew permitted his black brows to rise in a moment's astonishment, until he remembered. Then he smiled at the child. Miss Rachel thinks that Sara will never quite forget the tenderness of Mayhew's attitude toward scrawny, unbeautiful little

Clara, nor can she herself forget it. He put out a big hand in a friendly way and Clara came to him. "What all were you doing the night the lady died?" he asked her.

She looked up in bashful affection. "Sleeping, I guess," she said after a moment's hesitation.

Miss Rachel sat tensed in a shiver of dread. If the child were to hint that she knew something . . . She mustn't, for the sake of her own safety. "Don't tell him now," Miss Rachel begged silently in her thoughts. "Not here. Not with—whoever it is, looking on and listening." She glanced at the circle of faces. Behind which face waited the beast that pounced in the dark?

"Sleeping all of the time?" Mayhew prodded carefully.

The child's eyes met Miss Rachel's; they widened as Rachel gave a cool determined shake of her white head. It was a gesture that might have passed as a mere unconscious nod, but to Clara it was a command from a lady who was going to give her a kitten. "Just sleeping," she said promptly. Mayhew looked his disappointment. He had sensed from the beginning something reticent in Clara's attitude when she spoke of the night of the crime. He set her now to the floor, from his knee where she had climbed, and turned his attention back to the adult members of the group.

"Mrs. Turner?" He looked across at the tall spare figure of the landlady and wondered inwardly how she could be so infernally ugly and yet have been married. Above her long coarse nose her eyes met his unhesitatingly.

"This is absolute nonsense!" she pronounced loudly. "I've told you before that I was sewing. I sewed all evening."

Mayhew looked at Sara's mother. "Mrs. Malloy, I believe you verified Mrs. Turner's statement?"

She nodded. "Yes, I can verify it. I was sitting by the open window of our room, and I plainly heard the sound of Mrs. Turner's machine."

In the face of Mrs. Turner's open scorn Mayhew went on poking. "There weren't any long periods of silence—a half-hour, say—when the machine wasn't running?"

"Oh, no. It didn't run continuously, of course. There were stops such as a person makes to break thread, fix the material and such. I use a machine myself and naturally noticed the sound." Mrs. Malloy carefully refrained from mentioning her real reason for close attention to the sewing machine—her watch for Sara while Sara investigated her father's deserted room.

"I was hemming some new curtains," Mrs. Turner broke in. "The curtains are in dreadful condition. No one has taken the least care of them." She stared in deep animosity at her tenants, who looked individually guilty.

Now Mayhew must look at Sara, and Miss Rachel expected at least some sign of emotion. But he met the blue gaze of her young eyes as coldly as he had met the looks of the others. "Miss Malloy?"

"I—I had entered my father's room through the window that night. I was looking for some old letters and souvenirs that Mother wanted from his things. He had been gone so long we were afraid something might be missing. I went to look."

"And you believe you heard the murderer enter Mrs. Sticklemann's apartment?"

"I know that I heard her door open and close. After Miss Rachel went in—" She looked at the little old lady in gray; Miss Rachel's eyes were as sharp as a fox's. "After Miss Rachel went in, I heard the door open and close four times—that is, someone went into the room twice, and twice must have come out. At least, it seems to me that I remember it that way—someone going in, coming out . . ." Her voice died to silence in the crowded room. If she sensed the interested regard of the others she did not show it. Under the shining wings of her yellow hair her brow wrinkled in a small frown. "I've just remembered——"

Mayhew straightened a little. "Yes?"

"It's odd that I didn't remember it before! But it seems to me that there was a sound *in the hall—wait!*" She bit at the tip of an oval thumbnail in a gesture of concentration. There was complete silence from everyone else. "Yes, it was just after the second time the door was closed—that is, after whoever had first gonc in had come out."

"You mean between the two times that Mrs. Sticklemann's room was entered?"

She nodded, still with that quiet puzzled look on her face.

"And what kind of sound was it?"

"It——" She stopped, looking more puzzled yet. "I hardly know how to describe it, but I guess the best way—it was a kind of *mewing sound,*" she finished at last.

Mayhew looked openly annoyed. It was plainly not the significant fact that he had expected. But in Miss Rachel's breast a slow thudding had started. If she could have warned Sara beforehand—but she hadn't. And now the thing was out—spilled—and in some person's brain within that room, she had no doubt, a new wariness was growing.

She watched Mayhew, saw his disappointment at Sara's words and knew that she should have told him her theory of the case. Perhaps, she thought, it might not yet be too late.

But for Mayhew the conference was over, and as far as he was concerned he had learned nothing of great importance. Tomorrow he would check the alibis of these people as best he could.

He gave Miss Rachel a brief nod as he went out, and missed entirely the desperate entreaty of her glance. . . .

Mrs. Terry of the Ravenswood Arms met him in morning gown of lavender chiffon.

Yes, Mrs. Marble had been working for her the night of the crime. If one could call it work. Just puttering in the kitchen, really, though one had to pay . . . Wasn't it a dreadful murder? And what did he *really* think had happened? Wasn't the murderer—— But Mayhew dislikes fat women who wear red nail enamel. He got away with a minimum of courtesy.

Mrs. Terry has told her friends that Mayhew is big and good-looking, but brutal, my dears, simply brutal! His abrupt rushing departure surprised her. There are nearly two hundred pounds of Mrs. Terry to be surprised, but Mayhew managed nicely. His good-by, in reply to her chirruping one, approximated the growl which Leinster has said was all that he needed to be a bear. It left Mrs. Terry with her mouth open.

It was still early morning. He found the theater on the Strand wrapped in silence and darkness. By means of a small card tacked beneath the burglar alarm Mayhew learned the manager's name and address, and called on the man at his home. The manager was big, very dapper, and came in freshly shaved and wearing a red silk dressing-gown. It took Mayhew several minutes to recall to him the incident of Timmerson's counterfeit bill, but at last he remembered it well enough. This, while being no proof that the Timmersons had stayed the full time at the theater, at least verified a part of their alibi.

Mayhew could think of no way to check up on the statements of Leinster, who claimed to have been in the sunroom, or of Sara and her mother. But in response to a nagging hunch he visited a sewing-machine shop to discover if there was any known means of running a machine without staying with it.

The young woman who managed the shop was very stylish, very bright and intensely superior, and she was plainly not impressed when Mayhew informed her that he was a police officer. No, she thought, in reply to his query, there was certainly not any method she had ever heard of to manage a sewing machine—outside of putting a book on a foot control and leaving it down. That might do it.

Mayhew asked if such a procedure wouldn't give a continuous running, unlike the normal usage of a sewing machine.

The young lady laughed archly. Whatever trick Mayhew was up to, she considered it funny. Of course putting a book on the foot control would cause the machine to run on and on. She'd done it once, as a child, to annoy an aunt. No, it hadn't sounded like real sewing. Now—she wondered if he had seen these *new* models? Lovely little machines . . . She asked, ever so casually, if he were married.

Mayhew was overcome with the feeling that he'd better leave before he was sold a sewing machine when a new thought occurred to him. "What about repairs? Do you have a man who works with these things?"

"Indeed we do. We have a repair man." She seemed to be getting a little vague as to eye. Mayhew got the impression that repairs were chicken feed.

"Could I see this man?"

She looked briefly in the direction of the rear of the store which was walled off with fiberboard, painted gray, with a curtained doorway in the center. "He's back there." The sound of a machine's hum came suddenly from behind the curtain.

Mayhew found a little gray man in the rear. He sat in the

midst of dozens of parts of sewing machines with a dismantled machine before him. Mayhew greeted him pleasantly and explained to him what he wished to know.

The little gray man scratched a whiskered chin. Mayhew sensed uneasy reserve, a desire to keep still about something he knew.

At last he spoke. "It was a secret, like."

"This is police business, man."

"I know." The little man looked shrewdly at Mayhew from under bushy gray brows. "This was going to be a Halloween trick at some rich woman's party. She sent her chauffeur in to find out about it. Not that I had to tell him much—he was a smart feller in that way. Must have done electrical work, I figger, some time or other."

One word of the little man's narrative had caught Mayhew's ear. "Who came?"

"The chauffeur."

Across Mayhew's forehead stole out a band of sweat in fine beads. "Go on."

"It was a cute idea. I—I guess you want the details?"

Mayhew nodded dumbly.

"That's why I thought the feller must have done electrical work. He'd got this up in his head. I sold him the parts and gave him a pointer or two. He told me it was a secret, that his old lady'd be mad if I breathed a word of it. Not that I'd be afraid of a woman . . . Well, this was it: you take the cord that runs to the machine from the electric outlet. You split it apart—it's in two sections, you know—and you cut one section and join in a new line and a socket. A regular socket that'd hold a globe. Only under the globe you put a thermostat."

It sounded like magician's hocus-pocus to Mayhew, but he

was sure at last—so sure that he could scarcely endure to wait until the little man should finish.

"Now, when the electricity is turned on the machine will run for a minute or so. Until the lamp in the socket heats the thermostat to the point where it will switch off—then the machine would stop. The light would go off too, of course. For a while the juice will be cut off, a minute, say. Then, as the thermostat cools, it will click on again. It'd go on like that forever, as long as you'd like."

"Describe the—the chauffeur."

"He's a dark feller. Wore a big beaked cap. Needed a haircut too.

"Thanks," muttered Mayhew, making for the door.

The little gray man stared after Mayhew's hurrying figure. "Don't thank me," he said cheerfully. "The other guy thought of it first."

Chapter Nineteen:
The Footprints

At 7:30 that morning the telephone at Surf House had started ringing, and there seemed, oddly enough, no one interested in answering it. At the sixth or seventh rousing peal, however, Sara had rolled out of bed and gone to see about it. The hall was dim and deserted, filled unpleasantly with the recurring clamor of the phone. Sara lifted the receiver. "Hello," she offered.

Someone said, "Long distance. San Diego calling Miss Sara Malloy."

"This is Miss Malloy speaking," Sara told the phone.

There was a series of clicks then, as a connection went through, and a harsh voice burst in her ear. "Miss Malloy?" it demanded. "I'm Jasper Nicholson, your father's old friend. Do you remember me?"

"Oh, yes—very well indeed! Though it's been years . . ."

The voice grated on. "I've discovered some startling news concerning your father, Sara."

The girl raised on tiptoe in her eagerness, bringing her face closer to the telephone. "Is he—all right?"

"Yes, yes! He's fine," the voice assured her. "He wants to see you right away, somewhere where you and he can be alone."

"I'll come down right away, if he wants me," Sara said quickly. "I'll find out when the stages run to San——"

"Never mind," the other broke in with a great hurry. "It happens that my car is in your city today. I sent a friend home in it yesterday. You can come down in my car."

"But I don't drive." Sara hesitated. "Wouldn't it be better—?"

"There's no need for you to drive. My chauffeur is with the car. Let me know where he can pick you up—a downtown corner would be best—and I'll call the garage where the car should be, now. He'll be starting back. Could you make it by nine o'clock?"

Sara sensed the other's impatience and she made haste to agree. "Yes, I'll be ready. I'll be at the corner of James and Third."

At her quick agreement some of the hurry went out of the voice at the other end of the wire. "That's fine," it said a little more slowly, and then: "There's one more thing."

Sara listened attentively.

"Your father would rather that no one knew about this just yet. You see, the Sticklemann case has him in a bad light and he needs your help before he will feel free to come out into the open. Will you promise not to mention this errand to anyone?" At these last words the voice became almost pleading and some of its hoarseness vanished.

"I won't tell a soul," Sara said quickly. "Have your chauffeur pick me up at nine o'clock. I'll be waiting."

"James and Third?" the voice asked.

"James and Third," Sara assured it.

She went back to her and her mother's room. Mrs. Malloy was still sleeping, her small figure curled under the coverlets looking not much larger than a child's. She had wasted during this stay at Surf House. Her face was peaked with worry and fatigue and inability to eat and sleep as she should. Her eyes seemed sunken in shadow, their lids blue. Sara bent and kissed her mother lightly on her forehead, and then began dressing for her rendezvous. She watched her mother as she made her preparations, wondering what she should say if Mrs. Malloy awoke and asked what she was doing. But Mrs. Malloy, having drugged herself the night before with a sleep-inducer, did not wake.

At eight-thirty, hatted and gloved and at the door, Sara paused. Her mother would be worried if she woke and found her gone without a word as to her whereabouts. Sara was in a quandary as to what to do. At last she scribbled upon a card and left it propped upon the dresser.

"Dear Mother," she whispered, writing the words. "I'm on the trail of wonderful news. I'm going to San——" She stopped then and thought that perhaps his whereabouts was a point which her father would not want mentioned. A careful erasure took away the last three letters. "I'm going to see a friend. Don't worry," she filled it out, and signed her name.

Miss Rachel could not remember having slept a wink all night.

She lay stretched upon the uncomfortable bed, watching the dawn creep grayly into the window, watching the sunlight yellow the wall outside. Once in a while she sighed, and when Samantha made a scratching noise inside her basket beside the bed

Miss Rachel sat up suddenly, staring at the door. Then, placing the sound, she lay down again, shivering.

The telephone's ringing startled her, but she felt no desire to answer it. Telephones, she felt, should not ring so loudly in places like Surf House—a dull buzzing would be more in keeping with the atmosphere of the sinister place. Or a hiss. She tried to imagine a telephone hissing.

Sara's voice, muted by the length of the hall and her closed door, became audible. Without a scruple that she was conscious of Miss Rachel crawled from bed and opened her door a crack and listened. Sara's half of the conversation reached her, and she unaccountably didn't like it. She got back into bed again, very displeased and thoughtful.

Day grew broad and golden outdoors, and still she stayed in bed, feeling guilt for her laziness. Then she heard Sara leave her room, closing the door very softly after her. Miss Rachel became positively alarmed; she at once got up and dressed.

A tap at Mrs. Malloy's door brought no response. With an air of open shameless snoopiness Miss Rachel tried the door. It opened and she went quietly inside.

Mrs. Malloy was sleeping heavily, curled beneath the bedclothes. Miss Rachel looked at her carefully, but beyond a look of exhaustion could see nothing wrong. Then her gaze went round the room.

Sara's note brought a pucker of alarm to her brow. After she had read it she put it back in its place upon the dresser and returned to her own room. She stood for a long minute in frightened indecision, not knowing quite what to do and having a feeling that she was either delaying in something dreadful and urgent or else meddling in an affair which was simply none of her business.

There was, at any rate, one very decisive course of action which was open to her. She went down the hall to Mrs. Marble's apartment and knocked at the door. It took a while to rouse the work-weary woman, but at last she came, looking sleepy and surprised. Miss Rachel invited herself briskly into the room.

"I must talk to Clara," she told Mrs. Marble. Clara, having got up hours before to play, sat in her nightdress on the floor with two ragged dolls beside her.

"Have you got the kitty?" she asked Miss Rachel, circling her thin knees with her arms, watching the old lady with eager interest.

Miss Rachel was now so thoroughly become a sleuth that she thought nothing of a small falsehood for the sake of information. "Yes, I've bought your kitty. He's still in the store, however. We'll go get him this morning."

"That's good," Clara said noncommittally.

"And now . . ." Miss Rachel looked small, but very determined. "Now you must tell me what you know that happened the night my niece died." She sat down on a chair, not missing the start of amazement that shook Mrs. Marble's slight frame. Clara seemed undecided.

"You must tell me," Miss Rachel repeated firmly.

Clara looked up with a sly glance, but Miss Rachel's stern small face brooked no nonsense. "Come on, Clara."

"Well . . ." Clara's eyes shifted to her mother, then back to the little old lady in gray. "I wasn't asleep," she admitted cautiously.

Miss Rachel appeared not to be surprised at this information, though Mrs. Marble was showing signs of desperation.

"Clara," admonished the mother, "if you're making things up . . ."

Miss Rachel shook her head. "Go on. What did you see that night?"

Clara shot a quick guilty look toward the door to the hall, lowered her voice and muttered so that only her mother and Miss Rachel might hear. "I heard a kind of little noise. And I peeked out."

"And what did you see?"

"I saw Mrs. Turner coming out of her room. She had a little ax in her hand and she put her hand behind her skirt. She looked at the door for a minute. Then she left it open, as if she thought she wanted it that way."

"Could you see into her room?"

Clara turned her head sidewise, archly. "I creeped out when she was gone, and I peeked into the room. Her sewing machine was in there. It was running *by itself*."

Miss Rachel started. It was a moment before she found her voice. "What do you mean—running by itself?"

Clara stopped in bewilderment. "That's all. Just running all alone. There was a light close by, lying under the table. When the machine stopped for a minute the light went out." She shifted, to look at her mother. "Mom, you know the foot jigger that Mrs. Turner puts her foot on to make the machine run? Well, she had her big book on that, keeping it down. Her big book, the one with everyone's name in it."

Of the arrangement with the electric light Miss Rachel could understand nothing—but she saw that here was the heart of the matter, the very core of the crime. She got up suddenly, smoothing her taffeta skirt. "Let's go into Mrs. Turner's apartment," she suggested.

Mrs. Marble, her face white, put out a hand to Clara. "Not coming?" said Miss Rachel, seeing her fright. Mrs. Marble shook her head, speechless. "I don't believe she's at home," Miss Rachel went on. "I believe she's gone somewhere. With Sara Malloy." Miss Rachel stepped briskly across the narrow hall and beat a tattoo upon Mrs. Turner's door. There was nothing but silence inside.

Miss Rachel went in. A desk claimed her attention before she looked at the floor. Inside the desk was a letter addressed to *Mrs. Anne S. Turner.* Miss Rachel studied it for a long moment while a bitter gray line grew about her mouth, then she flung it from her all at once and looked down.

The floor was remarkably clean.

She was on her hands and knees, half under the bed, when a hard hand clutched her skirt.

"Come out, dammit!" Mayhew rumbled above her. "Where's the Turner woman?"

Miss Rachel had located what Mrs. Turner, for all her work with mop and brush, had missed. Dim through a layer of lint under the bed showed a faint cat track. Samantha, then, had covered the room pretty well before being caught and bathed. Miss Rachel shivered, backing away, remembering that here was a bit of Lily's blood. At Mayhew's touch she got up, looking very sober.

Seeing him, the thought struck her that Mayhew was a man-hunter. Something had tensed and brightened in his face, giving it a look of ruthless determination. "Where's Turner?" he growled again, through his teeth.

Miss Rachel's face was a study in pain. "We're late," she told him. "She's got away with Sara."

He flung about and went through the door in a hurry Miss

Rachel heard him beating on Mrs. Malloy's door before she had gotten into the hall after him. When she reached Mrs. Malloy's apartment he was standing at the window studying the card Sara had left. At his elbow stood Mrs. Malloy, inarticulate with terror. Both of them looked round at Miss Rachel's entrance.

"How do you know they're together?" Mayhew demanded.

Miss Rachel understood the cause of his belligerent doubt. He didn't want to believe that Sara was with Mrs. Turner. But carefully and sensibly Miss Rachel told him of the telephone call.

Still he looked disbelief at her. "But why?"

"Oh, that's pretty obvious. Sara knew something very important about the murder of my niece, and Mrs. Turner wants her out of the way before you get onto it."

He swung round, facing her with anger black in his eyes. "What does she know?" he demanded, and rushed on: "And why the devil didn't she tell me about it?"

"She did tell you," Miss Rachel explained hurriedly. Mayhew's hands clenched suddenly, his face going gray, but he said nothing. "Don't you remember in the sunroom last night that she told you she had heard a mewing sound in the hall?"

"And what of it?"

Here Miss Rachel shook her head. "We mustn't stand here talking. We've got to find Sara."

He came close and caught her arm in a grip that for once was not gentle. "Do you know where they've gone?" Miss Rachel, feeling the tension of his fingers, sensed the iron control that he was keeping over his nerves. She has said that it was just then that she became sure that Mayhew really was fond of Sara; which was nice to know, but gave no help at the moment.

"I believe I know the direction she has taken," Miss Rachel told him. "You see, in her conversation at the telephone this morning, she started to mention a town beginning with *San*—and she offered to come *down*. Doesn't that suggest going south—say to San Diego?"

Mayhew tore the note in a gesture of bewilderment and despair. "God, woman, there are thousands of towns in California that begin with that particular prefix. It's Spanish; it's——"

"I know. But it's a chance. What other have we?"

"None." Some of the frenzy went out of him as he said it slowly. He went from the room and up the hall to the telephone and called police headquarters. "Put this on the teletype, right away," he commanded. Looking up, he met Miss Rachel's serious eyes. "There's not much I can give them," he told her, cupping the mouthpiece with his hand. "We've no idea of the kind of car they're using."

"It will be a rented car," Miss Rachel told him. "But we haven't time to check the agencies."

Mayhew spoke suddenly into the telephone, giving them what he could—what Miss Rachel had heard of Sara's call, a chauffeur-driven car with a young woman in the back seat. Probably going south. When he had finished he looked at his watch. It was 9:40. "Damn! Now we just missed it!" he growled.

"Maybe we haven't—yet," Miss Rachel said briskly. "How's your car for speed?"

The same idea had been in Mayhew's mind but he did not relish a passenger. Women are inclined to scream at Mayhew's technique on curves. But Miss Rachel was gone to get her hat and a wrap, and she was back before he could get out of the door. "I'm going," she said coolly. It struck Mayhew all at once that from the beginning Miss Rachel had considered this case her own, and a wave of unreasoning anger rose in him in the face of her calm determination.

"You can't go," he told her suddenly. "This is police business. You're out of it."

She stood by the door, watching him in chill displeasure. "I suppose you know what you're doing," she remarked, and when he gave no answer: "You'll miss her. You haven't any eye for hats."

Mayhew was stung as usual by the unexpectedness of her words. "Hats?" he echoed, still angry.

"Hats," she repeated, and went on in the manner of a schoolteacher lecturing her most stupid and unruly pupil. "Don't you know that the best chance we have of catching them is by recognizing Sara's hat through the rear window? Do you think that that car will be poking along in such a way that you can drive up to it and look in at your leisure?" She stopped to put her chin out at him. "In case you don't know," she went on carefully, "Sara has three hats, and I'd recognize any of them."

He took her arm very quietly. "You win. Come on."

Sara had waited not more than three minutes at the corner of James and Third streets; then there had swung to the curb, out of the slow line of traffic, a long black car. A chauffeur, capped and goggled, had leaned from his place at the wheel to open the rear door for her. "Hello!" Sara had said, getting in. The chauffeur had merely nodded in reply, his attention on the car ahead.

The man was an expert and careful driver. Stop signs and traffic signals were obeyed with scrupulous precision until the open highway to the south was reached. Then they began to make time.

Sara studied the driver curiously. He was not a tall man, or else he was in the habit of driving slouched down in the seat, for all that she could make out from where she sat were the tips of his shoulders and an untidy stretch of neck beneath the cap. He needed a haircut most remarkably, Sara thought, and then, losing interest, she turned her eyes toward the blue dazzle of the sea.

The miles and the hours flew.

At a crossroad the car slowed and turned. Looking out, Sara glimpsed a tall archway with a sign hung above the road. "San Dimas Caves!" she exclaimed in the direction of the chauffeur. "Is this where I am to meet my father?"

For a moment the man in the front seat raised himself so that his face showed in the rear-vision mirror. Eyes looked through goggles into her own.

It was then that Sara began to be afraid.

"It's damnable," Mayhew was saying through his teeth, sidewise.

"Yes. And frightening," Miss Rachel said absently, watching the ends of a truckload of pipe upon which it seemed they were to be immediately impaled.

Mayhew saved them from being gored by the pipe with a last-minute flourish, like a conjurer, and they hummed round the truck and ahead of it. "It's a man, after all," he went on dully. "A guy who wears a chauffeur's uniform. Where does the Turner woman come in? Dammit—in spite of those hands—it must be Malloy. He could imitate a woman. He's been on the stage."

But Miss Rachel disagreed. "No. It's much simpler than that."

Mayhew's eyebrows went up.

"I think," she went on carefully, "that we'll find Malloy—today."

Chapter Twenty:
Miss Rachel Knows Everything

The coastline above San Diego, some ten or twelve miles from the city, has been broken apart, fissured and cracked, by the sea. Here there are chasms that split the rugged cliffs from their top to the level of the beach far below; here there are dangerous crumbling banks that sag outward; and all through the formation, like the cells of a honeycomb, are caves bored by the tide. The upper caves are mere dusty neglected holes in the earth. Those below, at the sea level, are famed round the world for the glimpse they give of sea life.

There was a cluster of parked cars at the entrance to the main trail, but the car which contained Sara did not stop there. It crept along a seldom-used weedy road that skirted the edge of the cliff, until it was out of sight of the cars belonging to the other visitors. Then it came to a stop, and there was a moment of dead silence during which the only movement that Sara was conscious of was the heavy thumping of her own heart. The chauffeur did not glance at her.

"Shall I get out here?" Sara asked, when the silence became unendurable. The capped head jerked in answer. Sara opened her door and stepped out into dry weeds and dust. The breeze that swept up off the sea was cool and held the odor of the tide. Sara faced it, breathing deeply, trying to down the terror that threatened to possess her.

"Follow me," the other said. The dark blue figure walked to the cliff's edge, surveyed the sheer drop through goggles and found a trail that slanted, almost invisibly, down the side of a chasm into shadow. But Sara held back.

"My father—he's really here, isn't he?" Her own voice sounded strange to her, lost in the emptiness of sunlight and silence.

The blue figure kept going and did not look back.

Sara looked about her. There was no other human being within sight, and even the enigmatic few-worded chauffeur seemed better comfort than the strange aloneness of this place. She made haste to follow along the rough almost obliterated pathway. "Wait a moment. I'm coming," she called. But again there was no answer.

The path dropped, then it turned, to round the face of the cliff above the beach. Sara looked down and clung to an outcropping of rough stone. Below, beyond a ribbon of gray sand, the sea boiled furiously among greenish rocks. The roar of it came up to her like the sound of a strong wind blowing, and fear came with the sound.

She found the chauffeur standing half in shadow in the entrance of a cave; the gloved hand motioned her inside. Within, it was suddenly cool and shadowed and smelling of earth. Sara turned when she had taken a few steps.

"Where is my father?" She tried to put confidence into her voice.

The chauffeur, without answering, began pulling off gloves, then goggles. The raised cap let a tumble of rusty hair fall from under it to cover the uniformed shoulders. Sara watched, dumbfounded, until it was finished.

"I don't understand," she whispered at last, feeling the damp wall of the cave thrust into her back as she pressed against it.

"Don't you?" said the other, harshly mocking. Something blue with a metallic glitter came from beneath the chauffeur's uniform; its barrel looked at Sara, trembling against the stone. "What would you like to know?"

"Where is my father?" she panted, looking everywhere but into the brilliant ferocity of the other's eyes.

"He's here!"

She looked about, bewilderment distracting her. "Where?"

"Behind you a little way. He's covered now by the earth. I wouldn't uncover him if I were you. It wouldn't be—pleasant."

Pain cut into Sara's whirling thoughts. "He's dead!" she cried into the echoing darkness of the cave.

The angular mouth opposite her smirked. "Very dead," it said carefully.

A new thought caused the girl to peer again into the recesses behind her. "Mr.—Mr. Nicholson!" she called, as if her need of him would summon the man.

Again smirking, again the flat harsh voice. "Mr. Nicholson was—shall we say?—impersonated. He doesn't know about our being here."

"But the phone call!" she cried, as though to insist would make it true. "He called me from San Diego. Or—someone did."

"No one called you from San Diego," the other corrected. "I called you from a pay station at the beach. It's fairly easy to give an imitation of long-distance calling."

The other was close to Sara now, the angular face under the

mop of rusty hair full of some kill-hunger—the lust to give death. Sara stretched her body against the stone. Pebbles rattled loose under the clutch of her hands.

"You know a little too much. Just a little," said the harsh voice. "Enough so that it's best to have you dead."

"Why did you—why did you kill my father? *Why?*"

"He intended to double-cross me about the Sticklemann woman. I arranged the marriage—I pointed her out to him at the beach. I told him how he could get hold of her. Then, when we had her, when we could have started milking her for her money, he wanted to back out. He saw that if they were really married he could have it all."

Slow tears started out of Sara's eyes, to creep down her cheeks.

"I arranged a meeting here between him and me. That was weeks ago. He came unsuspecting." Here a broad smirk, almost a grin, at the cunning displayed. "I knocked him out with a wrench. There was a chance of killing him, but I had luck. When he came to I—I *persuaded* him to write a will, leaving his estate to me."

The ferocious eyes flicked over her. "Persuading him was fun. I only wish I had a little longer to spend with you."

Sara drew breath in a slow gasp.

"Afterward I killed him with the wrench and cut off his hands. I thought that I could use them to plant fingerprints in the Sticklemann murder. Later, I found out. . . But no matter. I still stand to inherit the Sticklemann woman's estate, through your father. . . . I had a chance at you before, the night I choked you with one of your father's neckties. I had to get out through the attic entrance when Mayhew beat on the door."

A snarl of real anger came into the ugly face. "Your father

deserved all he got, because he was a double-crossing rat. I only wish he could be here to see what I'll do to you. *I* was the one who knew Lily. *I* knew how to manage her. Then at the end he turned——"

"*You knew Lily?*" Sara's breath took the words out on a long sigh. Her white face looked up, and suddenly, in the midst of her quivering fear, she stood quite still. "*Who are you?*"

"I——" The other stopped, something alert and watchful came into the face.

Miss Rachel glanced at the long row of parked cars, her eyes picking feverishly at each of them. "Not here," she got out breathlessly.

Mayhew's dark eyes narrowed against the sunlight. "There's a road going along the cliff. Looks deserted though—sure you couldn't have been mistaken?"

"No. I wasn't. It was the blue one with the red feather sticking up in back." By which Miss Rachel meant Sara's hat. "We'd better try that road."

Dust followed the car and dry weeds scraped the undersides of the fenders. "Nobody's been here for years," Mayhew was saying, when they rounded a hump of stone and found the deserted car.

Mayhew was out of the driver's seat very quickly and looking into the interior of the other machine. "No one's here," he shot at Miss Rachel, who was picking her way along a little broken pathway that straggled through the brush toward the edge of the cliff. She peered over, her tiny figure braced against the wind. Her taffeta skirt stood out like a sail. Then she was scrambling downward.

It was then that Mayhew got in too much of a hurry. He

lunged after Miss Rachel, and somewhere near the edge of the narrow chasm he stumbled. Miss Rachel saw his body go by, floundering in the midst of a great amount of rubble and dust. There was a sturdy-looking bush some few feet from the point where the break in the cliffside gave out upon the face of the cliff, but Miss Rachel could not wait to see if he was able to hold himself by it. She went round the pathway till she come to the cave.

She was obviously expected; but then, their approach had not been exactly silent. The nose of a wicked-looking automatic greeted her as she walked in.

Sara has said that at this moment Miss Rachel was positively superb. She cannot understand how so small and sheltered a lady could face a gun and appear coolly collected. But then, Sara did not see *The Purple Horror.* Miss Rachel thinks that if you haven't acquired aplomb after seeing a picture like that, you never will have it.

She ignored the pointing muzzle and looked beyond the distorted face above the blue chauffeur's uniform. "Sara!" she called. "Sara! Are you all right?"

Sobbing answered her, and a sobbing cry. "Go back!"

Miss Rachel deigned then to glance in the direction of the strange figure holding the gun. Her eyes snapped reproof. "You should be ashamed of yourself," she said with feeling. Then she leaned closer and openly studied the person before her. "You're an odd-looking thing now. But I think I know who you are."

There was a cruel joy in the smile that preceded the reply. "Do you?"

Miss Rachel straightened. "Yes. We've met before, you know. It's been in my mind these last few days who you should be. It's been so much the same kind of trick that I wonder I didn't guess long ago. Getting money out of Lily because the marriage wasn't regular . . . Who thought of it, you or Malloy?"

"I, of course. I saw Lily at the beach one day. She didn't see me but I followed her, learned where she was staying. I had just taken over the house at the beach. I was flat broke. My husband had been an acquaintance of Malloy's, and when Malloy came to get a room I knew he was the man I needed. His divorce not completed . . . You'd see how he fitted in."

"Yes, I see." Miss Rachel's composed gaze bored into the mad murderous eyes. "Anne Sticklemann—when did you marry Turner?"

The teeth bared themselves in a grin. "About a year after my brother died." The grin faded, and as though the mention of her real name had increased the other's anger the blue figure advanced. The trigger finger grew slowly white.

Miss Rachel seemed frozen; then, as if her ear had caught some sound from outside, her head flew round. So did that of the other woman. Miss Rachel ducked; when she came up the top of her head caught the other's wrist, the gun went spinning backward into shadow.

"Damn you," said Anne Sticklemann through lips gone suddenly white, and went after Miss Rachel with her bare hands.

But someone was really coming now. The dark blue arms were almost upon Miss Rachel's scrambling figure, when Mayhew's thunderous approach became audible. It sounded as if two or three people were on the path.

The blue figure rushed for the entrance and met Mayhew on the lip of the precipice.

Mayhew was caught off guard and the momentum of the other took him backward. He hung, arched and straining; then his hands had caught a grip on the blue coat. Sara tried to run but she stumbled over a stone and lay screaming. Miss Rachel picked up a piece of granite—she was to be amazed later at the size of it—and went warily toward the two locked and struggling figures.

Mrs. Turner displayed the strength of a madwoman.

The sunlight picked out Mayhew's square face—its lips tight, its eyes like fire above the shoulders of the other. The sea wind carried his hearty breathless cursing into the cave. Miss Rachel balanced her stone.

A small pebble shifted under the heel of the blue figure. It was a little thing, but it took her off balance for a second, a second during which Mayhew's strength showed itself. He had caught her, was holding her, but she tore loose. There was a scream like an animal's, fierce, high. Then the dark figure swam outward all at once, breasting the wind like a bird, and then plummeted downward all arms and thrashing legs.

None of the others watched. There was a moment that seemed a century before the other sound came—the wet heavy sound of a body's striking below.

Mayhew was breathing heavily like a man in an extremity of pain. His face and hands and clothing showed traces of his fall, of his creeping progress along the face of the cliff. He looked beyond the lax figure of Miss Rachel, who had let her rock fall, to Sara who was getting to her feet. The girl began laughing queerly. "You looked awfully funny," she said unsteadily, and of the three of them only Miss Rachel understood that she had no idea whatever of what she was saying.

Mayhew took two long strides to the mocking, shaken girl. He caught the front of her blouse in the grip of his brown fingers and slapped her full in the face with his other hand. "Damn you!" he exploded. "Getting us here, and then laughing at us. . . . You haven't got the sense of a hyena."

Miss Rachel started forward with a cry. "No!" She was almost up to them, and then saw that she was too late. Sara was gone too suddenly sober. Something freezing and scornful had drawn itself into her features. On her cheek a welt bloomed red.

Mayhew let go of her and rubbed his eyes with a weary befuddled gesture, and then went and looked out over the edge of the cliff. "Now I've got to get *that* up, somehow." He walked away and left the women in silence.

Mayhew found Miss Rachel busy in her room after dinner. She was packing her suitcase, setting things in neat piles, not forgetting anything. At Mayhew's knock she went to the door and let him in.

Mayhew made small talk at first.

"Sara and her mother are already gone," Miss Rachel said suddenly, in the midst of a conversation about the weather. Mayhew's face went dark. "You shouldn't have done that, you know. She'd been in there a little while with the—the other. You might try imagining a few of the things she said to Sara." Miss Rachel waited for a moment. Mayhew said nothing. "She had no idea of what she was doing or saying."

Mayhew poised disconsolately over a chair. Miss Rachel stopped packing to watch.

"I'm a fool," Mayhew growled, straightening up and thereby saving the chair. He wandered about the shabby room whose wallpaper still clung in uneven strips to the bare plaster.

"Not very wise, no." Miss Rachel went on with her job.

"Look at this." From his pocket, which bulged, he produced

a tightly wound length of electric cord and a socket with a lamp in it. "This was all apart, all of it scattered through the apartment. The thermostat's gone."

Miss Rachel glanced briefly at the contrivance. "Used with the sewing machine in some way, wasn't it?"

"Yes. The cord's been tampered with—the cord on the machine, that is." He stared at her gloomily. "It's a queer thing for a woman to know, this is."

"Not queer for Anne Sticklemann. She and her brother owned and operated an electric repair shop together. I'd think—she was like a man in so many ways."

"How long did you know that it was Sticklemann's sister?"

"I couldn't be sure until the last, there in the cave. Then I was sure, because at last I recognized her. Also, I had found a letter addressed to Anne S. Turner. That helped." She bent dreamily over the suitcase. "What about this man Turner whom she had married?"

"Died in an automobile accident two years ago."

"That would account for her being so hard up for money then. When she caught sight of Lily she must have thought at once of trying to get money from her again. Malloy was like the answer to a prayer."

"Lily must have known that Mrs. Turner was Anne Sticklemann."

"I don't doubt that she did. Some of the nervous fear she displayed must have been on that woman's account. Lily was afraid of the Scurlocks but she was also defiant toward them. There was something else, much bigger and more subtle and connected with Malloy—some fear that I sensed every time she spoke of him. It must have been her fear of Anne."

"Would your niece have been stupid enough to marry Malloy knowing that his divorce was incomplete?"

"I doubt it. She was bled white in the same way before. Malloy must have put up a good story to get her to accept him—especially with Anne Sticklemann in the background. But I've no doubt good stories were his specialty, with his training on the stage to give plausibility to what he told Lily."

Mayhew stood at the window, staring out into the gathering dark. "All of it, then, was in the hope of getting your niece's money. Malloy was after it on his own, having decided to ditch the Turner woman. We found the will made by Malloy. It—it was queerly written. As if the man could scarcely endure to hold the pen. It was in among Mrs. Turner's things. That seems to bear out the idea." Absently he fingered the dirty lace curtain at the window. "The San Diego police are digging Malloy out tonight. I've got to get down there."

"Good-by," Miss Rachel said briskly.

"Good-by." Mayhew paused at the door. "I don't suppose I'll be seeing any of you again."

Miss Rachel didn't seem especially interested.

"I guess you know that I'm crazy about the Malloy kid," Mayhew remarked, feeling for the knob. Under his tan he was somewhat pink.

"You haven't acted it," Miss Rachel said solidly. She glanced up at him. There was dismissal in her eyes. . . .

Miss Rachel poked a note under Mrs. Marble's door:

Dear Mrs. Marble:

I've just realized that my sister and I have needed a house-keeper for quite a while now. We're really elderly, you know, and a cleaning woman twice a week isn't a lot of help.

> Would you consider working for us? We'll make the salary satisfactory to you. And you can have Clara with you all of the time. Let me know by mail to my home in Los Angeles.

Miss Rachel's name and address were signed to the note in her meticulous, spider-track handwriting.

Miss Jennifer Murdock looked over her toast at her sister sitting opposite across the little breakfast table. There was faint acid in the tone of her voice, while Miss Rachel yawned. "I suppose," she said, "that since your retirement to private life things seem a little dull. No murders or anything."

The squalling of cats drifting in from the kitchen.

"No. Not dull," Miss Rachel answered, lifting her head to listen. A pleased look came into her face. "Jennifer, isn't it odd that Samantha should have had a family at her time of life?"

Jennifer let go her patience in an explosion of woe. "Rachel, how can you talk that way! It's perfectly obvious what must have happened—some dreadful tomcat! You didn't keep your eye on her."

Rachel leaned across to pat Jennifer's trembling wrist. "Don't be upset, sister. It really doesn't matter, does it? And Clara's awfully fond of the little ones."

Miss Jennifer softened a bit at mention of Clara and subsided to grumblings. "So many things happened down there, Rachel. I'll never get it all straight. Goodness! How *could* you stay there?"

"There wasn't enough happened to suit me," Miss Rachel said surprisingly.

Jennifer stopped eating breakfast at that one. "Not enough!" she cried. In the moment of silence that followed the sound of Mrs. Marble, working in the kitchen, was audible.

"No, there wasn't enough happened. That's what I said and that's what I meant. Sara and Lieutenant Mayhew should have made up their quarrel. They're really fond of each other. The other day Lieutenant Mayhew stopped by for a moment—you were upstairs, and I forgot to mention it later—but he looks really dreadful. Almost thin."

"Well . . ." Miss Jennifer cast about in her mind. "Do something about it, Rachel."

"I did. I asked him to luncheon next Thursday."

Jennifer looked her exasperation. "The man doesn't want *food!* That isn't why he's thin! He's in love with the girl."

Miss Rachel kept serene. "I know it. He'll get his girl."

"How?" said Miss Jennifer, with her mouth round.

"I phoned Sara. She's coming too. She doesn't know he'll be here, of course, but he will. And I think they've had time to get over their tempers." She buttered a slice of toast with pleased neatness.

A marmalade-colored kitten with a dark tail wandered in, mewing and twitching its whiskers. Jennifer regarded it puzzledly. "You're such a good detective, Rachel," she said forcefully, "that perhaps you can tell me who the father of these kittens is. Unheard-of colors . . ."

But Miss Rachel had no answer for that one.

THE END

DISCUSSION QUESTIONS

- What kind of sleuth is Rachel Murdock? Are there any traits that make her particularly effective?
- Were you able to predict any part of the solution to the case?
- After learning the solution, were there any clues you realized you had missed?
- Would the story be different if it were set in the present day? If so, how?
- Did the social context of the time play a role in the narrative? If so, how?
- What role did the geographical setting play in the narrative? Would the story have been different if it were set someplace else?
- If you were one of the main characters, would you have acted differently at any point in the story?
- Did you identify with any of the characters? If so, which?
- Did this story remind you of any other books you've read?